2

MY DRAGON MASTERS

KRYSTAL SHANNAN

My Dragon Masters

Sanctuary, Texas Book 2

Copyright © 2014 KS Publishing

All rights reserved.

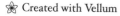 Created with Vellum

To my fabulous husband who helped me plot this story and survived me writing my first ménage.

CHAPTER 1

After thousands of years, I still want only one thing.
To be ruler of all the Veil and Earth. To be King.
—XERXES

B its of rock and brick crunched as I walked. I remembered when this roadway was paved and stunning. A smooth, red brick road leading into the heart of Orin. Now it was no more than crumbled bits and pieces.

The grinding of the gravel under each footstep reminded me of bones breaking beneath my paws in battles past, when I could fearlessly shift into my Lamassu form and tear apart my enemies with my teeth. Then walk across mounds of their bodies, my massive lion paws grinding them into the dirt.

I miss those days. It was kill or be killed. Winner take all.

Time had given the weak the ability to be strong in an annoying way. In the past, it had been easy to pit humans against each other and wipe out entire tribes or countries. Now, we had to play the humans' political games or the pathetic race might blow us all to hell, and both worlds along with it. The collapse began when an experimental drug exposed a half-dozen supernatural races.

Now "Others," as the humans called us, had to be more careful. We weren't worshiped or revered any longer. Instead, we were forced to hide our strengths.

It hadn't stopped me, though. I'd infiltrated and taken control of many global governments over the centuries. Humans were simple—their lives so short they were unable to see beyond the few decades of their existence.

It was the damn Drakonae that were giving me hell. They always had.

I stopped at the crest of a hill and looked down at the sprawling magnificence of Orin. The road might have gone to pieces, but the city shined like the gem it always had been—one of the greatest and most powerful cities in the Veil.

Eventually, it would be mine.

CHAPTER 2

DIANA

It was starting again. I could feel the beast inside me, slithering around like a serpent. Sometimes it would rage, cooling the air around me and coating the walls with ice.

Despite this, I was never cold.

There were no windows in my cell, just a few furs to sleep on, a drain in the back corner, and walls of ice. I didn't know how to stop the ice. It was always there when I awoke.

It would have been pitch black were it not for the torch that burned brightly across the hall from my cell door. There were three small holes in the top half of the iron door that I could peer through, if I stretched on my toes.

Strangely enough, with just that bit of light I could see perfectly. I tried using a bit of rock to mark time with each meal, but the broken piece of stone had worn to the size of a pebble and I'd stopped counting when I reached ten-thousand days. What was the point?

I never saw anything but the torch. The guards passed by from time to time, but never spoke. They fed me by sliding a plate of gruel under the iron door. Perhaps it was once a day. Perhaps not. When I finished eating the glue they considered food, I always slid the plate back out. If I didn't, they wouldn't feed me the next time.

Time had ceased to exist for me.

Even sleep held no peace. Two faces appeared consistently in my dreams. They were beautiful, identical men. Twin brothers, for sure. They had square jawlines, long wavy black hair, and honey-brown eyes that made my body thrum with desire. I had no specific memories of them, just a very strong attraction. They had been significant to me at one point. Of this I was sure.

Other nights I would dream of hearing a baby wailing, but there was nothing visual. I would wake sobbing and my cell would be coated with an extra thick coat of the glaring white ice. I didn't remember birthing a child, but something in my heart said the cries in my dreams belonged to my child.

Beyond those two faint memories, there was nothing. Who was I? Where had I come from? I couldn't remember my name. Just that I'd been here—wherever here was—a long time. In this cell.

It was different today ... or this time. Usually, I felt the same all the time. But when I'd awakened, I was feverish—so warm that sweat ran in rivulets down my temples from my straggles of greasy, blond hair. I stood from the furs and walked to one wall of my cell. I touched the icy bricks, laying my hands against them. The ice soothed only a little.

I pressed my cheek to the wall and droplets of water trickled down to the slick floor, melting fast from the heat my body was generating.

"Hello?" I shouted and moved to the door. I flattened both palms on the cold iron and craned my neck to look out of the three small holes. The familiar orange light from the torch was all I could see. I had no idea how long it'd been since my last plate of gruel had been delivered, but I burned with fever and my stomach cramped with hunger.

"Please. I'm ill." I called out.

No one answered.

My heart leapt at the sound of boots on the stone floor. Food? Or would they help me?

I flinched with each step as they approached. There were multiple sets of feet, at least four people—three more than normal. This was different.

Hope swelled in my chest. Maybe they were going to let me out. They certainly didn't need four men to shove a plate of gruel and a bowl of water under the door.

I took a deep breath and drank in their scent, confused by my instant arousal. My body trembled with excitement, as bile rose in my throat at the thought of any of them actually touching me. Moisture pooled between my thighs underneath the thin, linen shift that covered me. My breasts were heavy and my nipples puckered against the soft fabric. My body had a mind of its own and behaved more like a bitch in heat than a woman. I felt like I should know why my body reacted this way, but I hadn't a clue.

Just one more frustration.

Keys rattled on the other side of the door. The tumblers on the lock clicked and opened. "Back away from the door," a gravelly voice commanded.

I did as he said, more from the shock of hearing someone speak to me than the willingness to follow orders. I wanted out of this cell more than anything.

The iron door screeched as it swung open and three enormous men marched through the doorway. They towered over me. Their chainmail armor clinked with each step, and their red tunics were strangely familiar.

My gaze traveled to their faces. Solemn, but handsome. Strong jawlines and rich, dark brown eyes. Their dark, almost black, hair was long and braided down their backs.

I took another deep breath and released it slowly, trying to control my urges. They smelled delicious and I wanted them. All of them.

Shaking my head, I refocused, taking another step backward instead of forward.

One of the men, probably the youngest of the three, gave me a wolfish grin and made a crude gesture at his crotch. The other two did not appreciate his behavior. One shoved the young man and he sailed across the room, slamming into the icy stone wall with a painful *thud*.

"You know the rules, Aldan. Don't be a fool," said the man who'd done the shoving.

The younger man picked himself up and grunted his acknowledgement, keeping his head bowed and his eyes on the floor.

"Come with us." The third man finally spoke, and my gaze locked with his.

His brown eyes glistened with desire, but he held back. Smart man.

The second man, who'd dealt out punishment to the youngest, growled deep in his throat and I glanced up at him. Part of his top lip was curled into a snarl, though I felt his anger was directed more at his companions than at me.

Toward me, I felt the slightest hint of ... pity.

He spoke again, but this time to me. "Will you walk freely or should we bind you, Milady?"

What did I have to lose? I didn't know who or where I was. All I had were icy walls, a painfully hot fever, and a traitorously aroused body.

I took a deep breath and nodded.

"Edith, lower the wards," said the third man. "But just enough so that we can pass through the doorway with her."

A moment later, a rush of white-hot energy knocked me back against the far wall of my cell. Air rushed from my lungs with an audible *umph*. The ice on the wall behind me melted on contact, soaking the fabric of my dress.

The thing ... the beast I'd felt inside me moved again and a growl tore from my throat unlike anything I'd ever heard. Power within me surged forward and I leapt at the youngest man, knocking him to the ground. His body and clothing iced solid within moments and I jumped back.

My head was spinning. Had I killed him? There wasn't time to contemplate guilt.

I could hear shouting, but the words were garbled in my racing mind. The other two men were backing slowly toward the open cell door. I refused to stay here any longer. The entity inside me was being pulled. The burning arousal that plagued my body was a mere pinprick compared to the stabbing pain I felt now.

Freeing myself from this icy prison was my only objective.

I lunged and the two men dove to either side of the cell. Instead of pursuing them, I ran through the open door and swung it closed. It locked in place with a heavy clank and I breathed a small sigh of relief.

I turned, running headlong into a small woman. She fell to the floor, but jumped back to her feet quickly.

Her bright, red hair hung in loose waves only to her shoulders and she was dressed in strange clothing. A loose, waist-length tunic covered her upper half, but on her lower body, she wore tightly fitting breeches that extended to her ankles, where the strangest looking furry boots covered her feet.

"No! Don't leave. They'll kill me!" The redhead extended her hand and I observed her in suspicious silence. I started to shake my head. Whatever she needed from me, I would not give. She carried no weapon that I could see, yet the beast inside my soul wanted absolutely nothing to do with her.

"I need to go."

"Go where? You don't even know where you are." Her voice was like velvet and dripped with honey, the fear had disappeared.

She was stalling me. That I did know. I couldn't let her steal this chance from me. My gut told me there wouldn't ever be another. Whatever she'd done to allow me out of that wretched cell had awakened more than even I understood. It was as if everything around and inside me came to life. It was like I'd been unchained. Like magick.

The redhead took a step forward and I threw up a hand, gesturing her to stop. Within seconds, a thick wall of ice separated us. Her muffled curses followed me as I made my way down the long, dimly lit hallway.

I passed many doors. Dozens of voices called after me, but I stopped for none. The rough gravel on the floor bit into my tender, bare feet and I winced with each step. The floor of my cell had been as smooth as glass, every inch covered in ice. How I wished for that smooth, cold surface now.

With the next step I took, the gravel was gone. I stared at the ground and saw my terrified expression in the dark, glassy surface. By the gods! The floors had iced over. I lifted one bloody foot and then the next, wiping off the gravel. Then I wiped my bloody hand on the side of my damp skirt. The smooth, cool floor was heaven to my throbbing feet. Hopefully, the cuts would stop bleeding soon.

More commotion carried down the tunnel from where the ice had formed between the redheaded woman and me. There was thunderous hammering and yelling. It wouldn't be long before they hacked their way through the frozen wall.

Confusion swirled in my mind like a howling snow-storm. Common sense said I'd created the ice, but then again, common sense also said that people could not create something from nothing. *Gods!* My stomach twisted in pain. Heat flamed through me like I'd been tossed on a funeral pyre, and the throbbing in my sex was bordering on maddening. I couldn't remember *ever* having sex with anyone, but my body knew exactly what it wanted.

It didn't matter. Right now, all that did matter was getting out of this dungeon. So unless propositioning one of the guards chasing me was a viable option, sex was just going to have to wait.

The beast inside me growled in frustration and my breath fogged in front of me as I ran.

I leaned against the wall to catch my breath. "Just pull yourself together and help me get out of this place," I told myself. A new surge of energy buzzed through my body. All my nerves stood on end. My skin was *so* warm; the ice beneath my feet was melting into puddles.

I slipped along the bare stone wall and peeked around the next corner. There were several guards stationed at a gate that opened to the outside. Two guards stood on either side of the gate. How many were on the outside? I couldn't see anything past the glare of daylight. I'd been in the dark so long the light was uncomfortable. It was easier to focus in the darkness. In fact, the darker it was, the faster my eyes adjusted.

A bell sounded in the distance and the tunnel came to life. Dozens of guards poured in through the open gates and my heart dropped. I'd been so close. I could smell the fresh air, the scent of lavender on the breeze, and the tang of salt from an ocean.

Another emotion boiled from the center of my chest and the beast within pushed inside my mind. It wanted control and was refusing to give up. The single echoing thought in my head was *ice*.

Fine, then. *Take it.*

I stopped fighting the beast and let it guide me. I stepped out of the shadows and marched down the center of the tunnel. Several guards looked at me and then shouted. I raised my hands toward them and sheets of ice grew from the ground, trapping them. They hacked at the cold barrier with their swords, but it would take time for them to get free.

For a brief moment, I allowed myself hope. I threw up my hands and a wave of ice encased the group of men in my path. Running up the face of the frozen wave, I gasped, fear streaking along my spine as my fingernails lengthened into white claws. Though it made scaling the slippery face of the ice much easier, it further terrified my already confused mind. I slid down the other side and waved my arm to create more ice to smooth my descent. But I was a mere passenger in my body. The beast was controlling most of my actions.

A guard came out of nowhere and I threw him across the tunnel. His body slammed into the gray stone wall. My strength surprised me. The hit barely knocked the breath from my body.

No one was going to stop me. Not now.

I walked through the open gate unimpeded, drinking in the sights and scents around me. The salty breeze whipped through my long, white hair. I looked up at the azure sky and a roar tore from my chest that sounded inhuman. The beast receded, giving me full control once more over my body. My hands changed back to normal, claws retracted.

My eyesight adjusted to the bright sun and I scanned my surroundings. The landscape was eerily familiar, but no specific memories came to mind. I didn't know where I was or where I needed to go. The dungeon was isolated. I couldn't see a town or castle from this vantage point, but I could hear the tolling of the bells in the distance, raising the alarm. They were coming for me. I had to move.

The yearning inside me was stronger now. The call

that had flared to life when they entered my cell pulled me to the left. I emerged from the shadow of the tower I'd escaped and stepped gingerly onto the soft, grassy turf. The green grass cushioned my aching feet. I looked behind me, glad to see I was no longer leaving bloody footprints. At least that would make tracking me somewhat harder for the soldiers I'd left frozen in the tunnels.

I hitched up the skirt of my shift, not worried about showing a little leg. The pull inside me continued to grow; instinctively I knew it would lead me in the right direction. Every step I took pleased the beast within me.

Moments later, a large shadow passed over my head. I ducked to the ground. Terror clawed at my heart. I had no idea what kind of bird could make such a large shadow, but when I ventured a glance into the pure, blue sky, there was no bird. A creature that could only be described as a dragon had cast the shadow. It was big, reddish in color, and its wings were so large it easily could have covered an entire castle keep.

Where was I? And since when were dragons real?

The beast within me laughed and I shook my head. It could laugh all it wanted. There was no way I could stand up to a monster the size of a castle tower. The red dragon soared over the valley, exactly where I was headed.

Noises behind me pushed my feet into a run.

"Whatever gods or goddesses are out there, I could really use a hand right now." I half-slid, half-rolled down the face of a steep hill. I slipped through a thicket of trees and came out on the other side in time to see a man seemingly appear out of thin air inside a circle of large stones. A white mist hung in the air above the stones.

He walked out of the circle and looked around suspiciously. The mist vanished a few seconds later.

I flattened myself against a large pine and held my breath. Suspending my common sense, I realized this might be a good way to disappear. He was alone. Perhaps I could get him to take me away from this place. After singlehandedly escaping that horrid prison, one man didn't seem nearly as intimidating as he would have only hours ago.

I left the protection of the trees and walked toward him, taking a deep breath to try and calm my frayed nerves. The last thing I needed was him encased in a block of ice. I needed him to tell me how to escape. As I stepped closer, I noticed the odd cut of his clothing. He wore breeches that reached to his ankles and his coat only hung to his waist.

"Sir," I called out.

He looked at me and his eyes widened like he recognized me. But I had no knowledge of him.

The beast rumbled. Apparently, it recognized the stranger. I was the only one left in the dark.

"I need to leave this place. Can I go through the stones the same way you appeared? Where does it lead?" Only ten feet separated us now. Something about him gave me pause. Something I could feel surrounding him.

"You can't be alive. They said you died." He took a step forward and I backed up, keeping him at the same distance.

"I assure you I am alive, but I need your assistance to leave this place. I'm ill..." I wiped beads of sweat from my brow and refocused on him. "I need to go out the way you came. I cannot explain it." I could smell him now—his scent was masculine with a hint of cardamom. My senses were heightened and I could smell the moist dirt beneath my feet, the tangy scent of the grass. Salt hung in the air from an ocean I couldn't see. And then there was this man. Strange scents clung to his clothes—an unfamiliar musk of some type of animal. Sand? Perfume?

"You don't remember me?"

I opened my mouth to tell him I remembered no one, but then thought better of it. "I need to leave, sir. Those stones are a doorway. I don't know how or why, but they are, aren't they?"

He nodded and tightened his fingers around the handle of a small dagger he was holding. I hadn't noticed it before. It was short, no longer than the length of his hand. The blade was half that and triangular in shape. The hilt was gold, at least the part I could see. And his response to my question told me it was essential to using the gateway.

"If I let you out of the Veil, you have to promise to stay with me."

I narrowed my eyes and the beast within me pushed against my mind. The pain was so intense, as if someone were holding my face against hot iron. I screamed and fell to my knees. Something was happening that I couldn't stop. Ice flowed along the ground from me, spiraling outward in a circular pattern.

"Stop!" he shouted, running toward me with his hands raised.

An invisible force pushed on me and I screamed again. *He* was making the pain worse. Anger surged from deep within me and I stood, fighting through the searing pain and faced him. For a second, I saw hesitation in his pale gray eyes.

That was my moment. I lifted my hand and ice coated him from head to foot, except for the hand holding the small golden dagger. It amazed me that I could control this power with so little focus.

I should've been terrified, but instead it felt natural. The ice and the beast were part of me. I'd just forgotten them.

That was a problem for later. Now, I needed to escape and return to my life—a life I couldn't remember, but a life I wanted desperately to find. And those handsome twins from my dreams—perhaps they could tell me what happened to the baby.

The ice around the stranger began to crack.

I wrenched the dagger from his hand and ran to the stone circle. The mist didn't reappear. Nothing happened. I could see him breaking his way out of the icy coating one chunk at a time. It would take him only a few more minutes to free himself completely.

I frantically searched the stones for markings, running my fingertips around the smooth surface looking for anything that might tell me how to open the doorway.

There were none.

I ran from one to another and then to the large pillar in the center. A bloody handprint stared back at me from the far side. It looked fresh. In fact, the entire pillar was covered with worn and faded handprints. All in shades of red and brown. All made with blood.

My fingers tightened around the handle of the dagger. It was worth trying. Nothing about this world made sense. Why wouldn't there be a magickal doorway? I dragged the blade across my left palm, wincing at the first burn of the cut. Blood pooled in my palm. I closed my hand into a fist to smear the blood and then slapped it onto the face of the pillar.

Energy shot through my body and the world moved around me. The pillar was gone. In its place was a waist-high altar of stacked stones held together by mortar. The towering pillars around the edge of the circle were also gone. Instead of large, freestanding rocks, there were smaller rocks stacked together to create a dozen pillars in a circle around the middle altar. And instead of rolling hills of green grass, I stood in the center of an unfamiliar forest.

I dropped to my knees and dug a hole at the base of the altar. After wiping my blood off the small dagger, I placed it into the hole and covered it quickly. The man would most certainly come looking for it and instinct told me it wasn't safe to carry it around.

My palm still bled from the cut so I tore a strip from the bottom of my shift and wrapped it around my left hand. I hoped it would be enough to stanch the flow of blood.

I closed my eyes and turned, listening to a force I couldn't explain tell me which direction to walk in a land I knew nothing about. Bloody hell of a mess this was.

Taking a deep breath, I opened my eyes and took several steps. The ground was rocky and cold here, not grassy and soft. My feet were already tender from running on the sharp rocks at the tower. I couldn't last long out here without shoes, and the terrain was too jagged to ice the ground. I'd be on my bum more than my feet.

Choosing each step carefully, I climbed away from the hidden stone circle and picked my way through the dense, pine forest. The dead needles on the ground stuck into my feet like slivers of glass, but I had to keep moving. The sun was falling and it would be dark in a few hours.

There was no telling what might come out hunting under the cover of darkness. I could protect myself to a point, but I could not just freeze everything that came near me. Or maybe I could, but I didn't want to. There had to be someone somewhere who could help me figure out who and what I was.

Someone who didn't want to hurt me.

CHAPTER 3

XERXES

I stormed into the palace at Orin and glared down the center aisle at Kevan Incanti on his throne next to his brother, Leif. They were blond giants as men. Fire-breathing dragons. And liars.

Diana Karlson Blackmoor *was* alive. Her family and many others had been executed during the war in the Veil. I had helped the Incanti take power. I'd told them to kill every Blackmoor and they'd listened. Almost.

But their dicks had gotten in the way. The two brothers desired Diana, the Blackmoor princess—a rare prize in the Drakonae world after the civil war that tore apart the Drakonae race. She was one of the only ice-breathers left alive. Gorgeous, hair as white as the ice she created, and skin so smooth it was like porcelain. I would've fucked her, so I couldn't blame them for their desires.

The Incanti brothers had tortured the princes, Miles

and Eli Blackmoor, by chaining them to the two dragon-steel pillars in the center of this very room and flogging them until they couldn't stand. And then the Incanti had drugged and raped the Blackmoor princes' mate in front of them and the entire Drakonae royal court. What was left of it, anyway. It had happened over a thousand years ago, but I remember it as if it were yesterday.

When Diana hadn't collapsed after their assault, the Incantis sentenced her to life in the tower dungeon, north of the city. No one, not even the strongest dragons, survived there more than a dozen years. So how had she?

I walked down the purple carpet to the dais where the three stone thrones still sat. Strong and beautifully carved, the chair backs were fashioned to look like raised Lamassu wings. These were my people's thrones first, and they would be mine again once I acquired the Sisters of Lamidae —a race of semi-human women who could foretell the future.

Leif sat on the right and Kevan on the left. The center throne was empty. They must've killed their most recent plaything, again. There weren't that many female Drakonae to begin with, but these conceited reptiles used up women as quickly as water evaporated in a desert.

I only visited the Veil every century or so. And I'd yet to see the same woman in that center throne more than twice. There were whisperings that the Incanti brothers were mad. I was quite inclined to agree with them.

Most who knew me called me cruel and heartless, but Leif and Kevan Incanti were just as bloodthirsty, vicious, and barbaric as myself. We all enjoyed pain and torture for the pleasure of it.

But, I wanted to rule a world of people, not bones and

ash. When the Incanti took power, they slaughtered and burned half the population of the Veil.

At least they hadn't destroyed this beautiful city and the world around it. Only their subjects trembled in their presence, cowering against the walls like they'd forgotten they had wings, claws, and could breathe fire, too.

It didn't matter. Their fear would make them that much easier to conquer when the time was right.

The dragon kings' faces were grim, anger burning in their glowing, yellow-orange eyes. The warning bells still tolled from the tower east of the throne room. They knew they'd lost their prize. Unfortunately, they probably didn't know yet that she had escaped the Veil entirely, taking one of the four pieces of the key with her. Anger seethed in my chest. It disgusted me to ask them for another of the Shamesh daggers to replace the one she'd taken. But the Incanti only held the Veil because of me.

They owed me. They would give me another.

"Amir Xerxes Hilah," Leif's voice carried through the throne room. "It has been a long time. Though it always is."

"How is your vendetta?" Kevan asked, a grin turning up the corners of his mouth. "Has Rose bottled the last of your genies?"

I glared up at him and snarled. "Diana Blackmoor looked quite healthy on her way out of the Veil. I don't suppose her escape was on your agenda for the day?"

The heat in the room escalated. Kevan stood from his throne and walked down several steps to me. When his face was even with mine his I stared back at eyes swirling yellow and orange, like liquid metal in a forge. Sweat beaded on my forehead from the heat of his breath, but I wasn't concerned. The brat wouldn't try anything against me. I stood between them and the Blackmoors' vengeance.

"You opened the portal?" he said, heat from his breath blasting my face like waves from a furnace.

"Momentary lapse in judgment," I answered with a smile. "She froze my ass in place and took the key from me." Crossing my arms over my chest, I glared back at him until his eyes changed back to brown. "Odd thing, though. She didn't recognize me and was confused by the portal. Have you two been messing with her mind?"

Kevan snarled and stormed back to his throne, ignoring my statement and sitting with a huff. A slight hint of concern flashed across his brother's face, though.

Shit. They had wiped her memory.

I shook my head, irritated by their carelessness. She was a loose cannon on earth. A dragon out in the open without knowledge of history could be worse than the damn riots in the U.S. after the Lycans went crazy on that Instinct drug fifty years ago.

Leif and Kevan were psychopathic and vicious, but they weren't stupid. At least I hadn't thought so until now.

"Prepare the guard. She must be caught," Leif's voice thundered through the cavernous room. His voice echoed back to the dais, but still no one moved. His gaze focused on me and then fell to my hands. "Release them, Xerxes, and I will grant your request."

I smiled and dropped my fingers, releasing their guards from my paralytic hold. "You haven't heard it, yet."

"Speak it now and go. We're busy."

"I want another dagger. She took mine. I will get it back, but until then—"

He waved his hand to silence me.

Bastard.

His elder by thousands of years, I should be sitting on one of the stone thrones, not him. I bit my tongue. Now was not the time. This war would be won later.

"Bring the box." Kevan ordered. Two guards brought up a black trunk and lay it at the foot of the kings. He took a small, bronze key from around his neck, opened the box, and pulled out a gold dagger identical to the one Diana had taken from my hand. A cut from its blade and blood sacrifice was the only way to open the portal between this world and earth. The hilts of the four daggers connected to create the symbol of Shamesh, sacred to my kind. The complete set used to hang in the temple I guarded in Babylon millennia ago.

"You will return this dagger to us after recovering yours, Xerxes. Or the guard will be forced to come after *you* next."

I stepped forward and took the shining weapon from his hand. "Don't threaten me, Kevan. You aren't in a position to do so."

The dragon king's lip curled, but neither he nor his brother disagreed. They might be the kings of the Veil for now, but that position was precarious, at best. Still, something about their smug faces made me wonder what information they were keeping from me.

CHAPTER 4

DIANA

I stepped out of the forest onto a stone road and followed it south. The sun was setting on my right, but there was at least another half hour of daylight. The town below in the valley spread for miles. I couldn't believe how many buildings I could see. It was a wealthy city, indeed.

Every so often, metal carriages whipped past me on the road. If I'd not seen their wheels turning with my own eyes, I would have thought they flew. They moved so fast, although nothing pulled them.

As I reached the outskirts of the town, I saw many people. One old man with a long, white beard and long, oily, gray hair approached me. His clothes were dingy and smelled of feces. He held out a cup, but I shook my head and showed him my palms. I had nothing to give him. Shame filled my heart as the desire for his tattered coat crossed my mind. My shift was still damp and every time people stared, I cringed. The thin fabric clung to my every curve.

I passed by a small, brick building with a glowing sign in the window. It was a beautiful shade of pink. It was as good a place as any to start asking for help. Perhaps they could at least direct me to those in charge of the town.

My hand shook as I lifted it and knocked on the bright red door. A loud voice from inside yelled for me to come in. I did as told and yanked on the door until it swung wide open.

The booming sound of something that might pass as music hit my ears with the force of a storm. I winced and the beast within me shrank back at the sound of the tones and the vulgar lyrics. I couldn't tell where the music was coming from. No instruments or musicians were visible.

A man with arms the size of my thighs turned around and grinned at me. His full set of white teeth surprised me, as did the green stripe in his hair, and the ink covering his arms and bare chest. He was still handsome and I could sense his attraction to me immediately. How, I didn't know. It was as if I could smell it coming from his skin. The attraction consumed my mind, but fear of these strange surroundings kept me from being that forward with a complete stranger in a public place.

"Well now, what's a li'l bit like you doing in my shop?" He held a buzzing metal pen in his hand and a woman lay half-naked on a table at his side.

"I am so very sorry. I did not mean to intrude. I will leave you with your woman." The noise from the object in his hand was unlike anything I'd heard before. And the lights on the ceiling were brighter than any torch I'd ever seen, burning a bright white and illuminating the entire room without difficulty. But I couldn't see the fire or what was burning.

"My woman?" He raised an eyebrow in confusion.

I gestured to the naked back of the woman on the table.

His eyes widened with realization. "Oh, no, li'l bit. She's not mine. I'm just giving her a little ink." He held up the pen. "Were you looking to get a tattoo today?"

I stared at the pen and then at the half-inked woman's back. Realization struck and I shook my head. "No. I hoped you could tell me who runs this town."

"The whole town? I guess that would be the mayor."

That word was not familiar either. Where the bloody hell had I ended up? Or more importantly—when?

"This mayor, sir. Where would I find him?"

"I don't know. Maybe his house? I don't really keep track of politicians."

"Oh." I took a deep breath and sighed, not really understanding. This strange man wasn't going to be helpful. And the way my body was heating up from the inside out, I needed to get out quickly. I turned back toward his doorway and stopped when another man came barreling through the front door. He brushed past me as if I were not present.

"Jackson, you done yet? This'll be the last time anyone else mistakes my bitch for being available." He walked to the woman's side and slapped her backside hard.

Hard enough that I winced in sympathy.

She barely moved and didn't make a sound, but I saw tears well in her eyes.

The man looked at me next. His gray eyes were ice

cold at first, but then I saw something in them I didn't like. A primal hunger. He was dangerous.

"Thank you for your help, sir." I spoke politely and reached out to open the door. Before I could slip out, a heavy hand latched onto my shoulder.

"Where's a pretty thing like you going right before curfew? The soldiers will throw you in lockup if they catch you outside after sundown."

"I have to go," I said, twisting from his grasp. Ice started to spread across the floor from my bare feet and the air around me chilled. I sucked in a quick breath. "Please, just let me go."

The male hissed and pulled back his hand. His thick fingers were blue with cold. Instead of backing away, he struck out and I gasped as the force of his slap knocked me to the ground. Pain radiated out from my cheekbone.

He leaned toward me and I held up my hands. "No!" A moment later a wall of ice grew from the floor to the ceiling, separating me from the three strangers.

Scrambling to my feet, I yanked open the door and ran out. A loud horn on my left made my stomach leap into my throat. One of those horseless carriages was careening toward me. There wasn't any time to move.

I held up my hands and closed my eyes just as it was about to hit. Instead, I heard a loud *crunch*. I opened my eyes. Another ice wall had formed between me and the careening hunk of metal on wheels. I ran my fingertips up and down the slick wall, staring at the confused and irate face of the woman in the horseless carriage on the other side. The front of her vehicle was smashed beyond recognition and the clear glass over the front had cracked.

More loud horns blared and several other strange metal

carriages turned away from me. People screamed and pointed. There was no time to contemplate my abilities at the moment.

Angry men in black clothing, carrying glistening metal weapons, ran toward me. They raised the long, black sticks and explosions ricocheted around my body. Something struck me in the shoulder and I cried. Pain seared through my body like a fiery dart.

"Get on the ground. You're under arrest." One man shouted angrily and ran toward me.

I gasped for breath. My chest was on fire, but I would not give up without a fight. I threw up my hands, creating one wall of ice after another. It gave me a moment to run and it blocked the wicked projectiles their weapons were firing at me.

The beast within me writhed and cried out. So much pain. It burned from the inside out. I pulled back and let the beast take control. My body changed into something I didn't recognize—an animal of some kind. It came out and I withdrew.

The screaming of the onlookers only grew worse, but at least in this new form, the projectiles they fired just bounced off. My clawed feet tore the rocky ground beneath me with each step. I was massive. Bigger than the building I'd been in only moments ago. The people around me barely reached to the knee joint of my massive legs.

Air rushed around my face and an icy breath flowed from my mouth, coating everything in front of and below me with the same glacier of ice I'd been calling forth with my hands.

The shooting stopped and giant wings on either side of

me propelled my now-huge body forward. The people and buildings on the ground shrank from view.

I could fly? Bloody hell! What was I?

My wings pumped, pushing me into the clouds. I caught an updraft, allowing me to glide silently. I couldn't remember ever flying before, but it was easy enough, except for the ache in my right shoulder from the bleeding wound. I wasn't going to make it far, but I needed to get away from the commotion I'd caused. I needed somewhere isolated and quiet to rest.

Buildings flew past. Then trees. Hills. Mountains passed next. More people, towns, and unfamiliar land spread for miles.

Numbness began to spread through my body. Without warning, my wings became too heavy to lift. The landscape below rushed up to meet my face and the ground shook when I collided with it. Something shimmered around me and my arms and legs returned to normal. My white, iridescent, scaly skin was gone and I returned to human form.

I was naked, bleeding, and cold.

Why was I cold? I never remembered being cold in that icy cell. As fear took hold in my heart, ice spread around me and I moaned. It burned against my bare skin, but I couldn't stop it. The coldness swirled within me like a vicious storm.

Something struck my back and I moaned, praying to whatever god might listen to protect me. Instead, the white world around me faded as blurry images of people approached from the trees. Hands touched my body and I could hear the murmur of voices, but nothing was clear and I let myself drift into the blackness.

CHAPTER 5

XERXES

A new excitement grew inside me. Diana Blackmoor was alive. Those two idiots had kept her alive and locked away for thousands of years. It was obvious her mind had been damaged. There's no way she would've forgotten me, the man who helped steal the throne from her and her husbands' families.

They were all supposed to be dead, but those damn Blackmoor brothers proved to be harder to kill than the rest. With them in league with Rose, they'd been a bloody thorn in my side for more than a millennium. But with their mate resurfacing, they would be vulnerable.

I stepped inside the stone circle, sliced my palm with the small dagger then touched the center stone. A second later, I appeared inside an ancient circle hidden deep in the woods of Ireland. Lavender eyes peered at me in the dark, but no one spoke.

Diana had come through the circle. They should have had the sense to detain her. "Where's the woman?"

One man stepped out from behind a tree. "What woman, Master Hilah? You're the only one with a key."

My heart paused for a moment. Where the hell had that ice-bitch-of-a-lizard gone? I saw her disappear. She'd gone through the portal. They had to have seen her.

I advanced and grabbed one of the Djinn by the collar of his shirt. "You left your posts, didn't you? You let her slip through your grasp."

His purple eyes widened, fear making him sweat. "No, Master. We did not leave the ring unattended while you were away. No one came through. There was no woman." He stank of fear, but not of guilt. The Djinn wasn't lying to me.

I threw him to the ground. There was only one other explanation. "There are two sacred circles in North America. One outside of old Boston in the Washington Republic, and one in the woods of South Carolina in the SECR (South East Coast Republic)."

The Djinn opened his mouth to question me, but snapped it closed a half-second later. He nodded and spoke to his comrades. They left to begin the hunt and he climbed back to his feet and extended his hand, palm up. "Home, Master?"

"Yes." I clasped his hand and the world swirled around me like a hurricane. I hated the feeling of teleporting, but it was the most convenient way of traveling over extended distances.

When the world stopped moving, I snatched my hand away from the Djinn soldier and walked toward Cyrus' personal rooms. The Djinn king rarely left the palace we cohabitated in the middle of the desert between the Persian Gulf and Shiraz.

Several small villages were within walking distance, but no one ever bothered us. The locals spread stories of how people would disappear if they ventured toward the Palace of the Djinn. It worked out perfectly. The small, zealot groups that created havoc in much of the Middle East still feared the legends of the Djinn and stayed far away from what I'd come to call home.

I'd lived inside these stone walls for over a thousand years. Jeweled artifacts lined the hallways. Priceless rugs covered the floors. The best silks hung over the windows and doorways. Slaves in little more than bras and panties roamed the palace, making sure everyone was well taken care of. Then, of course, I had my personal harem. I'd grown to enjoy the lifestyle of ancient Persia, but I still wanted more.

A harem of women was not worth giving up my dream of ruling the world.

I turned a corner and shoved open the two, large doors. Both were ornately carved and leafed in gold. "Cyrus." I spoke his name loudly and took a deep breath. The musk of sex filled the air of his suite. My dick hardened in response. I should've visited my own rooms first.

Before I could turn to leave, several of Cyrus' concubines hurried forward from one of the back rooms and knelt at my feet.

"Where's your master?"

Without looking up, one of the women answered. "He is in bed, Master Hilah."

I could hear the sound of moaning and grunting coming from the far room even with the door shut. I licked my lips and twirled my fingers. The bitch who'd spoken gasped, but did not struggle as invisible fingers lifted her into the air and arched her back, which showed off her impressive rack hidden only beneath a thin, gauzy fabric. Her dark areolas were swollen and her nipples had pebbled. I could smell her arousal on the air, too.

These women were trained to be aroused on command. "Tell Cyrus to join me in my rooms for the evening meal."

"Yes, Master Hilah."

I flicked my wrist and let the magick fall away, dropping her to the floor. She landed on the soft carpets with a thud, but made no move or complaint. Perfectly behaved. They all were. If any misbehaved, Cyrus killed them.

I thought it wasteful to kill beautiful women, but the threat did keep them in line. So I had to give him props for keeping the palace in smooth running order.

⚜

I ENTERED MY ROOMS ON THE OPPOSITE SIDE OF THE palace, nodding to the two Djinn guards on either side of my doors. "No one disturbs me."

They bowed and closed the doors behind me.

Three caramel-skinned women approached. All with brown eyes, waist-length, shiny black hair and wearing nothing more than a few scarves attached to a jeweled belt. I forbade them from wearing any other coverings.

Their luscious breasts swayed with each step toward me, ringing the tiny bells that hung from the rings that pierced their nipples. Though their eyes were focused on the floor, I knew they watched my every move.

I crooked a finger at the girl in the center. The other two dropped to their knees instantly and prostrated themselves on the floor. Unless I commanded otherwise, they would stay in that position until I left. It'd been over a year since I'd had to discipline any of them.

The girl in the center raised her head just slightly, seeking instruction. I made an indication to a low couch a few feet away. She followed me to the couch and I sank into the soft cushions. Her fingers worked swiftly on the zipper of my pants, freeing my dick from the constraints of the soft wool. I lifted myself just enough to allow her to push down my dress pants. I enjoyed Lily's mouth and hands the most out of the three girls I kept and I always started my evenings with her touch.

When her warm, wet lips closed around my dick, I let the world fall away. I could just feel. Just take my pleasure and be satisfied for a single minute or two. It was the only time I ever truly relaxed my senses and let my guard down.

CHAPTER 6

DIANA

The smell of alcohol roused me from sleep, but when I tried to lift my head, I couldn't. It was too heavy. And the ringing between my ears was excruciating, making me long for the unconscious, pain-free existence to claim me again.

I licked my lips and tried to speak, but nothing came out. My tongue felt like it'd been wrapped in wool. Everything was so hot. My skin felt like it was on fire and sweat dripped down my neck. The sheet draped over my body rubbed and irritated my hypersensitive skin. I tried to pull it away but found even that slight effort painful.

I opened my eyes and looked around. This room had white torches affixed to the ceiling, but these buzzed annoyingly like a hive of honeybees.

The vibrations of approaching footsteps made my heart race. Who had found me? Were they taking me back to that prison? Where was I now?

I turned my head and tried to focus on the approaching figure.

"Hey there, you're finally awake. That's good, 'cause we've got to get moving again. The SECR forces are tracking your flight path." Her voice was calming and I trusted that for now. She didn't appear to mean me any harm. She smelled strange, though. And I noticed that I couldn't hear her heartbeat. Though until now, I hadn't noticed that I could hear something so faint until it was missing from the background.

My eyebrows scrunched and I tried to speak again. Instead, I coughed.

She reached for a glass of water on a table beside the bed. "You're not going to ice my arm if I help you take a sip, are you?" She grinned and sat next to me on the bed.

Her English was atrocious, but I gathered the meaning of most of her words. I mouthed a "no." She leaned forward and helped me raise my head. The glass was cool against my chapped lips and I greedily swallowed every drop.

"More, please," I managed to croak out.

"Yep, give me a sec." She rose from the bed and walked to the other side of the room. I listened to the wonderful sound of liquid being poured and licked my lips. Just that small drink had helped some already. But I still only understood one out of every three or four words she said.

Also, she was dressed like a man. Nearly like the soldiers I'd seen attack me in the town. A black tunic fitted to her upper body like skin, and the pants were the same—tight and form-fitting, made from leather by the scent of them. Her hair was tied up like a horse's tail and a sword was attached to her back. Several other blades were also affixed to her body by means of various straps. This woman, whatever she was, dressed as a warrior.

She returned to my side with more water and helped me until I drained the glass again.

"You lost a lot of blood, but hopefully you have some super healing powers tucked away in that Drakonae DNA of yours. When Charlie said she saw a dragon crash land out near Rodger's Mill, I couldn't believe my ears. I didn't think any of your kind still lived on earth." She set the cup down and stared at me, waiting for a response. "You were really stupid to shift in front of people, though."

I didn't know what to say. Had she called me a dragon? Though when I thought about how my body had changed, how big I'd become, the claws, the flying. It did make sense ... in a twisted, unnatural way. How could I be a dragon? That seemed like something a person would remember.

She could call me stupid if she wanted to, but this world was different than any knowledge I still possessed. How could I live in a world where nothing made sense and I didn't remember anything about who I was? I sucked in a quick breath and tried to calm my racing heart. The air chilled and ice spread across the bed.

The woman leapt from her seat. "Hey now!"

"Forgive me, I cannot control it well when my emotions are high." I took another breath, slower this time. My heartbeat slowed considerably and so did the spread of the ice. The chill in the air faded and my breath returned to a more normal temperature.

"We need to move in a couple of hours. I'll find you some new clothes and be back in a bit. Try not to ice the room while I'm gone. I promise you're safe here. The

Underground protects all of our kind, even the ones who are a little off the wall. And you qualify. Plus, you sound like someone from the Middle Ages. I haven't heard English used the way you've been speaking in almost a thousand years." She paused at the door and looked back at me. "My name is Eira, by the way. What's yours?"

"I do not know, but thank you for helping me Er--ra," I said, fumbling with her name.

She frowned at me and walked back to the bedside. "It's pronounced ēē-rah," she repeated, speaking both syllables slowly. "What do you mean, you don't know your name?" she asked.

"Precisely that. I woke up in a prison cell somewhere else. Somewhere with other dragons. I escaped from there by way of a magickal circle of stones."

"Wait, if you came through a stone circle, how the hell did you end up in North America?"

"I don't know what you mean by 'North America.' " I grimaced and tried to sit up against the headboard.

She reached under me and lifted my body and the pillows as if I weighed no more than a feather. "Better?"

I nodded. "The circle took me to another circle made of stone altars. It was in a thick forest, not too far from a town. In the town I encountered some unfriendly villagers and was accosted by several men. When I became frightened, the beast, or dragon I suppose, came forward and I flew as far as I could."

Her eyes widened. "Holy shit!" She jumped up from the bed and dashed to the door, her figure a blur. "I'll be back in a minute. I have to get Charlie. But, if you think you can eat, I'll have Chad bring you something."

"Thank you. That would be most agreeable. I cannot remember the last time I ate."

She chuckled and disappeared from the doorway.

I wasn't sure what she'd been talking about, but at least my pounding headache was dissipating. Unfortunately, the fever that had plagued me in the prison was coming back with a vengeance.

My body felt as though I'd been locked in a hot steam tent. The sheet covering me was nearly soaked, as were the linens beneath me. I experimented with my magick and waved my hand slowly over the sheet.

Nothing happened. Maybe the ice only came if danger threatened. I tried to remember how terrified I'd been when the stranger hit me inside that shop.

It worked. The whole bed iced over and the temperature in the room dropped considerably. I blew air from my mouth, amused that it turned to snow and fell softly onto the semi-frozen sheet covering my body. Unfortunately, my temperature was so warm the icy sheets started melting. Moments later, a wet sheet clung to my chest, outlining every line of my body.

Bloody hell.

An earthy smell tickled my nose and I took a deep breath. The fire inside me burned hotter and my sex throbbed. The scent was distinctly male and I wanted nothing more than to have it all over me. My body was practically begging to be used.

He appeared in the doorway a moment later, carrying a wooden tray with some covered dishes. "Hungry?" He took a step forward and then stopped. His nostrils flared and his eyes glowed yellow.

"What's wrong with your eyes?"

He shook his head and the glow faded, his eyes returning to a natural shade of brown. "Sorry, I ... you—" He took a deep breath and started again. "I wasn't prepared for my wolf's reaction to you. I apologize." His eyes lingered on my chest a few moments longer than necessary and warmth pooled between my legs. I licked my lips and nodded. Hunger gnawed at my insides like a feral animal. And not just a hunger for food.

What was wrong with me?

"I'll just leave this at the foot of the bed." He inched closer, his heartbeat increasing and his breathing becoming more sporadic.

"That would be good. Thank you, sir—"

"Chad Fallon. No need for sir. We're all friends here, right?"

"Of course."

My breaths had been reduced to pants and I leaned forward, holding the wet sheet in place over my bare breasts and body. Even though he could see *everything*, it gave me a modicum of propriety. His dilated eyes and behavior told me he had noticed my arousal and was more than a little uncomfortable. To his credit, he didn't rush me like a drunkard with no impulse control.

If only the room would stop spinning, and my shoulder wasn't shooting fiery-darts-from-hell up and down my arm, I would be rubbing against him like a tavern wench. The image mortified me and I closed my eyes, trying to refocus my brain on anything other than him. I might not remember who I was, but I knew I wasn't a common barmaid.

I could not be that.

Chad took another step closer and his earthy musk

filled my lungs. He smelled better than the food on the tray he'd set at my feet. My grip on the sheet loosened as I contemplated dropping it away from my upper body. Would he accept the invitation if I did? Did I want him to?

A familiar female voice broke the moment for both of us. I leaned back against the headboard and Chad rushed backward several steps.

"So …" Eira entered the room, carrying a large bag. Another tall, lithe brunette followed her. "This is Charlotte Mason. She goes by Charlie."

They could have been sisters for all I knew, except Eira's eyes were the same brilliant blue as the sky outside. The second woman had brown eyes, more like Chad's. I thought I saw a flash of the same golden glow when our gazes met for the first time. Her scent was similar to the male, who continued to edge his way closer to the door.

"Is something wrong with you Chad?" The woman named Charlie turned her head to stare at the handsome male.

"She's emitting something." He paused. "It's making it very difficult to … remain in control."

Charlie's brows knit together and she looked back at me. "Emitting what, Chad?" She addressed him, but kept her hard gaze trained on me. "I don't sense anything."

He took another step into the doorway and nodded his head. "I would recommend informing all the males in our squad to give her a wide berth. She's in some kind of heat."

A laugh rippled from Eira's lips. "That actually makes more sense than her being ill."

Charlie waved and Chad disappeared. Then she pulled up a chair to the foot of the bed and sat. "I need to know everything you know. And you need to keep a lid on the dragon. No shifting. Do you understand? It's not safe."

I swallowed. The temperature in the room dropped again and Charlie shivered, her breath fogged in the air.

"Hey, D. Relax. No one here will hurt you." Eira approached the bedside with her hands outstretched. "I promise. You don't have to freeze anyone. We're all going to help get you where you need to go."

Ignoring the annoyed look on Charlie's face, I met Eira's glance and took a deep breath. "I like 'D.' It feels natural."

Eira grinned. "I just figured D for dragon, you know?"

A small laugh rolled up from my chest. The air in the room immediately warmed.

"So, Charlie would really like to hear your account of what went down before I found you in the woods," Eira said, reminding me of her friend's first question.

"There's not much. I escaped a stone prison using magick I didn't know I possessed. Then I saw this man appear in the center of a ring of stones. I took the dagger he used to cut his hand and mimicked his actions. When I touched the rock with my bloody palm, the world shifted and I found myself in a different place. A different circle."

Charlie's eyes widened. "Do you still have the dagger?"

I shook my head. I'd hidden it carefully in case I needed it again. Even if these were friends, I'd known them less than a day. "No, I lost it in the commotion in the village."

"There's the spot up in Boston that witches used to use, but I'm guessing it was probably the circle in South Carolina. I don't think she could have flown from Boston to the western border of the Appalachian with a bullet in her shoulder." Eira leaned against a table across the room and folded her arms over her chest.

"I want to send people to search for the dagger. Do you know how important that could be for us? If it's really one of the ancient keys to the Veil, we could use it to leave and live off-world." Charlie looked back at me. "What do you remember of the place there?"

"Nothing except the prison. It was tall and made of stone. The guards were dressed as knights, but I did not recognize their crest. The land outside was grassy, but I did not see a town." I glanced back to Eira. "Did you find anything I could wear? This sweat seems to be a constant condition for me, but I cannot continue to be naked. I'm afraid I made Chad quite uncomfortable."

"That old dog will survive," Eira answered, a smirk crossing her face. "I think he might've been more worked up than you."

"Worked up?" I grimaced. Our language differences were trying my patience.

"He says you smell like you're in a heat cycle. Which explains—"

"Like an animal?!"

"Sweetie, you're a dragon shifter. Animal tendencies kinda come with the territory."

Charlie moved from her chair. "I'll let the guys know to keep their dicks to themselves. Find her some clothes and see if she can move around. There's no way she doesn't have soldiers coming after her. We don't have any time left." She slapped the doorframe and waved as she disappeared into the hallway, leaving Eira alone with me.

"Eira, may I ask you something?"

"Sure," Eira answered, bending to dig in the bag she'd

brought with her. She pulled out several pieces of clothing and offered them to me. They were black and looked a lot like the clothes she was wearing—long breeches and a skin-tight tunic without sleeves. "Here, I grabbed these. I know from the tunic-dress-thing you were wearing that these are strange, but we need you to blend in, not stick out. Plus these are enchanted by a siren, so they self-clean. Very helpful for the sweating, and they should shift with you. Though we've never tested them on a dragon. The Lycans swear by them. But try not to shift, okay? Wolves are much easier to play off as normal beings than a lizard-shaped Mack truck."

A what? My earlier question about her lack of a heartbeat fled my mind. I didn't understand half of what she said. "Lycans? Meaning wolves? First, I find out that I am a dragon. Now, there are wolf people, too? Are there any ... humans left anywhere?"

"Sure there are. They all want us dead. At least most of them do. Which is why I'm telling you, no shifting." She laid the clothes on the bed and I pushed myself up, surprised I already felt stronger than I had an hour ago.

I hadn't eaten anything; the tray sat untouched at the foot of the bed. Some type of meat and lettuce smashed between layers of bread. It smelled good, but I'd never seen food made like that before.

"So the people firing at me in the village wanted to kill me because I am this dragon creature?"

"Yep."

I grabbed the piece of clothing that most resembled a shirt. It was squarish and had no shape, but the fabric was a beautiful midnight blue and smooth as silk, though much thicker and more durable. I grimaced when I raised my arm and pulled the top down over my head. A tingle spread over my skin and the fabric began to change.

"Bloody hell!" I pulled at the tunic, trying to get it off.

"No, wait." Eira pushed back my hands and jumped back when my breath turned to frost again. "I told you, the clothes are enchanted. It's just sizing itself to fit you."

"Oh." I took a deep breath and calmed my racing heart. Looking down, I watched the tunic gather and shrink, the neckline changed several times, like it was trying to decide what I preferred. It finally settled on a form-fitting shirt with a high wide neck. It was beautiful and the fabric had a stunning luster to it that reminded me of the incandescence of an abalone shell.

"You're small enough to go without a bra, but I highly recommend panties." She pointed to the scrap of black lace on top of the breeches. "They help keep certain areas from getting rubbed the wrong way."

I had no idea what a bra was, but the panties intrigued me. The lace was a beautiful design. I slipped them on and the same tingling sensation surged through them and they shrunk in size to perfectly fit. I picked up the pants next, surprised by how big they looked, but understanding now that they would shrink to fit. The idea that they would self-clean was amazing, too. Slipping my feet into them, I pulled them up slowly. The fabric was as soft as the shirt material, but a little thicker. And instead of the deep midnight blue, it was as black as a raven's wing.

They pulled and shrunk, fitting snugly to my waist and thighs and a little looser below my knees. It was a strange look, but comfortable. It was quite similar to what Eira wore herself. The colors were identical.

"Were these yours, Eira?"

She nodded. "Yeah, I had an extra pair I hadn't worn yet. Hopefully you don't mind dressing like me." She laughed gently, handing me a pair of stockings and boots. "The enchantment only bonds to one person, so these clothes will only fit you now."

"They are lovely. It is a fabric unlike anything I've ever seen."

"Calliope is known throughout the supernatural community for her amazing clothes. She lives in a small town called Sanctuary in the Texas Republic."

"Sounds like a nice place. And the clothes are lovely. I can't thank you enough and when I am able, I will pay you for them." I pulled on the black stockings and then the boots. Moments later, they fit like a glove. I burned with fever, but it was comforting to be fully clothed once more. And as snugly as they fit, the clothes were extremely comfortable.

"They're a gift," she answered, smiling.

CHAPTER 7

MILES

"She's here, Rose!" I slammed both palms down on the counter, hard enough to make sure Rose felt the frustration and anger that surged through my blood like a fiery inferno. "We've got to go look for her."

"After a thousand years, how can you be sure it's really her?" Rose's voice was soft, but her strength was not to be underestimated. I could feel the soothing effects of her power washing over me as we spoke.

"Stop. Just stop trying to handle me."

"You can't leave. You and your brother are the biggest threats to Xerxes, besides me. The Sisters would be left vulnerable without you."

"Then perhaps just one of us can go." My brother spoke softly from the barstool next to me.

Rose stood on the other side of the counter. Her gaze

traveled back and forth to each of us. She wasn't going to let us go. I could see it in her steely gray eyes. She was only about five and a half feet tall, but in human form, I didn't have a shot in hell of walking out of this town unless she wanted it to happen. No one would've ever guessed this petite brunette ruled the town of Sanctuary like a fierce warrior.

The Lamassu were unlike any other supernatural and were as powerful in human form as they were in their shifted guardian form. Magick didn't affect my dragon, but turning into an ancient, medieval creature the size of a couple of semi-trailers to go against her would not be appreciated by the town, though at this point that's exactly what I wanted to do.

I could feel Diana's dragon. Our mate was here. She was on earth. We'd always known she was alive. And now she'd escaped the Veil.

Perhaps it was a trick. It was possible Xerxes was behind the whole thing. Rumors circulated that he'd been seen near the sacred stones of Beara in Ireland on more than one occasion through the centuries. Eli and I had many friends throughout the world. Every few years, someone would visit the Castle and report what they'd seen or heard.

The heat of Eli's gaze burned into my temple. I turned and met his dark eyes and nodded. If she would let one of us go, I would stand down. Both of us had dreamt of Diana last night and both of us had awoken at the exact same point. Her dragon had been crying out to us, in pain and in need.

If she was entering her heat cycle, she would become

volatile until she found both of us. Even if she managed to find a male to sleep with, it wouldn't be enough. She was bound to us. Only sex with one or both of us would satisfy the primal need to mate.

"We have to find her soon." I hated to imagine what they'd done to her five centuries ago when she experienced her last one. Nothing short of torture and a lot of powerful magick would put down a Drakonae female in heat.

Eli nodded. He knew.

"Rose," Eli started again, "Let me go. The Sisters will be safe with you and Miles here."

Rose shook her head. "I need you both here."

"Fuck you, Rose!" A vicious growl tore from my throat. "If you had a chance to have Naram back in your life, you would take it." I jumped up from my seat at the counter and stormed from the diner, not giving her a chance to respond. The whole building shook as I slammed the door behind me, the glass from the French doors shattered.

Fuck the Sisters. Fuck Rose. I would have my mate back one way or another.

The oath wouldn't mean anything if something happened to her.

The pixies cursed at me for the broken door, but I didn't care. I crossed Main Street Circle and took the shortest path back to the confines of the Castle. Eli could clean up after me. He was the more rational one anyway. Our fathers had always called him the peacekeeper, though the few fights he participated in, he always won. Including pounding me into the floor a few times.

I, however, Miles of Blackmoor, first heir to the throne of the Veil, was the one who enjoyed a good fight and often went looking for one. Eli would rather find a different way to solve the problem.

My oath to Rose kept me from leaving without her permission and she knew it. Right now, I hated her for it. But I wasn't anything without honor and I would always stand by my word. Eli would, too. But maybe his shrewd perspective would find an option I'd overlooked.

CHAPTER 8

ELI

I sighed, watching my brother cross the circle and disappear from view. Rose touched my hand and I yanked it back with a snarl. She might think me less volatile than Miles, but really I just hid it better.

Rose's eyes flashed white for a brief second and I saw the hint of fangs behind her small, pink lips. Magick was tense in the air and I knew if pressed, she could easily overpower me. But mostly I could smell her fear. She worried that we would leave her. Leave the Sisters.

"We gave you our oath, Rose. Doesn't mean we aren't pissed as hell about it right now, but we will always honor our word." I ran my hands through my hair and tried to stifle the growling roar rumbling in my chest. "Send someone else. At least send Bailey and Erick, or a couple wolves up to the Underground checkpoint in Ada. If anyone has heard anything about her, they would've."

"The bond will pull her here. She's a dragon for gods' sake, Eli."

"She's in heat, Rose. Her mind will not be right. She could expose herself and others without realizing it or being able to control the dragon inside her. Our females, when they're in heat, seek out the bed of *any* male, but unless they join with their bonded mate or mates, they can kill out of frustration when the need is not sated. She will burn with a hunger for sex, not unlike a starving vampire seeks blood."

Understanding finally filled her big brown eyes. "Your brother isn't going to do anything stupid, is he, like turn into a dragon and fly away?"

I chuckled and shook my head. "I haven't seen him this pissed since the day we escaped the Veil and realized Diana had been snatched away from the circle at the last second. But, no. He won't endanger the town or go against our oath. Our honor binds us to the House of Lamidae until they need us no longer or we die."

"Dragons are as close to immortal beings as I am. You're not dying anytime soon."

Shaking my head. "Perhaps. But if she dies, our human hearts, our humanity, will die with her."

Rose's gaze snapped up to meet mine. "What does that mean, Eli?"

I lowered my voice to a whisper. "Let's just say, Miles and I have been living on borrowed time for centuries. Our father believed in the old magick of the Drakonae and we were bonded heart and soul to Diana when we wed. It makes for a stronger, more powerful mate connection. We've wondered for centuries why the Incanti brothers hadn't killed her and ended our human lives."

"You'll die?" Her eyes widened, genuinely surprised.

"Only our human halves. The dragon will emerge to take its vengeance, killing everything in its path until the lost mate is avenged or the dragon is killed. That's why there are stories from the Middle Ages of knights fighting dragons in caves."

I frowned, remembering those dark times. "Those were the fallen, the ones whose humanity was lost when their mates died or were killed. They were cast out of the Veil when Kevan and Leif Incanti seized power." Several of the fallen had been close family members. There was nothing to be done for them. A full-sized dragon could only hide on earth for so long.

"I had no idea," Rose uttered.

I shrugged. "You were busy with your own problems. You found us shortly after and we never looked back, knowing they had all four daggers. It was either hide and wait to lose our humanity, or go with you and help as long as we could. We knew if we became like the other fallen, you were powerful enough to kill us."

"So you never said anything?"

"After centuries passed, we suspected that they'd imprisoned her for whatever reason and didn't plan to kill her. Then when the Sisters said she would return one day, we allowed a little of our hope to return. Plus, by then we knew Xerxes had one of the keys. Our eyes and ears around the world couldn't get close to him, though, and he never removed the dagger from his person."

Rose propped her elbows on the counter and leaned forward. "Just reminds me that after all these years, the world still has many secrets." She sighed and then looked back at me. "I will find someone willing to connect with the Mason wolf pack running the Underground out of Ada. You and Miles have given your lives to help me protect the House of Lamidae. I hope you know I will do everything I can, short of letting you go after her yourselves. Miles just—"

"I know."

A purple-haired pixie sidled up to Rose's side and smiled at me. "Y'all done fightin' yet?" Maven spoke gingerly, probably afraid one or both of us would snarl at her.

"We're good, Maven. Thank you," Rose answered before I could.

"Good." Her eyes brightened. "I don't like it when family fights. Bad auras floating around are downers." She flicked her wrist toward us and a cloud of iridescent pixie dust filled the air around our faces.

I snorted and stood from my chair. "Maven," I growled. "I don't like that stuff."

"Your auras do. Both of you are already a brighter, cheerful yellow." Her grin spread wide across her face.

Rose shook her head and smiled before walking into the kitchen.

The pixie turned her attention back to me and I held up a hand. "No more." I could already feel the first dose seeping into my skin. Its magickal cleansing warmth spread across my skin and I sighed. For a supernatural, pixie dust was like a mega dose of dopamine. Stress would just melt away. "Thank you, Maven."

The pixie darted from behind the counter and threw her arms around my waist. She was barely five feet tall, but packed a wallop if you pissed her off. I squeezed her shoulders gently and ran my fingers through her silky purple hair. It smelled like spun sugar and felt like the finest Asian silk.

She stepped back and I looked down at her sparkling blue eyes filled with love and compassion. I'd slept with Maven a couple of times over the years. Nothing serious, but we'd become friends. She'd always known my heart was taken.

Touching her hair made me remember Diana's fine, white-blond hair and her lilac-scented skin, but I couldn't remember her face. It'd been so long. Those memories were cloudy. My hands clenched and unclenched. I took a deep breath and frowned.

"Diana is a lucky woman, Miles. Everything will be okay."

"When she's safe in Sanctuary, perhaps." I answered, running my knuckles down Maven's cheek. "Thank you for saying that, though."

The bell on the door rang. Travis and Garrett McLennon walked in and nodded to Maven and me. I dropped my hand from her face and moved around them to the door, stepping carefully around the pile of broken glass.

Travis had lived in Sanctuary for years, but his brother, Garrett, had only recently arrived. The two guys said hi to Maven and sat at the counter where Rose and I had been. They proceeded to flirt and tease Maven while she served them each a mug of coffee.

Pulling open the door, I nearly collided with Erick Thorson's little mate, Bailey Ross, or D'Roth as we found out during her Protector ceremony. Her Caribbean blue eyes sparkled with life and she flashed me a demure smile.

"Eli," she said, "I'm so excited to hear about Diana.

Rose sent me to get Travis and Garrett. She's sending them to Ada to find out if the Underground has heard about her whereabouts."

I raised an eyebrow. "Really?" For some reason, I'd assumed she would send one of the Protectors rather than Lycans. The sun-proof vampires could move fast during the day or night, making them nearly invisible to the human eye. Wolves were strong and fast, but no match for a healthy vamp.

"Yes, really. Erick and I offered to go, but one of the Sisters said that the trip would be more productive if Lycans went."

"Why?"

Bailey pursed her lips.

"Is it because of Astrid's vision?"

Her blue eyes widened in shock. "How did you know?"

The Sisters always kept them in the loop. They were their first line of defense and privy to everything that happened inside the Castle, whether it was related to something personal or magickal. Arlea, the current Oracle of Lamidae, was beginning to feel her age. The visions of a new Protector were the herald of her passing. I knew we would lose her soon.

"We know everything that happens in the Castle," I said, rolling my neck to loosen the knot forming at the base. "Especially when it involves the impending loss of a dear friend."

Bailey nodded and frowned. Her pulsed raced and I detected a more than a hint of anxiety. Arlea's illness was no doubt hitting her hard.

"It's time, Bailey. She has lived a good, long life. She's ready to rest."

"I've lost so many people. It's hard to accept. I wish there was something someone could do. There seems to be a spell or magickal something for almost everything in this town."

Truth be told, there probably *was* a spell that could save Arlea, but I couldn't break Bailey's heart and tell her the old woman wanted to pass on. Arlea had already let go of the visions that would lead the Sisters to the next Protector. That was the first step in her ritual to step down as the Oracle of the House of Lamidae.

And Astrid had already picked up that mantle and was wielding it like a pro. She'd had two visions repeatedly over the last week—both about new Protectors. The entire Castle was abuzz with the news. Strangely enough, Astrid wasn't the only one who'd been having visions. One of Astrid's nieces had been having visions for several years already, but she was only seven and too young to take on the mantle of Oracle.

The Sisters hadn't been this excited in centuries. With Bailey taking the fifth place in the spell that would protect them permanently from Xerxes' advances —or so they told us. Only Rose truly knew the details of the spell. My brother and I were merely guards and facilitators of safe procreation for the Sisters. With two more Protectors being located in such a short timespan, everyones' hopes were riding high. Perhaps, just perhaps, the spell to free the Sisters would be completed soon.

With the spell's completion, mine and my brother's oath to Rose would also be fulfilled. Not that I didn't enjoy running a BDSM club that facilitated an unconventional way for a group of supernatural oracles to continue having baby girls, but it would be nice to travel the world again. We'd been in Texas a very long time.

I looked down at Bailey's expectant expression.

"Everything happens for a reason, Bailey. Arlea will live on in our hearts and our minds. Nothing will ever erase her shrill, nasally voice from my memory," I answered, chuckling. "Or her dry sense of humor."

"This is true," Bailey answered, a hint of a smile turning up the corners of her mouth.

"I know she would enjoy a visit from you."

The suggestion made her cheeks color slightly. She'd gotten better at hiding her emotions. Erick was doing an excellent job training her, but when something was really bothering her, Bailey was an open book.

She nodded and looked away.

I patted her shoulder and left. The little, gold bell jingled as I closed the front door and stepped into the nippy, winter air. Yesterday's rain had shifted the weather and now, instead of a steady southern wind, we were getting the first hint of a frost.

Winter wasn't here yet, but it was coming soon.

CHAPTER 9

DIANA

"**G**lad to see your dragon DNA speeds up the healing process," Eira commented as I followed her down a narrow hallway. "You seem to be moving okay, which is good. The whole pack is about ready to move. We have several guests, other than you, in tow and need to get on the road now that it's dark."

I wiped my forehead with the back of my hand and sighed. My arm did feel a lot better, but this fever would be the death of me. And every time a male passed, I had to hold myself back because the beast inside wanted to leap on him. Each one smelled so good—just enough musk and spice to make my legs quiver and my heartbeat race.

By now, I also wished I'd eaten that strange meal Chad had brought earlier. My stomach growled. I had no idea when my last meal had been.

Eira dug in her bag and produced a small, rectangular bar wrapped in paper. "It's not much, but it should tide you over until I can find you something a little more filling."

I took it from her and smelled it. The scent of honey and oats came through the paper and my mouth watered. I ripped the wrapper at one end and slid the bar out. It looked like horse feed, but it smelled delicious. There were little chunks of something brown in it that smelled sweeter than the honey. I took a bite and moaned.

"Don't go making love to the granola bar," Eira giggled. "We'll find you a proper man to take care of those needs."

I took another bite as we rounded a corner. "I don't think that's a good idea. The last man that touched me ... his hand turned blue. I think I may have frozen it."

"Note to self. Do not touch D without warning her first." She pushed open a heavy, steel door and we found ourselves outside under a starry sky.

About fifteen people stood in the group. They were all wearing dark clothes and most of them had on heavy coats. Eira and I were the lightest clothes of the entire bunch. Neither of us even wore sleeves.

I leaned closer to her. "Why aren't you cold like everyone else? Does it have to do with the fact that you have no heartbeat?"

She chuckled. "You noticed that, huh? Yep, I'm a vampire. Blue eyes, fangs." She flashed some sharp teeth and I gasped in surprise. "Don't worry. I won't drink your blood without asking. I was kinda wondering what a dragon might taste like, though."

I took a step back. "You drink blood? Instead of eating? Are you a demon?"

She turned back to me sharply. "Not that I know of, but I can be bitchy if insulted enough."

"I apologize." I did not mean to insult the only person on this earth I considered a friend. "Please forgive me. I'm ignorant of this world and my surprise clouded my judgment."

She sighed and pointed me toward the right side of the group. "It's okay. I just need to eat and it will be a while before the group stops and I can hunt. They don't really like to share with me."

"Share what?"

"Blood, sweetie. No one in the group fancies getting bitten. But, there are farms along the way, so I'll find something quietly later on tonight."

"Strangers just let you drink from them?"

"No, I have to persuade them."

I decided I really didn't want to know how she persuaded them. But the idea of allowing her to drink my blood did cross my mind. I certainly owed her for saving my life out in the woods.

"Does it hurt?"

She paused mid-step and turned back to me. Her blue eyes were ringed with a tinge of red now. "The bite?"

I nodded.

"A little. But it doesn't last." She stared at my neck and then back to my face. "I can't take the chance, though. But, you're sweet for even considering it. Your body's defense system might kick in and deep freeze my face." She patted her cheeks and smiled. "I like my face just how it is. Frostbite can be a bitch."

The corners of my lips turned up at her colorful speech. I only understood about half of her words, but I got the general idea. I couldn't blame her for not wanting to risk it. Still, I felt bad because I really didn't know how to control the power within me. I knew it was tied to my emotions, for the moment. Hopefully, I would be able to control it better in time.

"Stay in pairs and stay in sight of the pair in front of you," Charlie's voice carried across the still chilly air. We will keep a steady jog for as long as D can hold the pace. Then we'll drop to a walk."

Eira briefly touched my arm and we headed down the road and away from the dark building. There were several pairs ahead of us and several behind. Everyone stayed about fifty paces apart. Strategically, it was smart. If something happened to one pair. The others would have enough time to assess the situation and either help or run.

I prayed to whatever god might be listening to protect us on the journey.

⚜

HOURS PASSED. AT LEAST IT FELT LIKE HOURS. MY LEGS felt like lead weights, but I refused to be the reason the group had to stop. My beast needed to figure out a way to keep going for me. All I received was an inner growl and the temperature around me plummeted instantly. The cold air soothed my overheated skin and breathed new life into my aching limbs.

The ground around Eira and me started to frost over. The pine trees along the edge of the road began to sag under the weight of icicles.

"It's feeling a lot like Christmas around here all of a sudden. You okay, D?"

"I feel much better now, thank you. My inner dragon is just helping me out a little. What is Christmas?" My heartbeat had slowed and my breathing was even and unlabored. The icy air invigorated me and once again, I was able to keep up with Eira's long, ground-eating stride. She hadn't slowed once since we started.

"Oh ... well, nobody I know really celebrates it anymore. But technically, Christmas is in five days. It's an old tradition that humans once celebrated. We'll be on the road still." She sighed. "I used to really enjoy all the decorations during the Christmas season. That's mostly what I miss. Anyway, it will take twenty days to get to Ada. We'll run about eight hours every night and hole up in a hotel during the day. A big group of us traveling together in broad daylight is too suspicious. I have a ring, but I'm still way more comfortable in the dark and so are the wolves. We're used to living in the shadows."

"A ring?" That statement hadn't made sense.

"Vampires can't go out in the sunlight, unless they have an enchanted bit from a witch to protect them." She flashed her left hand toward me and I caught the glint of something gold on her first finger. "I'm pretty good pals with a couple of witches in Ada and they hooked me up with this little charm. So no bursting into flames for me."

"So you would burn in the sunlight?"

She nodded.

"That's scary."

"Not when you've been dealing with it for over a thousand years. I've only had the ring about a hundred. So, darkness and I are still best friends. I'm glad Charlie and the others choose to make their runs at night. It's harder for the soldiers to track us in small groups on foot. We tried cars for a while, but it attracted too much attention in the towns. Too many video feeds."

Again with the language barrier. Or time lapse ... how long had I been in that cell? "What is a video feed?"

"It's a machine that captures a streaming picture."

I shook my head.

"It's hard to explain. Just think of it as eyes watching you from far away. I'll point one out to you when we get into a town. Always avoid looking directly at the cameras. The governments can track you through them and the SECR is a kill-first-don't-bother-with-questions type of place."

We crested a hill and I saw a lake on the distant horizon. The road curled back and forth a bit before curving off to the left toward a group of sparkling lights.

"How are the fires so bright from so far away?"

"They aren't made of fire. It's electricity. Like the lights in the building where we were."

"The white torches hanging from the ceiling."

A soft snicker bubbled from Eira.

It might be funny to her, but it was frustrating to me.

"How old are you, Eira?"

"I've lost track. Maybe eleven-hundred."

My mouth formed a surprised o-shape. "How old do you think I am?"

"From the way you speak, I'd have to guess at least eight- or nine-hundred. You really remind me of England, pre-Norman invasion. Plus that's when most of the shit went down with the Drakonae taking over in the Veil. It would make sense that your impression of history would end there. But I could be wrong. Usually as most supernaturals age, our speech patterns change to fit where we live." She took a deep breath. "Makes it easier to move on."

I wondered who she'd lost, but now didn't feel like the

right time to press her with more questions. Instead, I focused on the road ahead.

A scream from behind jolted me from my thoughts and I almost tumbled to the ground. I still ended up on my bum after Eira pushed me off the road into some shrubs. She was gone from my sight before I could speak.

A loud *crack, crack, crack* in the distance sounded like the weapons the soldiers had fired at me in the town. My shoulder ached at the memory, but the beast within wanted me to stand up and fight. Something told me cowering behind plants was not typically my response. *It* certainly hadn't been when I escaped that prison tower.

More screams came from down the road. Several wolves passed me, headed toward the pandemonium. Their eyes were bright yellow and glowed in the moonlight. They were bigger than any wolf I'd ever seen. Their backs were easily level with my waist.

I crept from behind the branches. Ice spread across the ground in front of me as I walked. My breath was frosty and I could feel the magick tingling in my fingers, waiting to be released.

Growls and shrieks filled the air.

These people had saved my life. I could not stand by and do nothing. Breaking into a run, I followed the sounds toward the mayhem. The *crack, crack, crack* of those weapons ripped through the din of the fighting.

I turned a corner and came face-to-face with an unfamiliar soldier dressed in black. He raised the black metal weapon and I threw up my hands, covering him in a solid block of ice before he could fire at me. My heart lurched in my chest. I could hear him screaming from inside the ice. The terror in his voice was hard to stomach. But he'd made my choice for me when he'd raised his weapon. His heartbeat raced and then slowly faded and stopped.

He was dead. I'd killed him. Just like the others before him who had threatened me. Their weapons were strong, but not as strong as the magick I wielded. I could help these people fight. Help them escape to a better place. That is what Eira said they were doing. Merely moving supernaturals from one land where they were hunted to a land where they could live in peace. This was an honorable fight and these soldiers were on the wrong side of it.

CHAPTER 10

DIANA

I moved swiftly through the darkness. After the first encounter, my vision had changed, allowing me to see clearly in the dark. The inner beast had come forward somehow and now I could see clear outlines of everyone in the roadway.

They wore strange-looking masks made of metal and other materials I wasn't familiar with. Their weapons were unlike anything I had ever seen. In the dark, fire seemed to spew from the mouths of the metal pipes, but the projectiles that fired from them were too small and too fast for her to see.

I froze several more men with their backs to me and tried to ignore the cries that echoed from within the frozen blocks. The ice wasn't enough to freeze them instantly; instead, they suffocated, slowly running out of air.

There was nothing I could do. I didn't understand my

powers enough to change my fighting tactics. It was all I could do to keep the beast in check and not shift again. The dragon wanted to, but I feared that if I did, I wouldn't be able to tell friend from foe.

A heavy body slammed into me from the side and air whooshed from my lungs. I tried to cry out, but instead, a blast of icy air exploded from within me and knocked the person away. I rolled to my stomach and glanced up at him. A tall soldier dressed all in black like the rest. His mask had been knocked off and he was feeling around blindly for it. I crept forward, grabbed the mask, and crushed it in my hand. His weapon lay a few feet in the opposite direction.

I reached it first.

"I saw you ice my buddy a few seconds ago. We will find you, dragon bitch, rest assured. Even if every single one of us dies. Now that they know you exist, they will never stop looking for you."

My heart climbed into my throat and I bit back a growl of frustration. I shouldn't have to kill to survive. They were making me into a murderer.

Another form floated past, moving so fast I barely saw her except when she paused behind the speaking soldier and snapped his neck. I shuddered and backed away from his fallen body. She disappeared a moment later.

The moonlight reflected off the smooth cheek of the fallen man. Barely a whisker. He was so young. It wasn't right that he had to die. But it was them or us.

Eira had spared me from having to take another life that evening. For that, I was grateful.

The sounds of the fight died out shortly thereafter.

The *crack, crack, crack* of those terrible weapons had ceased. The night was still again. Quiet.

The wolves shifted in front of me and I gasped in amazement. Eira told me they were shifters, but seeing it in person was so much more ... real. It wasn't a story anymore. These were people who lived, fought, and were willing to die so that I and the others they were smuggling might have a chance in the place they called the Texas Republic.

I recognized Chad's scent before he approached. He paused about ten feet away and I felt a rush of desire flood my body. I burned on the inside, but ice spread across the ground turning the pavement and grassy area where we stood white. It was such a contradiction. The hotter I felt, the colder everything became around me.

"You okay?"

Taking a deep breath, I nodded my head.

"Thank you for helping. I know stepping in with strangers couldn't have been easy. You saved lives tonight. It was a big unit and we were having trouble covering everyone. They still got one of the guys we pulled out of Monroe. Silver bullet to the head," he added.

"One of the soldiers was just a boy." My voice was flat. The coldness around me faded as I remembered the man Eira had killed before he could shoot me.

"A lot of them are young. They're conscripted at age eighteen. A four-year service term is required by law." Chad shoved his hands into his pockets and rolled his neck from side to side, popping joints with each movement.

"So they are all young?" I swallowed bile. "Where are the trained warriors? They shouldn't be sending mere boys out to fight for them. Cowards."

A soft chuckle slipped from between his lips. "Those are fighting words. I bet you were a hell of a spitfire in another life."

My mind drifted to the strong, handsome men I'd seen in my dreams before escaping that cold cell. Two men—both with dark hair and eyes that glowed like living flames. I never woke from those dreams feeling afraid. Only longing. And love.

"I wish I knew," I finally answered. "Eira says I could be eight-hundred years old. What if everything I knew is gone? Everyone I might have loved ... or who loved me ..."

He took several steps closer and I held my hand up to stop him. His scent was already making me wet between my legs. I didn't trust myself not to leap on him if he came any closer. Whatever this heat was that had taken hold of me had progressed to the point where I barely had the ability to think clearly around a man.

"Sorry," he mumbled and stepped back.

"It is not your fault that I am taken over by ... whatever this is. But you and your friends sheltered me and fought for me tonight, too. Helping was the least I could do. Was anyone else hurt?"

He shook his head. "No, just the one."

Charlie approached him from behind and Eira blurred to my side a moment later.

"I told you to stay down."

"I guess I don't follow directions very well."

She shrugged. "You probably don't, since someone had you locked in a tower in another dimension."

I couldn't stop the corners of my mouth from curving upward at her sarcasm. But as more people gathered, the severity of the situation robbed me of humor. Bodies littered the ground. My ice had coated them all with a thin layer of frost and their faces were haunting.

"Will they come back?"

"You mean rise like zombies?" Chad snorted.

I frowned, not understanding his question.

"That's not what she meant, idiot," Eira snapped. "She doesn't even know what a zombie is."

"Yes," Charlie spoke, finally answering my question.

Focusing on her, I took a deep breath. "Because of me?"

She nodded. "You're something they've never seen before. A creature only found in stories from mythology and in books that were burned decades ago. The general population doesn't know what dragons are."

"So people *used* to know?"

"Yes." Charlie answered and then turned to Chad. "Gather the rest. We run together the last five miles. We have to get to Lake Kentucky before morning and get settled into that small hotel off the highway."

He sprinted off and Eira pointed me toward the road. "We're almost there, D. Then we can rest."

"And do it all again tomorrow night."

"Yep. Though hopefully without the soldiers. It should take them at least two days to regroup, collect their dead, and send another task force," Eira said, breaking into a full run.

I struggled for a moment to keep up until I remembered the trick with the cold air. Calling on something inside me, my breath became icy cold and the air around me once again held the bite of a new frost.

"Damn, girl. If I didn't like the cold, I'd be freezing my ass off."

"Sorry, I just can't keep up unless—"

"Don't worry. It's a pretty nifty power to have. I'm guessing you don't breathe fire though," she laughed. "That's something I've always thought would be cool to see. Never met a dragon face-to-face. Even way back, they were pretty private."

We ran quietly for a few moments before I finally managed to speak the words I'd been holding back. "The heat is getting worse, Eira. And I keep seeing these two men when I close my eyes. Well, the same man, but there are two of them. I think they are twins. My body is so hot it feels like I'm on fire."

"So it's a memory. That's good," she exclaimed. "Maybe these guys are still around somewhere. It's highly probable that they're dragons, too. I've heard of supernaturals occasionally mixing with humans, but it's very rare."

"But if all the dragons are in the Veil where I came from, I should try to go back there. Not stay here."

"You can't go back," she said, touching my shoulder. We both stopped and I caught her blue gaze. "You have to have the dagger to travel between this world and the Veil."

I knew that. What I truly wrestled with was continuing on this journey. What if I should be going back the way I came? In addition, my presence put these people in extra danger because soldiers were hunting me.

Averting my eyes, I began jogging again. She loped along at my side and whispered. "Don't tell Charlie or anyone else in this group that you know where the dagger is. Do you understand me?"

"Yes." Somehow she'd guessed. I hadn't told anyone I hid the dagger, but she knew, and she wouldn't tell.

"There's enough going on in this world. The last thing

we need are a bunch of dragons coming after us too because a pack of werewolves thought it would be cool to invade. At least humans get old and eventually die. If you're any example, I have a feeling dragons hold a grudge for a really, really long time."

CHAPTER 11

DIANA

"Shit!" Eira's voice rang through my ears.

I opened my eyes. The hotel room was white. An inch of frost clung to the walls and ceiling. The bed was a block of ice and the floor looked like a frozen pond.

"I leave for a couple of hours and you turn this place into the North Pole. This is not good."

I sat up and wiped tears from my face. The other dream had come back this time.

"What's wrong?" She tiptoed across the sheet of ice and sat on the edge of the hard, frozen blanket.

"I didn't tell you before, but I've had another dream."

"So the two hot guys aren't the only men in your life?"

"I don't believe the men are overheated in the dream. They appear—"

"No, no, I mean handsome. Hot is an expression for

appealing. Sorry, what was the dream? You look like you were crying."

"I was in this dark room. I can't see any faces, but I hear a baby crying. I ask for the baby but no one answers me. The crying gets fainter and fainter, like the baby is moving farther away from me. It just repeats over and over until I wake up." I took a deep breath and looked around the room again. Everything was coated with ice, just like the inside of the cell I'd escaped.

"The cell where they kept me was covered in ice like this. So thick I could barely see the stones on the walls or floor any longer." My mind was spinning so fast. "Eira, I should remember having a child. That's not something I could forget, is it? I would know if I had a baby." I wiped another tear from my cheek and shuddered.

"Sweetie, I'm so sorry."

Eira tentatively wrapped an arm around my shoulders and I turned to lean into her. The tears flowed down my cheeks and froze solid once they left my skin, clinking against the frozen blanket covering the bed.

"Even if I did have a baby. It's been a long time, hasn't it?"

"Probably so, but I'll help you any way I can. Maybe my friend in Ada has a spell to help you get back your lost memories. Just hang in there and try not to freeze the whole hotel. Those wolves down the hall might have fur, but they'd rather not sleep in it."

Always trying to lighten the mood, Eira was definitely good for a smile. She was cheerful, sassy at times, but no-nonsense—an interesting combination and a welcome companion.

Eira was tense when it came to touching me, not that I

could blame her, but she genuinely seemed unafraid that I was a dragon. In fact, I think she may have liked me more because of it. I was this fantastical creature she'd never encountered in all her centuries of life.

The idea that there might be someone out there who could help me piece together my memories made me want to get to Ada even more.

I pulled away from her and stood. "When do we leave?"

Eira chuckled. "That got your antenna up, didn't it?"

I cocked an eyebrow and she grinned again.

"Sorry, I meant it attracted your attention," she replied.

"Oh ... then yes. My antenna is up."

"We can't leave until dark. Plus, this is the second check-in for Manda. She popped in at our last stop and Charlie had a short conversation with her dad about you, via Manda's teleportation, before we headed out that night."

"Who is Manda?" I wasn't even going to ask about teleportation.

"A Djinn who works with the Mason pack. She helps keep us one step ahead of Xerxes' and the SECR soldiers. Although after last night, I wonder if they suspect her alliance with us."

"Who is Xerxes? And what is a Djinn?"

"A Djinn is a supernatural that can appear anywhere in the world with the snap of their fingers. No walking or running. Just poof and they're there."

"That sounds like a pretty helpful power to have."

Eira nodded. "Xerxes is an evil, supernatural badass who wants to rule the world. He's slowly and successfully infiltrating the human systems of government with his own lackeys and putting down supernaturals that don't support him."

"I take it that you, Charlie, and the others in this group are against him ruling the world."

"Yeah, big time. He's an ass and has something up his sleeve that we can't quite put a pin on. All of the Djinn work for him, but Manda has gone rogue and helped us out of a huge jam on more than one occasion. Whatever her reasons are for betraying the Djinn king, Cyrus, and Xerxes, we don't know, but we'll take the help."

"What if she is toying with you?"

"Then life will suck donkey balls when she finally betrays us."

I snorted at the image and shook my head.

"For now, the Masons are semi-careful. There are measures in place in Ada and some of the other larger bases to slow down the Djinn, should they ever show up uninvited. But, you're right. Mostly it would be a shit-storm and a lot of people would get hurt, or worse."

"Are Charlie and Chad wed?"

Eira glanced up, catching my gaze. "Stay away from that dog. He and Charlie aren't an item, but he'll sleep with you and then sleep with the girl down the hall the same night. You don't want any of that," she said, waving her hands toward the door. "I don't care how horny you get. We're gonna find those two hotties you keep dreaming about and you can do them to your heart's content." Her vocabulary still perplexed me, but I knew what she meant this time.

She walked to the door, cracked it open slightly, and peered out. "We should find you something to eat. Can't run all night on an empty stomach. Although, I have to give you props for last night. With your wound and mental state, I didn't think you would keep up."

"My wound is healed. I can barely see the mark where it was. Did you eat yet, Eira?"

Eira shut the door and licked her lips. As she turned back toward me, I could see a narrow ring of red around her blue irises.

"You haven't, have you? How long are you going to starve yourself to protect me?"

"I'm not." She closed the door and turned the deadbolt.

I frowned.

"Okay, fine. I am. You're a dragon. Everyone wants you. Even Charlie's dad, Randall. They want to interrogate you when we get to Ada. I've got to make sure you stay safe. I claimed responsibility for you when we pulled you out of that ditch where you crash-landed. Technically, they can't take you from me without a fight because I claimed you as my ward."

"I'm not a child. I can protect myself."

"I know, but you looked young at first and so beaten down. You were naked and covered in blood. Every mothering instinct I never had shuffled out to stake a claim."

She pretended to be all tough and hard, but I could see through the chinks in her armor. "Thank you."

Eira shrugged. "I protect people. I always have. You're just my newest stray. I brought in Chad, too. That's why he does what I say and—"

"The real reason you don't want me to sleep with him."

"You know, for a gal who can't remember anything, you're quick."

This crazy world I'd been thrust into so violently wasn't all that bad with Eira to guide my way. But I had a feeling life might get ugly if I ever lost her. I moved to the dresser where a clear cup sat with some white paper packets in it. I dumped them out and touched the hilt of the large knife she'd given me to wear strapped to my thigh. Pulling it from the sheath, I pressed the sharp blade to my palm until it cut through.

"D! What the hell?" Eira blurred to my side and tried to grab the knife, but surprisingly I held my own. She swore something I didn't understand under her breath, but stopped trying to pull the knife away.

I raised my hand over the empty glass and let my blood trickle into it, filling it at least halfway, before she started protesting that it was too much. Opening my hand, I held it up and blew ice-cold air across my bloody palm. The bleeding stopped almost instantly and the cut began to knit back together.

Eira sucked in a quick gasp beside me and leaned closer to my hand. "How did you know you could do that?"

I really didn't know. It'd felt almost like muscle memory. "Instinct I guess," I replied.

"Thank you for the blood, but you really didn't have to do this. I can go weeks if I need to."

"But you don't need to. And since we don't want to freeze your pretty face off, I figured this was the next best way."

Eira laughed out loud and held up the cup. "I never thought I'd get to taste the blood of a dragon. It's an honor."

"You are welcome. I hope it helps."

She nodded and took a long drag from the cup. I

grimaced watching her, not able to imagine the taste of blood being pleasant, but she certainly seemed to be enjoying it. A minute later she was draining the cup of the last drop and licking her lips.

"Well? What does dragon blood taste like?"

"Better than a thousand-dollar bottle of wine. Holy mother of the gods, you taste like pure energy."

I smiled and dabbed my forehead with the back of my hand. My heat was getting worse again. And I could smell every single male in this establishment. Chad was two rooms away. But there were ten other males on this floor with us and I wanted all of them. By the gods indeed, there had to be a way to get this to stop. I eyed the closed door and then let my gaze flick back to Eira.

"Your heart's racing. D, what's wrong?"

"It's the heat cycle, it's building again. It's a pain worse than starving. I know I can't give in, but I keep considering it. I'm afraid the pain will overrule my will."

Eira set the cup on the table by the window. "Just lie down and count the dots on the ceiling. I'll be back shortly with something for you to eat. Do. Not. Leave. This. Room."

I walked back to the iced-over bed and sat down, the blankets crunched under my weight. It was ridiculous. How hard was it to sleep on a bed without freezing it into a block of ice? "Bloody hell."

"It will get better. You will figure out your powers or we will find someone who can help." She said, slipping from the room.

The door closed with an ominous snap. I listened as her footsteps became fainter. I wanted to leave, but I wouldn't. Being shot at again or taken by someone was not on my agenda for the day. Still, it was hard for me not to leave the room and explore.

But, every time I stared at the closed door, I remembered the screaming and yelling of the people in the streets, and the pain and terror I'd felt when the soldiers started firing at me with those metal weapons. Eira told me they were called guns and could strike targets from a long range.

I'd never seen anything that shot a projectile besides a bow and arrow. I found it strange I could remember tidbits about how life should be, but nothing specific to my life. It was like they'd taken my memories of my life and the people I knew and left me with only factual information. But even the facts were foggy.

I pressed my lips together tightly, closed my eyes, and screamed on the inside. When I opened my eyes again, the whole room had another layer of frosty ice covering every surface—the furniture, both beds, and the mirror in the washroom. *Bloody hell!*

The only thing not covered in ice was me. And because of this horrid mating heat, the ice covering the blankets beneath me was melting. How could I be so warm and yet still able to cover an entire room with ice the moment I felt frustration?

CHAPTER 12

DIANA

The door to the room squeaked and shuddered on its frozen hinges as Eira pushed it open. She stepped into the room and her feet crunched on the frosted carpet.

"D! Really? Again?" Her voice was filled with more annoyance than usual. She closed the door and yanked one of the chairs free from the floor, shaking it until all the ice broke free. Then she sat at the frost-covered table and dropped a brown paper bag on it. The smells coming from the bag were greasy, but appetizing. My stomach rumbled hungrily at this point, willing to eat anything.

I followed her example and cleaned off the other chair next to the small table by the window. After brushing away as much ice as would come loose, I sat down and sighed.

"I am sorry. I didn't mean to do it."

"They will be able to track us because of this. The hotel will report it."

"I can leave. You have all done enough already. I should not be putting you in danger because of my lack of discipline." I started to stand, but she put her hand on mine and then jerked it back.

"Damn, girl. For all this ice, you're burning up. Kind of an oxymoron, you freezing the room, yet scorching to to the touch like an overfed furnace."

"I don't know what you meant by half of that, but yes. I am confused by the conflicting elements. On top of that, I feel as though I will go mad if I do not find a man to ... satisfy me soon."

"Don't you dare. You'll end up icing them or the whole hotel."

I grimaced. She was right, but it was so hard to hold back. "I can smell them. Chad is only two rooms away and there are ten other males in this establishment right now. I know exactly where they are. Their scent calls to me like—"

"Like nothing, dragon lady. You need to keep your icy breath and fiery skin to yourself until we get to Ada and talk to my friend."

"What will your friend be able to do?"

"Hopefully break whatever spell is messing with your memory. I've never met a supernatural who didn't have control of their powers. Whatever's missing in your brain has to be affecting your abilities." She opened the bag and handed me a warm bit of food wrapped in brown paper.

I unwrapped it and took a bite of the strange conglomeration of meat, cheese, and bread. It was not unpleasant, but it certainly was not delicious, either. My stomach couldn't care less and I ate it quickly, relishing every greasy bite.

Licking my fingers, I eyed the strange-looking yellow strips Eira was putting out on a napkin in front of me.

"Guess I don't have to ask if you liked the hamburger," she said, smiling. "Try the French fries. They're the best around here, so I've been told. We're heading out this afternoon to try and get a jump start on the next stopover."

"That thing did not taste like ham." I stated, before biting into one of the soft yellow strips she'd called French fries.

"That's probably because there's no ham in it. It was beef."

"Oh. Why do they not call it a beef-burger then?"

"Good question, D. I don't know." Eira's face contorted into a suspicious smirk.

After finishing the strange meal, I returned to the now-soggy bed and sat down. The mattress squished beneath me and I wrinkled my nose in disgust. At least the enchanted clothes she had provided would dry almost instantly when I stood again.

"I'm going to go talk to Charlie. Stay in the room."

"Of course," I answered, waving as she disappeared out the door again. I couldn't blame her for wanting to go. The room was cold, wet, and covered with layers of ice and frost. It was terrible and I didn't want to be in it, either. It couldn't possibly hurt to sit outside in the fresh air.

I stood and walked to the door, pulling it open a crack to listen. No one was outside my door, so I stepped outside into the chilly air and took a deep breath. The fresh air was invigorating and I sat down on the lip of the walkway outside our door. The inn was secluded. In the distance I could see a large body of water, possibly the lake Eira had mentioned last night.

Footsteps to my left made me turn my head, but I already knew it was Chad from his scent on the breeze. I stood and moved back to the cracked doorway, not trusting myself with him this close. He stopped and nodded, tipping the strange, wide-brimmed hat he was wearing. He was so handsome. But it was really his scent that made my entire body weak with want. It filled my lungs and I dug my fingers into the wood trim of the doorway to hold myself back. I wanted him. In my room. In me. Wherever I could have him, actually.

"How are you doing, traveling with Eira?"

His question caught me off guard. The tone of his voice wasn't unfriendly, but he seemed upset.

"I am well, thank you. Eira is an excellent companion."

"Did you feed her?" His voice was accusatory. "She looked perky this morning. You shouldn't, you know. It's dangerous to let one of them get attached to you."

"I've saved your ass on more than one occasion, so just put a sock in it. As far as Randall and Charlie go, I'm as old as dirt and know a lot more about this world than they do," Eira said, appearing suddenly at the door next to Chad. Her eyes were ringed with red and she looked cross. "I told you to stay away from her. Her powers are unstable. Would you like to be turned into a human Popsicle?"

He glared at her before turning on his heel and walking off, his boots thumping the hard stone-like ground like a fuming bull.

I swallowed and turned my gaze back to Eira. She narrowed her eyes and came toward me. I moved and allowed her into the room.

"I asked you to stay in the room."

"Why would he care if I fed you?"

She slammed the door. Sheets of ice shook loose from the walls and crashed to the floor. "Look ... as a rule, wolves don't like vampires, but they need me. I can jump the Republic fences and they can't without me. Makes crossing the borders much stealthier. They won't let me drink from any of them because they fear that I'll bond to them or some such shit. Which is only true if I drink from the vein."

"What kind of bond?"

"A sexual one."

I raised my eyebrows. "But I cut myself to feed you. You didn't have to bite me. Why would they care about that? You do look much better. Your color and everything is brighter."

Eira sank into the chair by the small table and frowned. "They're just stubborn, superstitious, and most of the pack only tolerates my presence because Charlie and I are friends."

"How did you come to befriend a werewolf, if none of them like vampires?"

"It's an interesting story and one that ends with me saving her mother's life a long time ago."

"Yet, even Charlie will not allow you to drink her blood?" I didn't understand. How could she deny this person what she needed to live if she owed her mother's life to her? Why didn't the whole pack adore Eira?

"I can see the questions rolling through your brain. Just forget about it. Even though we are friends, Charlie still grew up believing that vampires are evil, bloodsucking monsters who enslave the people they drink from. Needless to say, I normally have to go a week or two between feedings. It's hard to find people out alone these days in the country. Humans have been educated to be a little smarter and I prefer to drink from people who take care of themselves, rather than the homeless and sick who live on the street."

"I do not mind sharing whenever you have need. It is the least I can offer for you stepping in to save my life and explain this strange world I find myself thrust into." I sat down in the chair opposite her and she smiled at me.

"Thank you, D. Though I would like to have some every day, I really won't need more for several days."

"It is yours when you wish it. You need only ask."

"I really hope my friend in Ada can help you. I'm dying to know who you really are underneath all that well-mannered tactful speech. Because the woman fighting last night was a badass, not the proper and fancy lady-in-waiting type."

I gave her a quick nod. I hoped for the same thing. Even more, I wanted names to go with the faces of the two men, the twins who haunted my dreams. I wanted to know why I would awake in the middle of the night, sometimes sobbing, and hear the cry of a baby in the recesses of my mind. But deep down, I really wanted to know who had stolen my life from me so that I could take my vengeance on them. So the beast inside me could rest from its relentless pacing and fury.

CHAPTER 13

DIANA

Day after monotonous day passed. The group moved steadily west each night and I continued to feed Eira every third day. She tried to say it was too often—an unnecessary risk—but I didn't see it that way. I saw it as something I could contribute to this group. Because nothing I had done so far was making this trip any easier.

My body was hot to the touch, yet I iced everything around me when I slept. I'd taken to sleeping in the woods instead of the hotel where the pack holed up during the daylight hours. It was better than continuing to raise alarms when I ruined one hotel room after another. I hated that I inconvenienced Eira, but she said spending the night outdoors was nothing new to her and that my winterization didn't bother her at all.

She speculated one evening while we were walking that perhaps all the ice was simply my powers trying to cool the fever that raged inside me from the heat. I wished I had an answer for her, but I did not. I saw it as torture. The desire to touch and be touched coupled with the knowledge that it could never happen. The heat within me was burning hotter than ever. Now, I would burn anyone who touched me. Even Eira refrained from touching me now. She joked that even in the middle of winter, one could fry an egg on my stomach, whatever that meant.

I looked up at the rising sun in the distance. Seeing the pinks, purples, oranges, and yellows every morning had become a moment I treasured. I knew I'd been in that tower a long time. But there had been no windows, no way to measure the passage of time. Now witnessing the rise and fall of the sun each day was a blessing I would never again take for granted.

"It's beautiful, isn't it?" Eira spoke next to me, her voice quiet and almost mournful. "I was trapped in the dark for so long before I got this ring." She rolled the gold band around her finger and sighed. "It's little moments like these that remind me why I want to keep living. Keep fighting."

"I do not know how long I resided in that prison tower. Most likely centuries. I know nothing about myself or my kind and neither do you because they all disappeared off the face of the earth." I kept walking and waited for her response.

"No matter how long you were there, you have to focus on the here-and-now. You're out and free. Don't dwell in the past. I did that for a long time and I can tell you, it sucks."

"Donkey balls?" I asked, trying to stifle a giggle.

She laughed. "Yes, it sucks donkey balls, you crazy woman."

A howl echoed through the cold night air, making the hairs on the back of my neck stand on end, sending the joviality I'd felt skittering away. Since the night we'd been attacked, several of the group had taken to patrolling in wolf form to try and keep soldiers from being able to sneak up on us again.

Eira tensed beside me and waited. I watched the muscles in her jaw flex as she tried to decide what to do.

Another howl joined the first, followed by several short yips.

"Soldiers?" My voice was no more than a breath of cold air, but Eira nodded.

Footsteps sounded behind us as the group gathered. We moved off the road together into the dense trees and overgrowth to our right. A shot rang out, cutting through the night and one of the wolf's songs was cut short.

I whimpered and Eira covered my mouth with her hand, then drew it back again with a hiss. She'd forgotten the slightest contact burned like a live flame.

"You have to be quiet, no matter what," she whispered.

Others crouched nearby and the tension in their bodies was nearly unbearable. I could feel their anger and their sorrow over losing one of their own. Yet they didn't move. How could they stay here and—

Another shot ended the remaining howling. Silence made the night air empty and stagnant. The breeze had died down, too. Both wolves were either dead or dying and we were all hiding.

I did not like it.

The beast within me did not like it.

It was not right.

Everyone looked to Eira, but she shook her head. Charlie was only a few feet away and she nodded to the vampire, agreeing with her assessment. I could hear noise in the distance. Voices. Conversations. The rumble of the large machines they called vehicles.

"Why aren't we doing something?"

Eira shushed me and glared. "There are too many. We're only twenty people. They have at least a hundred in this regiment. Can't you hear them?"

I nodded. I could, but I still wanted to fight. Being stopped by these men was not an option. Answers waited for me in Ada. At least I hoped they did. Two wolves had possibly already given their lives tonight. Did they expect to hide in these trees and never be found?

Crawling forward slowly, I peered up and down the empty road. I could hear them coming, but it would be several minutes before they arrived. Eira crept up beside me and hissed. "Stop. What the hell do you think you're doing?"

"I'm going to fight."

"You're being ridiculous. You can't even control your own sweat, how are you going to fight twenty or more highly trained soldiers?"

"You know this heat I'm in is not my fault," I shot back. "The beast wants to fight. It doesn't like hiding. I don't like hiding."

"Well la-de-dah to the beast," she growled. "I would rather not die because you have a sudden hero complex."

"We beat the last group that attacked us."

"There were only about twenty soldiers and they didn't have heavy artillery vehicles with them. You hear that rumble and metal on metal sound. Those are guns. Big guns. Bigger than the ones that shot you the first time. These guns will blow your whole arm off."

I sucked in a quick breath at the thought, but it didn't change my mind. Or the mind of the dragon inside me.

"I can do this," I growled low in my chest. The beast stirred and I could feel it rising to the surface. My vision changed first and then I fell to all fours as my body began to morph. At least this time I knew what was happening.

"Shit." Eira hissed and backed away to give me space.

I shook my head and took a step. My body felt unfamiliar, but powerful and strong. Terror didn't grip my soul this time. This time fury burned hot. I instinctually crouched and moved as stealthily as possible being taller than most of the trees surrounding me. The dragon pushed for dominance in my mind and I gave in, becoming a mere passenger. She, the dragon, knew what to do and wanted to do it.

A blur to my left caught my attention. Eira was moving along the tree line with me, her face no more than a faint creamy outline in the moonlit night.

A male voice shouted an alarm and I sprang into action. My breath iced everything in front of me and my feet smashed the vehicles. Several guns sounded and I felt glimmers of pain in my side, but continued on. My huge tail swung around to my side, sending vehicles and people flying in every direction. A terrifying roar came from my throat and I lunged at a group of soldiers preparing to fire a large, metal weapon at me. Eira reached them before they fired, ripping all five of them to pieces. The weapon lay on the ground and I stepped on it, crushing it in my enormous white claws. The metal pole snapped like a twig, giving me a delicious sense of satisfaction.

"Get the other car!" Eira's call caught my attention and I swung my long neck toward her. Another group of soldiers had taken up residence in a large, brown vehicle with another of the bigger guns on its top. A flash of light and then burning pain ricocheted through my chest.

I roared again, covering everything around me in a swath of ice. Wolves came racing from the edges of the forest. They began picking off the soldiers still firing at me one by one. I sent the offending vehicle and soldiers flying dozens of feet into the air with another swipe of my tail. The wolves fell on the rest and I stumbled.

Breathing was difficult. I gulped in the cold winter air, but it did not help much. That last shot must have hurt me worse than I realized.

Everything around me began to fade. My vision blurred and then changed. My body shifted back to human form and I flickered my eyes open and closed. Wolves rushed back and forth around me, then I finally saw Eira's pale blue eyes and heard her voice telling me to suck it up, that I "wasn't allowed to die on her." And something about "being a stupid, stubborn dragon."

If I had more energy I would have laughed at her, but at that moment, I really wanted to sleep. My heavy eyelids closed again and the voices around me faded to silence. I really hoped all the soldiers were gone.

☙❧

THE BUZZING, WHITE TORCHLIGHT GREETED MY EYES AS

they opened. I squinted and turned my head, hoping to see a familiar face. It was. Just not the face I wanted to see.

Instead of Eira's friendly blue eyes, Charlie's dark brown ones met my gaze. Her eyes widened when she realized I had awakened. She rose from her chair and moved to my bedside, wiping my forehead with a damp cloth. It felt like a cool drink of water to my burning skin.

"Where is Eira?"

"She's meeting with a mutual friend of ours. Apparently there are two wolves from Texas looking for you in Ada. We're trying to figure out how they even know about you."

I licked my dry, cracked lips and swallowed. My chest hurt like I'd been run through with a broadsword. Pain shot through me like fire every time I drew a breath. "I need to see them." I struggled to move even a fraction of an inch. Visions of the men in my dreams flashed through my mind. "Were they twins?"

A growl rumbled in Charlie's throat. "Stay still. That 55 caliber put a couple of holes in your chest. You need to lie still and rest while your body rebuilds itself." She paused for a moment. "Manda didn't say if they were twins. Just that they were two wolves from Texas. Why?"

"Please. I want to speak to them," I groaned and tried to move again. There had to be a connection. Why else would they be looking specifically for me? "Please," I said, holding back a wheeze.

"If you promise to stay in bed, I'll send in Eira. Deal?"

I nodded, wincing again. All the talking made me breathe deeper and it hurt so badly tears were running from the corners of my eyes.

She stopped at the doorway and turned back to face

me. "Thank you for risking your life for the pack. You saved lives that night. We owe you a debt and I promise we will help you in any way we can." She started to say more, but didn't and slipped out the door.

I had earned their respect and gratitude. Something told me that was no small feat.

Lifting my head slightly, I raised the sheet covering my body and bit back a whimper. My ribs were wrapped in layers of gauze. Spots of red stained the white bandage in three places.

Three wounds. No wonder I felt as though I'd been run through. I glanced around the room, bare white walls, no windows, and the floor looked like stone. All of it was covered in a thin layer of clear ice, of course. Even wounded and unconscious, I couldn't keep from icing everything around me.

I tried to draw a deeper breath and hissed through the pain that burned in my lungs. It was unbearable and I wished unconsciousness would come back to claim me.

CHAPTER 14

MILES

"**R**ose!" Eli and I both yelled as we stomped into the cafe at four in the morning. The French doors shuddered behind me, slamming back into place. A little harder and I probably would've broken the glass—again. I didn't care.

Diana was in trouble and we were bound to this place out of honor.

I could feel her pain and confusion like it was my own. I knew Eli could feel the same and it was driving us both mad. She was much closer now, but she'd gotten hurt again. This time worse. This time she was struggling to heal.

She needed us. If the wound was severe enough, it would take all three of us together to heal her. We could lose her if we waited too long.

"Yes?" She poked her head out of the kitchen, her eyes

wide with surprise. "Y'all are here awfully early for breakfast."

"You have to send Travis and Garrett again. They have to bring her back with them somehow. She's close. Maybe a couple hundred miles. She has to be in Oklahoma." I gripped the edge of the counter and forced a deep breath. Diana's pain ran through me like flames racing along a trail of gasoline. It was as if every breath she took caused her agony.

"Rose. She's dying," Eli growled, saying aloud what I'd been unwilling to admit.

But I knew it and my dragon did, too. He paced and pushed and it took every ounce of my strength not to shift and fly straight to her side. Our bond acted like a homing beacon. Knowing she was fewer than three hours away was tearing us apart at the seams. We'd been snapping at the Sisters for days and now they scurried away as soon as they saw us.

I released a deep breath and it raised the temperature in the cafe by a good ten degrees.

Rose wiped her forehead and narrowed her brow. "Are you sure? Travis said the smuggler they spoke to knew about the dragon shifter, but not where she was. If they were bringing her to Oklahoma all along, wouldn't they have told them?"

"Who did they speak to?" Eli asked, pacing the length of the counter.

"Her name was Eira."

"That's it?"

"That's the only name she shared. They did say she was a vampire and able to walk in the sunlight."

Rose came around from behind the cafe counter and

stood before me. She looked up and met my gaze with her soft brown eyes and some of the anxiety in my heart faded a little. I knew she would do her best for us, but it was so hard not to do it myself.

"I will send one of the pixies to fetch Travis and Garrett." She touched my arm, but withdrew it quickly. My body temperature was high right now and uncomfortable for anyone but another dragon to touch.

"The vampire is old then and has witches for friends. I wonder if Meredith or her sister knows her." I released the counter and tried to calm the fire rising within me. No need to melt the wallpaper if I could help it. She'd make me replace it.

"We will find her, old friend. I promise." She looked past me to my brother. "Eli, please."

He stopped pacing and looked up.

"I promise you. We will find her. If she's in Oklahoma, then she's almost home." She spoke with such certainty that it was difficult not to take her at her word. But the radiating pain in our chests said we were racing against the clock. Diana didn't have much time. Travis and Garrett needed to hurry.

Rose disappeared into the kitchen, calling Maven's name. Rushed footsteps upstairs said she'd been waiting for the call since we had arrived. The back door of the cafe slammed and I turned to my brother.

His eyes were glowing orange. The flames of his dragon were pushing to the surface. He frowned and sat himself at one of the closest tables.

"How are you keeping your dragon at bay? Mine is clawing at my insides."

I shook my head and walked to him, sitting in the chair

across from him at the small square table. "Mine is the same. We've been battling it out since we felt the first shot of pain days ago. I just keep reminding myself that she's alive and close. We will have her in our arms soon, brother. We will be united once more. Our fathers' legacy will continue and the House of Blackmoor will have a chance to reign in the Veil again one day."

"You think she has one of the daggers of Shamesh?" Eli's eyes shifted back to brown. The distraction had worked.

"There's no other way she could be here. Those four daggers are the only way in or out of the Veil. After all these years ..." It had been so long. My heart broke at the thought of Leif and Kevan torturing her for centuries. Eli and I had watched them hurt her when the House of Blackmoor fell, helpless to protect Diana or any of our family. They'd slain our mother and our fathers without remorse.

Then when escape was within our reach, Diana been snatched from our grasp at the last second. Another reason we fought with Rose against Xerxes—he was the one responsible for taking our mate from us and leaving us trapped in the earth realm, unable to save her.

Eli reached across the table and touched my shoulder. "Vengeance will be ours, brother."

"Yes." I nodded, grimacing through the phantom pain in my chest. "They will *all* pay with their lives."

I looked up at him. His eyes were completely brown again and glassy, though not one tear rolled down either of his cheeks. "I need to hold her, Miles. It's been so long. She needs us and we can't go to her. We could lose her if those damn smugglers don't give her up," Eli growled low in his chest.

The front door burst open and Travis appeared. "Won't happen. My brother and I will find her. I give you my word." Garrett entered a moment later and nodded. He'd only been in Sanctuary a few months, but the two Lycan males understood my brother and me better than anyone else in town. They knew what it was to share a mate ... and lose her. Theirs had been killed, along with most of their pack, after the riots of 2046.

Sharing a mate was uncommon among Lycans, but not unheard of. For Drakonae though, it was customary. Drakonae brothers shared and treasured one mate for their lifetime. No one outside of the Drakonae race, other than Rose Rose, knew how permanent the bond really was.

Eli and I would literally cease to exist in out human form without her. And that would leave Rose and the Sisters of Lamidae unprotected and vulnerable to Xerxes... and even more vulnerable to our dragons. A fallen dragon, one missing his human half, cannot help but terrorize anyone and anything in its path.

If finding Diana wasn't at the top of Rose's priority list a week ago, it was now. Diana's death could spell the end of Sanctuary and everything we'd fought for centuries to protect.

CHAPTER 15

DIANA

The door across the room shuddered and finally sprang open. Bits of ice flew across the room and I struggled to open my eyes. I still burned with the heat, but exhaustion had weakened me to the point that it didn't matter. The entire male half of the pack could stroll through my room and I would not bat an eyelash. Tremors racked my body with each labored breath. Death was reaching for me.

Eira came in and sat on the edge of my bed. I blinked a few times before trying to smile at her.

"I'm so sorry, D. I wish there was something I could do."

"I need t-to remember who I am, Eira. Please. You said y-you had a friend. A witch." Even if I died, I wanted to know the truth of my past. Who was I leaving or who had I already lost?

The vampire shook her head. Her blue eyes were

despondent. "Hannah is staying in town right now and already came by while you were sleeping yesterday. She said you're too weak to do the spell. It requires more energy than you can give. It was all she could do to stem the flow of your blood. Your wounds aren't healing, D."

I ignored her last statement. "We are in Ada?"

"Yes." Eira nodded. "You saved the pack. We found an old van and got you here as quickly as possible. The rest of the group will be here in a few days."

They'd risked exposure crossing into the Texas Republic in a vehicle to try and save me. But death was embracing me quickly. I could feel the life slipping out of me. Even the beast inside me was heavy and sluggish.

"Please. Ask Hannah to come back." I tried to lift my hand, but it didn't budge. My arm felt as though it was made of stone.

Hurried footsteps in the hallway led my gaze to Charlie in the open doorway. "Those Lycans from Texas are back. They're demanding to see her." Charlie's voice was low, but I could still hear every word. *They were back. Someone who knew something about me.*

"How do they even know she's here? Manda wouldn't have told them we were bringing her to Ada." Eira growled and her eyes brightened.

I gasped for another breath. "Eira, let them in. Please," I begged. "It is not like they can make it any worse for me."

"Fine." Eira waved to Charlie and the Lycan female hurried off.

Moments later, two large males entered my room and approached my bedside. When they were about six steps away, Eira motioned for them to stop and they did, though neither looked pleased to be ordered about. They were handsome men. Not the ones that haunted my dreams, but pleasant nonetheless. They both had shaggy hair the color of wheat and enough scruff on their chins to be considering a beard. Their eyes were blue-gray and I saw flashes of gold appear the second I caught their gaze.

"My brother, Garrett, and I have come from Sanctuary to fetch you." The man on the right spoke first. "Your mates, Miles and Eli Blackmoor would've come themselves, but cannot leave their charges unguarded."

"Mates? Charges?" Eira's lip curled, showing a hint of fangs. "You're not taking her anywhere. She can't be moved. She's too weak."

"That's exactly why Diana must come with us. If she doesn't, she will die. Miles and Eli were quite clear—her injuries will be fatal if they are not allowed to heal her through their mate bond."

"Diana?" I let the name slip between my chapped lips. No matter how much water they gave me, I sweat it out within minutes. Even the ice I continued to throw off was barely cooling the room anymore. Most of it had melted.

"I guess we were on the right track calling you D, huh, sweetie?" Eira dabbed my forehead with a cold cloth and I took another shuddering breath.

Miles and Eli Blackmoor. The names didn't mean anything to me. The name Diana didn't, either. I needed to see their faces. If they *are* the men in my dreams, I would know for sure I had found a piece of my missing past.

The other Lycan shifted his stance and frowned. "What do you mean? Right track?"

Eira turned to the werewolf. "She has no memories.

She didn't even know she was a dragon until she turned into one."

"She shifted? Did anyone see her?" The first man sucked in a breath and came closer.

"Of course they did," Eira scoffed. "Why do you think she's lying here with three 55-caliber holes in her chest? Only a fully shifted dragon could take those hits."

I opened my mouth and tried to speak, but only a whisper left my lips. "I have to go, Eira."

She turned back to me and growled. "You can't be moved. I won't let you die because these two wolves think you're their pals' long-lost mate. They don't know for sure. Miles and Eli should've come themselves if they were so worried."

"They would move heaven and earth to have come, but they couldn't. They are bound by an oath. They sent us to bring you back, Diana."

"No." Eira stood, and her eyes flashed red. "The trip would kill her."

The one who called himself Travis spoke again. "She will die for sure if she doesn't and then we will have two very pissed off dragons in Sanctuary. I don't know how scary this one is," he said, throwing a thumb in my direction, "but those two fire-breathers can cause more damage than you *ever* want to see."

"T-tell me what they l-look like." Speaking was getting harder and the pain was starting to make me lose consciousness again. I could feel myself slipping back into that dark hole.

"They're identical twins, both as big as a brick house with long, black hair and brown eyes that turn to flame when they're upset. Believe me, honey, they're about as upset as I've ever seen them. It's driving them mad knowing you're only three hours away and they couldn't come to you." Travis took a breath and knelt to the floor beside my bed.

I glanced at Eira. She nodded. She knew.

They had described the men in my dreams perfectly.

"I go with her. She's been in my care this whole time. I want to make sure everything's as you say," she said, glaring at Travis who was at eye level with her now.

"Good. Let's go. There's a bus parked a few blocks away. We can lay her out in the back so she's comfortable."

"A bus?" Eira frowned.

Travis chuckled. "Cops rarely bother to pull over buses, so we usually travel that way."

"I see."

"What's with all the ice in the room?" The other Lycan, Garrett, spoke from behind Travis.

"She does it. And get ready for more. We get a thick layer every time she falls asleep or slips into unconsciousness," Eira answered.

"She's an ice-breather?" Travis asked, standing.

"Yep. Don't touch her, though; she's burning up with a fever like she's made of fire right now. We have to carry her using the bed sheets. I'll tell Charlie we're leaving," she said, hurrying from the room.

Both Lycans stared down at me and I fought for enough breath to speak, but couldn't manage it.

Travis leaned down to touch my sweating forehead and pulled his hand back quickly. "Damn, that vampire wasn't kidding. She's too hot to touch, even for us."

"Is she going to make the drive?"

The other wolf thought he was whispering too quietly for me to hear, but he wasn't.

"I hope so, for all of our sakes. I know Miles, Eli, and Rose are hiding something. I get the feeling if she dies, we're all in for a shit load of trouble in Sanctuary," Travis replied.

I refused to die, yet. Answers were so close. At least now I knew my name and that the men I remembered from my dreams were still alive, but I wanted more.

"Travis, what's that scent? She smells so—"

"I think she's in heat.

I nodded my head and glance up to meet Travis' gaze.

His blue-gray eyes were filled with compassion. "We will get you to them. I promise. Just hang on. Do you hear me?"

I nodded again and tried to swallow, but my mouth felt like it was stuffed with wool. He reached for the cup on the bedside table and put the a slender hollow stick up to my lips. Eira had called it a straw. It was strange to suck water from the reed-like thing, but it did allow me to drink without straining and for that I was grateful.

The cool water coated the inside of my mouth and throat as it slipped down. "Thank you."

"This vampire, Eira, do you trust her?" Travis asked, leaning closer.

"Yes," I murmured.

"What about the female Lycan? The one in charge called Charlie?" Travis continued, helping me get another sip of the ice cold water.

"Yes."

I hadn't at first. But after Charlie's heartfelt admission

and thanks, I did. She and the others really were trying to save people. Nothing more.

My eyes fluttered and I struggled against the black spots filling my vision.

"Diana." Travis' smooth voice rumbled beside me.

I opened my eyes again.

"Fight," he ordered. "You're a freakin' dragon. You can fight this." Travis set the water glass on the table and stood as Charlie and Eira appeared in the doorway.

The three Lycans stared at each other for a moment before Eira began barking out orders on how to move me from the bed. But I'd seen the flaring nostrils and I could smell their arousal when Charlie had entered the room. No wonder they hadn't been interested in me, even with my heat, they were already focused on Charlie.

I grimaced as they lifted me from the bed, using the sheets as a sling to keep from touching my fiery hot skin. Each took hold of a corner and they carefully walked me outside and up into a large vehicle. One bigger than I'd seen, yet. At least there were no metal weapons fixed to the top of it. I'd had quite enough of those.

CHAPTER 16

DIANA

They situated me at the back of the vehicle, propping rolled up blankets around my body to help keep me in place as the vehicle started to move. Eira was arguing with one of the Lycans. I couldn't tell which one, but their faces betrayed their emotions.

I knew Eira was worried, but I had no intention of slipping away until I at least saw my mates. *Two mates? Husbands?* Who in their right mind would marry two men at once?

My mouth felt as though I'd swallowed sand. "Eira—" I gasped for a breath, but what I really needed was water.

She was by my side in an instant; whatever she'd been arguing about with the Lycans was forgotten.

"Water?"

I nodded.

"She's sweating it out faster than she can drink it," the Lycan named Garrett said from his position behind Eira.

"Damn, why is the air conditioning on so high?" He rubbed his arms and visibly shivered.

"It's not the bus, it's her. Remember her room?"

"Yeah, but you said that was when she was unconscious. She looks awake to me."

"Unconscious just means it ices faster. She can't control her powers so she's constantly throwing off ice and cooling the air. Look at the windows." Eira inclined her chin above my head.

I couldn't see the windows, but I knew what they looked like. The Lycans' eyes widened with understanding.

"We need to hurry," Eira said, her voice heavy with concern.

The male turned and walked to the front of the bus. I heard him tell the driver to "step on it." It must've been a signal to go faster, because I felt the vehicle accelerate and shudder as it was pushed harder. The noise of the road beneath me became soothing and drowned out the voices of my companions.

I knew I might die. I didn't need to hear them argue about it for the entire three hours of the journey. Eira roused me from my semi-conscious state every few minutes, urging me to drink as much water as I could.

Even as my energy waned, I could feel that same pull I'd felt when I first crossed through the ring of stones. The closer we came to the place the Lycans called Sanctuary, the stronger that feeling became.

It had to be them—Miles and Eli. They had somehow felt my presence in Ada and sent their friends to get me. I knew we were heading in the right direction, too. I'd just been too ill to really notice it through the heat that consumed my body and my injuries. But now ... we were so close. Even the beast within me struggled and fought against the darkness that was closing in on us.

Every bump in the road sent pain shooting through my aching body. And with each jolt, my tension grew and I felt the temperature drop further inside the vehicle.

"Her heartbeat's slowing! Tell the driver to hurry." Eira's voice growled from my side.

"We're ten minutes away. I'm calling them now. Do something."

"There's nothing to do. Even my blood didn't help."

My eyes fluttered open to a familiar vision. Frost coated the inside of the bus. Small icicles hung from the ceiling and the air around me felt icy. It was comforting. Peaceful even, were it not for the yelling echoing around me. The two Lycans were arguing with someone and Eira was ... yelling at me? I tried to focus on her face. I could see her mouth moving, but the words were lost. It was almost as if I'd slipped beneath a body of water.

CHAPTER 17

MILES

Travis had just called. They should be here any minute. Darkness had fallen and the old street lamps were glowing all the way around Main Street Circle. I took a deep breath and pushed back my dragon. It took every ounce of strength to keep from changing and flying toward the bus I knew was only a mile or two away. We couldn't risk it, though. The Protectors worked hard to keep Sanctuary off the human radar. If dragons were sighted flying through the Texas sky, we'd have a whole new set of problems.

My brother, Eli, stood next to me shifting his weight back and forth from one foot to the other. He wasn't doing much better. In fact, his eyes would flash orange every few moments. His dragon was as agitated as mine.

I knew he could feel the same thing—her life slipping away. With it, our humanity would also go. Nothing would hold back our dragons if Diana died. And Rose already knew she would have to kill us before we burned Sanctuary to ash.

The sound of a diesel engine rumbled over the hill and down the main road to the circle. We leapt into a run, crossing the grassy area in the center of town in a few strides. Eli was quicker. He wrenched open the bus doors before the driver could pull to a stop and I followed right behind him.

Travis and Garrett stayed in their seats as we hurried down the aisle of the frost-covered bus. Our dragons turned on the heat and everything began to melt. My brother's back blocked my view, but I knew she was there.

A snarl and a hiss from the back seats made my brother roar and the temperature in the bus rose higher, making it feel more like an oven than an ice box.

"Get out of the fucking way, Eira. Miles and Eli will roast you alive if you don't." Travis' voice bellowed out the warning from the front of the bus.

A small, brunette woman, a vampire by the scent and lack of heartbeat, stepped to the right and Eli knelt next to Diana, releasing a howl of agony that made my fiery blood run cold.

I leapt over my brother and landed gingerly on the seat cushion above her head.

"You can't touch her!" The vampire cried out. "She's burning up."

I turned my head and snarled.

The vampire backed away and followed Travis and Garrett, along with the driver out of the bus.

"Miles, I can barely hear her heartbeat." My brother looked up at me, his eyes swirling with orange flame. His voice conveyed the pain I felt. We could still lose her. She was climbing the steps to the afterworld at this very moment.

Pulling the small, dragon-steel dagger from my waistband, I sliced my palm and then one of hers. Then I pressed my palm into hers so our blood would mix. Eli took the dagger from me and did the same with her other hand.

"Ready?"

Eli nodded and we began to chant the old blood magic spell together. It'd been so long since I'd seen the spell done. I hoped and prayed to the gods it would work.

"Mitt blod er ditt. Blodet ditt er mitt. Vi kaller på den magiske vår obligasjon til å helbrede. Mitt blod er ditt. Blodet ditt er mitt. Vi kaller på den magiske vår obligasjon til å helbrede. Mitt blod er ditt. Blodet ditt er mitt. Vi kaller på den magiske vår obligasjon til å helbrede ...

We repeated it over and over.

Diana's body trembled and more ice formed around us, cocooning us and the bus in a solid glacier. I could hear shouts from the outside, but quickly turned my focus back to our mate. Eli's and my dragon's heat kept the back of the bus clear of ice through the entire spell and the curved walls of ice that'd formed around us ran with water, melting almost as quickly as it had formed.

Her body stopped shaking and both of us blew across our palms to heal our cuts, doing the same for her. Even though she was an ice-breather, our warm breath could heal her because she was our mate. The cuts on her palms closed and I kissed the newly healed skin, drinking in her sweet scent. She'd always smelled like the lilac flowers that bloomed on the hills above Orin in the Veil. I took another deep breath and looked up to meet my brother's gaze.

"The spell has taken hold," he said, his voice deep and relieved.

I nodded.

He peeled back the bandages wrapped around her torso. The open wounds were gone—completely healed, as if they'd never existed. The injury was still there and she would need time to mend on the inside, but the process had clearly begun. She would live.

We had our mate back. After a thousand years apart, it seemed almost unreal.

Eli continued to unwrap her, inch by inch. She was completely naked, but for a pair of lacy, white panties.

Gods, she was gorgeous and just as I remembered her. Legs that stretched for miles and luscious breasts with ... large, dark pink nipples begging for my mouth. *Wait.* I remembered her nipples being lighter, smaller, and more delicate.

I reached forward and caressed one breast, then pulled my hand back. She was injured, in pain, and had nearly died in front of us, and yet I groped her like a man who'd never seen a naked woman.

"They look different, don't they Miles?" Eli said, then stood and turned toward the solid wall of ice blocking our exit from the bus. He placed his hands against the frozen wall and it began to melt quickly. We would only need a few minutes to completely thaw the entire bus.

Pulling off my shirt, I tugged it over her head and down her bandaged body. It was so much bigger than her that the hem reached about midway down her thighs.

"They do," I said, finally answering my twin brother's question.

Eli looked back over his shoulder at me for a second. "Do you think ..." The crack in his voice was the same one I felt in my heart.

My vision blurred. I blinked the unshed tears away and nodded.

She'd had a baby.

CHAPTER 18

ELI

My heart lurched in my chest. Questions raced through my mind about what had happened. Her breasts had changed enough that Miles and I both had come to the same conclusion.

She'd had a child. But what happened to him or her? And who had fathered the child? Was it mine, or Miles', or ...

A murderous growl rumbled in my chest at the ugly memories being sluiced up from the recesses of my mind. Rage I hadn't dwelt on in centuries bubbled to the surface. My brother and I had been whipped with dragon-steel-tipped cat-o-nines and chained to the pillars in the center of the throne room. Then they'd taken one of our fathers' swords and made us watch as they beheaded our fathers, Gareth and Konrad Blackmoor, and their mate—our mother, Adria.

No sooner had the bodies of our parents been cast off

the dais, the Incanti bastards had dragged our beautiful, strong mate up onto the platform, thrown her over the same rock, bloody from the beheadings, and raped her in front of us.

Diana's cries had haunted my nightmares since that day. We'd been powerless to do anything, held in place by dragon-steel chains enchanted to withstand our strength and our heat.

Instead of killing all three of us right then and there, we'd been locked up in the prison tower west of Orin. The Incanti wanted to torture us indefinitely, but one of the few guards still loyal to the House of Blackmoor helped us escape a few days later. To our horror, Diana had been snatched from the ring of stones by Incanti dragons, just before she placed her hand on the center rock. Miles and I had tumbled through to the earth realm without our mate and had been cursing fate ever since. The only way back into the Veil was with a piece of the Star of Shamesh. Diana had been holding our family's dagger when she was taken from the circle.

A few centuries later, Rose found us in a tavern drinking ourselves into oblivion and gave us a new purpose. The Sisters had given us new hope. Each appointed Oracle through the years always told us the same thing.

She will come to you.

Now here she was.

Over a millennia had passed and she had finally come back to us. I continued to move forward through the bus, melting the ice with each step. Water ran down the sides of the frozen walls, pooling around my boots. I focused the heat through my palms and in another thirty seconds,

I stepped through the door and off the bus. Miles walked behind me carrying Diana.

The little vampire jumped toward me, but Rose froze her in mid-air.

I nodded to Rose and she flicked her wrist, releasing the lionhearted woman from the clutches of her Lamassu magick.

The vampire showed no signs of fear, even after being handled by Rose. Her gaze narrowed and her gemstone blue eyes ringed with a dark scarlet red. Then her fangs descended menacingly and she blocked my path. As if she thought she had any chance at all of stopping me. The corners of my lips curled upward just a hint.

"Who are you? Where are you taking her? And how is the brute behind you able to touch her without pain?" Her questions fired at me like a repeating revolver.

"My brother and I thank you for your zealous care of our mate. I assure you, she's safe with us. She needs only to be put to bed to heal. As far as the fire in her skin, it does us no harm. We're her mates, vampire," I said, huffing out enough flame on my breath to make her jump back in surprise. "We are of fire."

My brother turned and walked around the semi-frozen bus. His only thought, like mine, was to get her safely into the Castle—into our home and tucked into bed to rest. Everything else could wait.

Diana was in heat, but she would remain in a hibernation state until her body was completely mended. The spell we'd cast would make sure she rested in peace.

I turned to watch Miles cross the dark circle of grass and then looked back to the vampire who I knew wasn't going to take no for an answer. She reminded me of several of the younger Sisters—stubborn as a three-legged mule.

"She has been in my care for nearly three weeks. I would like to know where you're taking her and how she's being treated. You can claim to be her mates until the cows come home, but she will be terrified when she wakes up and I intend to be there." She waved her hand toward the Castle behind me. "Unless you want your stone fortress over there to turn into the first Texas glacier."

The glacier threat didn't concern me in the least. Now that she was with us, her anxiety should be much less and she shouldn't create any more deep freezes. It was strange that she would've frozen the bus that badly, but even that could be overlooked because of her injury. What caught me off guard was the vampire's claim that she would be terrified when she awoke.

"Why?" I started. "Why would she be afraid of her mates?"

"Because she doesn't remember anything. She has some form of amnesia." The vampire explained. She waved her other hand at the cafe and storefront to her right. "You might also want to let your neighbors know to expect unwelcome visitors."

"Why?" Rose stepped to my side. "Who was following you?" Erick, Bailey, Sita, and Calliope also stood by, just a few yards away, ready to spring into action should the unknown vampire female present a real threat.

The strange female's blue eyes flashed and she turned to Rose. "Soldiers. Two attacks on our way from Clarksville to Ada, both from SECR soldiers. They have video of her as a dragon in the first town she popped up in, somewhere on the East Coast. She called it a village, so it had to be one of the smaller towns outside Charlotte. But it still would've had street cameras."

"She wouldn't have shifted in front of humans," I growled. Diana wasn't stupid.

"She would if she didn't know she was a dragon and jumped a millennia into the future without realizing it. Like I said, big guy, she's not quite with it."

I took a deep breath and tried to tamp down the anger flowing through my body. Our mate had been hurt worse than we'd ever dreamed possible. The Incanti had taken away more than her life, but her memories as well. Rose touched my arm, bringing me back to the present. The little slip of a brunette continued to speak.

"Anyway, our best guess on where she came out of the Veil was somewhere close to Charlotte. Makes sense because of the sacred circle in the mountains north of there. Government's been tracking her ever since. I wouldn't put it past them to slip into the Texas Republic unannounced and try again."

"We will speak to Diana when she wakes. Until then, can you find a spare room for our guest?" Rose's hands clenched at her sides, but her face remained calm. "I think it would be wise to keep ..." She looked to the brunette and waited.

"Eira ... Eira Rennir. And you are?"

"Rose Hilah."

"Hilah?! As in related to Xerxes, pain-in-my-ass, Lamassu freakin' Hilah?"

I snarled at the mention of his name. Even Rose's fangs descended and she tensed, anger breaking through her smooth veneer. The others around us tensed in response and stepped closer to Eira.

"What business do you have with that man?" Rose snapped.

Erick, Bailey, and Sita crouched, ready to react to the slightest provocation. Even easy-going Calliope had inky black eyes and her razor-sharp claws extended.

The female vampire's shoulders squared instead of shrinking in fear. She definitely didn't intimidate easily. Which meant one of two things—she was old or stupid. I didn't think it was the latter.

"I don't have any business with him, all right? No need to tear off my head. He's a thorn in the Mason pack's side. He's come close to catching us before. Well, not actually him. I should say his soldiers."

"The Djinn?" I asked calmly. "I wouldn't call them soldiers."

She whirled back to face me. "No, the soldiers. You know he practically owns the SECR, right? Give him a few more years and he'll own the Washington Republic." She raised an eyebrow. "Why did you think his soldiers were Djinn? They would be killed on sight if found in the ranks of the SECR."

"Because we've been fighting them for centuries. The Djinn are his lackeys. The entire race does his bidding." Rose loosened her stance and withdrew her fangs. She motioned to the others to stand down.

"Not all of them. One of them owes me and she helps keep us ahead of Xerxes when she can. We know most of the big moves inside the armies patrolling the SECR before they happen. She's helped us get a lot of supernaturals out safely." Eira pointed to the Castle. "We can exchange war stories later. Right now, I would like to make sure my little ice dragon is safe and sound like you and your twin promised."

I glanced to Rose. She nodded and turned away.

I started walking toward the Castle and the rest of the group followed Rose into the cafe. The petite vampire fell into stride next to me, though she had to take two steps for each of mine just to keep up. Her long, brown ponytail swished back and forth over the guard of the sword strapped to her back. It reminded me of the blades the Elvin masters used to make. The hilt was wrapped in a turquoise cloth and had an old, Norse emblem affixed to the end.

"I've been here a couple of times before. Bought some clothes from the siren, Calliope. Damn ... I didn't know her game face was that scary."

I glanced over at her and sighed. Chit-chatting was not on my agenda.

"Never visited the Castle, though. Calliope invited me last time I came to town, but I'm not really into kink." She growled low in her throat. "You're not going to talk to me, are you? Just tell me one thing. If Diana is so important to you and your brother, why didn't the both of you come looking for her instead of sending those two Lycans?"

My temper simmered just below a boil and it took everything I had to keep from turning and snarling in her face. Instead, I calmly answered her.

"You don't know a damn thing about this town or my brother and me. We have no interest in educating you, either. We're eternally grateful for your care of Diana. I know you wish to watch over her, but there's really no need for you to stay. I'm sure your Lycan friends in Ada miss you."

She chuckled. "You're not getting rid of me that easy. My *Lycan* friends are chilling in Ada for the rest of the winter. We won't make another trip east until spring. So I'm all yours."

I rolled my eyes. *Great.* We approached the front door of the Castle. I pushed it open and stood aside for her to pass.

"Nothing's going to eat me inside here, right?" she asked, stepping into the dimly lit foyer and glancing around nervously.

I couldn't help the chuckle that rolled up from my chest. "That, Eira, is entirely up to you."

She whirled around and frowned. "I told you I wasn't interested in this stuff. I'm too old and set in my ways. I quite prefer my rolls in the hay to be unrestricted and without rules to follow, or chains."

I lifted my hands in mock surrender. "As I stated, the Castle is open to your exploration. However, our personal wing is off limits without my or my brother's supervision."

"I suppose that's where you've stashed Diana?" She crossed her arms and took a quick glance around.

The stairways on either side of her led to the public second floor. Farther back in the building, the Sisters had their own private quarters, below ours. Another added layer of protection we'd devised when designing the place. It was full of secret rooms and magical components.

"She is," I finally answered. "You will have full access to the public areas of the Castle. But there are more people here that require their privacy than not, so please be discreet when exploring."

"I don't want to explore, you big oak tree. I want to sit

next to Diana's bedside. I'll sleep on the floor. I don't care, but she's under my protection."

"She's my mate, vampire!" I roared, walking past her. Several wisps of white figures flitted past outside in the courtyard and through the adjoining halls. The Sisters knew to avoid an angry dragon. This crazy vampire didn't.

"Eira, my name is Eira. Not vampire." She corrected me, her voice riding an even keel.

Frustration burned through my body. *By all the gods! This woman just wouldn't leave it be.*

"She's my responsibility," she continued. "I saved her life. The Mason pack kept her out of the soldiers' hands. You should be grateful, not harping at me about where I can walk."

"Harping!" I growled. "I'll introduce you to a harpy if you want to see some harping. Of course we're grateful, but you're not a Lycan. Quit acting like they're your pack. What's a vampire even doing with a wolf pack? Plus, Diana wanted to come to us. Our mate bond is a homing beacon."

"First of all, I seem to remember Lycans being the ones helping you out. Weren't they called Travis and Garrett? And I saw a few vampires in your welcoming party, though no one introduced me. So I'd say they coexist pretty damn well when the need arises."

I should've just kept my mouth shut. Being surrounded by women day in and day out, I should've known better. But the Sisters didn't require a lot of our attention. In fact, other than overseeing the pixies who monitored the club dungeon, we rarely conversed with them. Maybe I didn't get as much practice as I thought. My brother and I were quite the shut-in reclusive bachelors, except for our jaunts in the club with visitors from time to time. It wasn't my fault Eira Rennir didn't get the red carpet treatment. She'd arrived with my wife nearly dead.

I rolled my neck, cracking a few vertebrae. How on earth was I going to stand being around this know-it-all-pain-in-the-ass? *Here comes more.* Sure enough, her mouth opened again and started slapping me worse than the sting of my childhood tutor's cane on my knuckles.

"Second, I couldn't care less that she was being drawn to you. She doesn't remember who you are and the both of you look primed and ready to jump her bones. And by the way, she's in a heat of some sort and I've been keeping her from humping every male that crossed her path for the last three weeks." Her footsteps stopped, and suddenly she was no longer walking beside me.

I stopped and turned around. She was standing in the middle of the dim hallway. Her black leather clothes blending into the shadows, but her blue eyes sparked angrily.

"We can take care of her. We don't need you to do it for us," I roared. Heat rolled off me in waves and even Miss nothing-phases-me grimaced as the blast hit her face.

"Maybe not, but I doubt it," she replied, her voice still calm. "The Diana you remember isn't the woman your brother carried off the bus a few minutes ago. She doesn't remember anything about either of you. I," she pointed to herself, "have been with her for the last three weeks. Who do you think she'll feel more comfortable waking up to? Two horny, big-ass dragon-shifters from her cloudy dreams or a familiar face?"

My blood ran cold.

No memory ... of us?

I vaguely recalled Eira mentioning it just minutes ago, but my adrenaline-filled brain hadn't registered exactly how much she'd forgotten. Though not remembering you're a dragon and shifting in front of humans should've been a clue.

"Didn't you hear me earlier?"

"Shut up!"

She hissed.

My dragon roared again, this time shaking the walls of the Castle. My vision changed for a second and I knew my eyes had blazed flame orange. I pushed the angry reptile down and shuddered, a sick feeling growing in my stomach. My brother didn't know any of this yet.

"Please, just shut up and follow me." I didn't wait for an answer. I just turned and continued down the hallway to the wing of the Castle that housed my brother's and my living quarters. She could either follow or not. I didn't care.

A few moments later, I heard her light footsteps behind me.

CHAPTER 19

XERXES

An annoying *rap* at the door roused me from sleep. I pushed Lily's arm off my chest and nudged Iris and Roshanna's sleeping forms away from my legs.

"What?" I hollered across the vast bedroom suite, really not interested in leaving my soft bed unless necessary. My three girls had done an excellent job last night of taking my mind off the fact that Diana Blackmoor had slipped through my fingers, yet again. The last task force had been found weeks ago. Some of the soldiers had been slaughtered by those damn Mason wolves, while the rest were reported to have been flash-frozen. *Fucking ice dragon.*

"Mandana Farrok has requested your presence in the great hall."

Cyrus' daughter. *Finally*. That bitch had a tendency to fall off the map for months before reappearing in the palace with a report. I only gave her the freedom she had because she was somehow able to gather good information on the supernatural movements in the former U.S. She wasn't stupid. The woman led the Djinn race the entire time her father was imprisoned. That's why I didn't yank too hard on the leash.

If any Djinn presented a threat to my overall plans, it was her. Especially after her father lost his temper and killed the husband she'd taken in his absence. She hadn't spoken to Cyrus face-to-face since.

Manda, as she preferred to be called now, was a master of disguise and blended exceptionally well into the human population. She was also one of my most valuable assets within the SECR government. I'd worked diligently, made payoffs, and coerced just the right people to get her high into their ranks. She now held the position of Director of Defense. Nothing happened in that republic that I didn't know about well in advance.

It still hadn't helped me catch Diana. How a lost dragon in heat managed to avoid detection across several thousand miles of government monitored country astounded me.

I grabbed my watch from the table next to the bed and glanced at the time. *Almost noon.* The women on the bed stirred briefly before climbing over each other to get to the floor first. All three were prostrate before me in moments and I smiled.

"Find me something to wear and have some light food readied to serve outside." I pointed to the dining area outside my suite. "Ten minutes. Then have Ms. Farrok escorted in to dine with me."

The three slave girls fled from their positions on the floor as if I'd lit them on fire. One returned a moment later with a white linen set of clothing, soft and comfortable. Exactly what I preferred to wear when staying at the palace. I had no reason to venture into the chaos of the outside world unless Manda brought me news of the missing Drakonae female.

I slipped into the clothes, choosing to remain barefoot. Iris followed me to the table in the sunroom and poured a glass of cold water, adding several fresh slices of lemon. She set a bottle of my favorite red wine, already opened to breathe, in the center of the table with two goblets. Only a few minutes later, Roshanna appeared with two large trays of cold fruit, cheese, bread, and meat.

The blue desert sky was cloudless and the beige landscape stretched to the horizon. The village a few miles from the palace could only be seen from the west side. My suites were on the east. I preferred the sunrise and morning light to the glare of the sunset and blistering afternoon sun.

I used the delicate silver tongs to move a few pieces to my plate and began nibbling on the food. Another few minutes passed before I heard the *clip clap* of boots on the marble floors of my bedroom suite.

A vision of female perfection stepped from behind the curtains to the veranda area. Manda was what people would call jaw-dropping. High cheekbones and beautiful lavender-gray eyes that made a man's dick stand at attention. Her long, silky black hair was wasted on a tightly braided bun pulled up at the nape of her neck. She was tall and lithe with legs that stretched for miles. Curvy in just the right places. She wore knee high, leather, high-heeled boots over painted-on black pants. Her blouse was sheer ivory silk beneath a fitted red jacket.

If she hadn't been Cyrus' daughter and queen of the Djinn for two-thousand years, I would've fucked her the first time I had her alone. As it stood, she was one of the only women who knew I wanted her and relished the fact that I couldn't force her. At least that's what she assumed.

Even though she was too proud to truly serve as a slave in all aspects, it was a role her father had taken up graciously when I'd freed him. Cyrus Farrok ruled the Djinn in name alone and I pulled those puppet strings.

She frowned at the spread on the table, but removed her jacket and sat across from me anyway. "I don't plan to stay. And you know I hate meeting in your suite."

"Hello to you as well," I replied, not affronted at all by her curt tone. "I prefer to keep these meetings as private as possible and that means staying in my wing of the palace."

She snatched a grape from the tray in front of her and popped it between her red satin lips.

"Get your mind out of the gutter, Xerxes. I have places to be and people to deal with if you don't want to hear my report right now." She leaned back in her chair and crossed her legs.

"By all means, please share." I flashed a wide smile and continued with my meal.

"As you already know, both units sent after the Drakonae female failed. I lost some of my best men to her frozen breath and two-ton claws. I didn't realize how fucking big dragons were until I saw her footprints."

I nodded. Older Drakonae were the size of small jets and more powerful than any other supernatural, besides me. Unlike other shifting races, the Drakonae dragon continued to grow in size for several millennia, even after the human side was full-grown.

"Did your men manage to kill any of the Mason wolves? Those pain-in-the-ass Lycans are always causing trouble in the SECR."

"Only two. Wolves are strong, but it's nothing a few well-placed silver bullets can't manage. However, this group has a vampire working with them."

"Vampires do not work with Lycans." I bit off a piece of soft, smoked cheese. The flavor was excellent and the smooth texture made me want to smile. My girls knew exactly what I liked to eat.

"This one does. There are rumors that she saved Charlotte Mason's mother. Her name is Eira Rennir. Do you know her?"

Yes and damn it all to hell and back. Another fucking Viking.

Darius, one of my better assassins, had gone and made it personal with one of Rose's Protectors, Erick Thorson. The Viking warrior had been around for centuries and I'd never been able to kill him. Now he was part of Rose's little circle of Protectors. As a rule, vampires weren't that difficult to handle, but when you ran across the really old ones, the fights could get messy. She was just as old as Erick Thorson and just as deadly. Eira was a woman who a man never forgot meeting.

"Yes. I've been trying to kill her a long time."

Manda raised an eyebrow, but didn't respond.

"Where are the Masons now?"

"Most of them are safely tucked away in what used to be Oklahoma for the winter. They rarely leave the Texas Republic once the cold weather hits around Christmas."

She leaned forward and snagged a piece of pineapple from the tray in front of her.

"And Diana? Is she still with them?"

She shook her head. "Nope. Two wolves showed up from Sanctuary and hauled her off. Eira left with them. I do have to tell you though, Diana was not looking well. My boys got a couple 55-caliber rounds into her gut."

"Keep your ears open for anything concerning her. She took something of mine that I want back."

"Did you not hear me? I said she was dying." Her voice held more arrogance than it should.

I snarled and she flinched in her chair. Not much, but just enough to show that I'd rattled her. "Do not speak to me that way. You may have more freedom than any of the others, but what I give I can take away."

She narrowed her eyes and stood from her chair. "A threat is always my cue to leave." Picking up her jacket, she blinked away before I could say another word.

Damn Djinn. If her father hadn't murdered her husband, she'd be easier to control. But Manda Farrok had nothing to lose.

It was becoming a problem.

CHAPTER 20

MILES

I ran my hand along her brow, moving a silky tendril of her snowy blond hair from her peaceful face. She was everything I remembered and more. The most beautiful woman I'd ever laid eyes on. The only woman who had ever held my heart, and she still did.

To have her here—lying in my bed, nestled among the scarlet red sheets, breathing, and safe—was like a dream. I don't think either of us ever really thought the Oracle's words would come true. Not that we'd given up on Diana. We knew she was still alive; we just had no options left to pursue.

Fate had bound us to Rose for now, but with Diana safely returned to us, the House of Blackmoor would rise again. In time, nothing would stop us from finding a way back through the gate and back to our rightful home.

Taking a deep breath, I stood as my brother entered

through the dark-stained, oak double doors across the room. The warrior-woman of a vampire who'd arrived with Diana walked quietly behind him. Neither made a sound as they crossed the room on the plush, ivory carpet.

Eli walked up next to me and bent down, pressing a kiss to Diana's cheek. The female stopped at the foot of the bed.

"Miles," Eli spoke softly, "I need to talk to you in the other room."

I growled and shook my head. "I'm not leaving her side."

"Eira will watch her. You know the spell will keep her under at least a day or two. It's important." Eli urged, but the hesitation in his voice made fear tighten its hold in my chest.

The vampire he'd called Eira regarded me coldly. She was pissed, but it wasn't directed at me. That was a first. I tended to be the one accused of gruff, unfriendly behavior. Eli tended to be more charming and witty.

"Fine."

We walked together, crossing my large bedroom quickly. Eli closed the doors behind us and then we entered his suite of rooms across the hall. We'd shared a bedroom in Orin, but always with Diana. Without her, we preferred our own rooms.

Those arrangements might have to change soon and I couldn't help but smile at the thought of the three of us finally being back together. My brother and I had shared a few women through the centuries and found our pleasures individually, as well. We'd become masters at being Dominants in the process, but no woman had ever remained in our bed more than a few days' time. Nothing and no one could ever fill the void Diana had left in our hearts. Now it didn't matter. She was here.

But something was off. Eli was far too serious.

I didn't like this. "We have her back. What could possibly be wrong?"

Eli shut the doors to his suite and leaned against them. He looked green.

"Spit it out." I sank into one of the large, leather chairs in the sitting area. It felt as though I might need to be seated for this conversation.

My brother walked to the chair opposite me and sat—his body stiff and tense. "She has no memory of us, Miles. Eira said our faces came to her in dreams, but she cannot recall who we are or were."

It was like a sword through the heart. I didn't want it to be true. But I knew it was. Eli might like to joke around and keep the mood light, but this was no prank.

"Are you sure?"

He rolled his head to the side. "That's what the vampire said. She doesn't really have any reason to lie. And it does explain why Diana allegedly shifted in front of humans."

"She did what?" I stood from my chair, fire burning at my core. Not only had the Incantis stolen precious memories from our wife, now the human governments knew dragons existed and were probably headed straight for Sanctuary. The Texas Republic border would only slow them down. It wouldn't stop them.

"If she didn't know, we can't blame her. These beasts within us are strong. It never occurred to me how different the world would look to her if she ever escaped from the Veil. It had to have been terrifying. Her dragon would only have tried to keep her safe." Eli waved a hand at my empty chair. "Just sit with me, brother. I'm still processing what this means for us. If she has no memory of us or what happened—"

"How do we explain that she's wed to us both? How do we ask her if she had a baby? What the fuck do we do? When she wakes up, she won't be able to deny her dragon's heat cycle. The need will consume her until it's fulfilled."

"In the meantime, we need to find out just how much Eira knows," Eli said. "I just wanted to give you space to absorb the shock of—"

"You mean the loss." I snarled. "We got her back only to have her taken from us again. Kevan and Leif are bastards who don't deserve the air they're breathing. They did this to her on purpose. Stole her past ... and our future."

"Don't lose hope, brother. If magick did this to her, it's possible we can find the right magick to undo it as well. I'll speak to Meredith as soon as she gets back into town. Between her and her sister, Hannah, they will be able to come up with something. They're two of the strongest witches in the country." Eli stood. "We should check in with Rose and see what plans of defense need to be discussed. Soldiers will be here in fewer than seventy-two hours."

"Let them come," I growled. "I'll burn them all. Problem solved."

Eli smiled a menacing, bloodthirsty smirk—the I'm-going-to-kill-them-all look did not often appear, but when it did, it was usually before a killing spree. The last time we reached the point of combustion was during the American Civil War.

"I completely agree, brother."

CHAPTER 21

ELI

We left my room and returned to check on Eira and Diana.

The vampire turned at the sound of the door opening. Her face and neck were visibly tense. *Too bad.* This was our house, and Diana was our wife. She was just going to have to get used to us or leave.

"How are you keeping her from icing the room? Every time she was unconscious previously, we had ice forming on the walls and across the floors within an hour." She gestured to the pristine room around her.

Classic artwork hung on the dark, paneled walls. The merlot-colored, crushed velvet drapes hung open just enough to let some light drift across the bed. The rays caressed Diana's milky white skin, giving her an ethereal glow. Between her absolute beauty, the fact that I hadn't seen her in over a thousand years, and the maddening scent of her heat, I wanted nothing more than to lie next to her in Miles' bed and forget about everything else around me. My brother's face betrayed that his thoughts were running along the same carnal line as mine.

"Well?" Eira asked again, impatience sharp in her voice. "What did you do to her?"

Miles huffed and walked to the side of the bed to kiss Diana's cheek. He moved aside and let me do the same. Her scent filled my lungs and just that tiny taste of her skin helped to control the beast within me.

"It's part of the spell we cast using our bond to heal her," I responded, straightening to my full seven-foot height. She didn't bat an eyelash. I wasn't sure what would intimidate this vampire, but apparently two seven-foot men capable of breathing fire wasn't on her list.

"The magick puts her into a peaceful hibernation until her wounds are healed. From the look of her injuries, I don't expect her to wake or be disturbed by anything for at least twenty-four to forty-eight hours." Miles crossed his arms over his chest and frowned. It was his normal look.

"So, she's not dreaming?" Eira asked, a flash of concern crossing through the Caribbean blue depths of her eyes.

I shook my head.

"It's like a magickally induced coma?"

"Yes," I answered.

She sighed and sank into the high-backed, leather chair against the wall near the bedside. "At least she's finally getting a break. Her emotional roller coaster is bad enough without all the soldiers and shooting coming at her from every direction. Though I have to say she handled herself pretty damn well for a woman with no memory. Her dragon can kick SECR ass." A grin tugged at the corners of the vampire's mouth. "She's one tough cookie."

"She always was," Miles said softly.

"Will you stay with her for now?" I asked, hating the idea of asking her for any kind of favor. "We need to speak with Rose about the possibility of a human assault force headed toward Sanctuary."

She nodded. "I was afraid you were going to try and get me to leave."

I wanted to. I shook my head. If she was the one person Diana trusted through all of this, the last thing I needed to do was alienate the vampire. "Do you need to feed? I can bring you back blood from the cafe."

"They have it on tap?" She half-snorted, half-giggled. "I should visit here more often."

I couldn't stop the grin tugging at my mouth. Perhaps she wasn't going to be quite the painful irritant I'd thought at first. "We have five vampires living in town. We're well-equipped to handle the demand."

"If it's cold, I'll just wait. She fed me last week. I can last—"

A snarl tore from my brother's chest and I caught his arm a second before he lunged at the little female. "You fed from Diana! You bit her!?"

The little brunette blurred past my brother and me, but paused at the door. Her eyes were wide and she watched Miles' heaving body as if her life depended on it. Which it probably did. I'd held back my brother's lunge, but I wasn't pleased either at the thought of her biting Diana. A vampire drinking directly from a being, human or supernatural, created a bond. One that was impossible to completely break.

"I didn't bite her," she spoke gingerly, her voice laced with a fear I hadn't heard yet. And I rather enjoyed it. At least I knew something could spook her. She might be a bit on the mouthy side and not willing to back down from a challenge, but this proved she wasn't stupid. When a pissed-off dragon-shifter lunged for her, she'd run.

"Miles," I growled, wrenching his arm back until he snarled and shook off his initial upset. "She's our guest."

"I don't give a shit."

I couldn't believe what I was about to do, but I turned back to face her anyway. "Please forgive my brother, he overreacted."

She gave me a suspicious glare and came out from behind the bedroom door that had hidden most of her body from view. Her movements were graceful, but strong like a person trained for combat. She placed her feet well and circled the furniture, giving us a wide berth as she made her way back to the opposite side of Miles' bed. She was a fighter. Of course the samurai sword on her back and smaller blades strapped to her thighs should have made that an easy guess. They seemed to be a part of her. Not flashy accessories, but items she probably always carried.

I walked to the bar cabinet across the room and removed a wine glass. Setting it on the marble top, I pulled open a drawer. The knife we'd used to cut our palms for the spell lay shining in the shallow, black-velvet-lined drawer. I picked it up and drew the sharp dragon steel blade over my palm again, holding my hand above the glass. My blood ran freely from the wound. When the glass was half full, I blew a focused stream of my warm breath across my palm, sealing the wound.

Taking the glass in my other hand, I approached her and offered her the glass. "I was a bit on the grouchy side earlier and I apologize as well. This has been a difficult day.

Being able to feel the life of your mate slip away without any recourse is—"

"Beyond terrible," she finished, accepting the glass from my hand. "Thank you for this." She raised the glass. "But you didn't have to."

"It was and is the least I can do for now, Eira. You helped to protect her. For that, there's nothing my brother and I wouldn't give to repay you. You're our guest. And if what you've said is true, we will need you present and on our side when she wakes."

She nodded. "I just want her to be happy. She's never at peace, awake or asleep. It's as if the weight of a world clings to her shoulders."

I backed away a few steps, then turned and walked back to my brother's side. Miles' hands were at least unclenched now and his breathing had returned to normal. Pulling out my mobile phone, I texted Rose's number, letting her know we were headed to the cafe.

"Don't you know they monitor everything? Why are you using a mobile phone?" The vampire's voice raised in pitch, her anxiety about the phone clearly evident.

"Ours are special. The only thing the government hears is static."

Her eyes widened. "How?"

"It's a town secret." I gave her a quick wink and looked back down at the screen. Rose had texted back to hurry. "We'll be back shortly."

She nodded and returned to the leather chair, her gaze falling gently to Diana's peaceful face.

I inclined my head toward the door and Miles moved ahead of me hesitantly. He exited first and I gave Eira and Diana one last glance before closing the door behind us.

"I don't like it, Eli."

"Don't like what?" I asked as we walked down the hallway to the main foyer. The lights were dim and moonlight flooded the hall at each window. It was like walking through a cave of shadows. I could hear the *da thump, da thump* of the music in the basement below. There were six guests in the club right now and they were all in the excellent hands of our faithful pixie dungeon monitors. One less thing we had to worry about right now. The only thing we wanted on our minds was Diana.

"She could be lying about everything. What if she did drink from Diana? We have to kill her, Eli."

My eyes widened in surprise. I hadn't seen that coming. "I believe her, Miles. Give it a few days. Diana will be able to answer that question when she wakes." I lifted the heavy beam barring the front doors and set it against the wall of the foyer.

Miles yanked the heavy door open and I followed him out into the cold, December evening. Something wet touched my face and I huffed out a foggy breath, shaking water droplets from my hair. It was a wintry mix of rain and snow. Just the kind of mess that fell every year about this time. None of it was sticking to the ground. It wasn't cold enough, yet. But come late January in Sanctuary, usually there would be a couple of inches of snow. When the white blanket covered the ground, it was the only time I let myself remember *home*. I hadn't lived in the Veil for millennia, but for some reason, snow always reminded me of the Brechin Mountains above Orin in the winter.

The door closed behind me and I glanced to my brother. He wiped his face with one hand and sighed. The steely glare and stoic face he showed most of the time was crumbling away. I could see his worry and concern. His brown eyes were glassy from unshed tears and my eyes watered in response. Rarely was he ever this worried about anything. Facing him, I placed both hands on his shoulders and he met my gaze squarely.

"She's going to be fine. We're together again," I said, trying to convince myself more than him.

"I'm fine," he grumbled. "I just never thought we'd get her back. Now that she's here, I can smell her, taste her, and that snip of a vampire's telling me she won't remember anything about our life. Nothing."

"Then we make her fall in love with us all over again."

"What if she doesn't want both of us?" His bass voice cracked and my heart dropped to my stomach.

I hadn't considered that.

CHAPTER 22

MILES

It was still dark as Eli and I crossed the town circle again. A cold wind blew through my loose hair and I took a deep, cleansing breath, allowing the chill to tamp down the fire inside. The street lamps illuminated the sidewalks, giving the town buildings a soft, ethereal glow. The old brick and chipped paint made most of the town look like it was from the 1940s. We purposefully kept the old town look to discourage anyone from thinking they needed to stay in Sanctuary. Visitors who fell in love with its quaintness were quickly influenced by one of the vampire Protectors and put on the next bus out of town.

Here and there, visitors trickled in to buy merchandise at Calliope's shop. They were all supernatural and knew the moment they met Rose that staying in Sanctuary was not an option for them without explicit permission. Our other visitors stayed in the Castle, and several of the pixies in town took care of all their arrangements. We were only called on when and if things escalated.

It didn't happen often. The pixies could be convincing when they needed to be.

Eli pulled open the cafe door and I frowned at the jingle of the little bell Rose insisted stay above it. I hated that little thing and always had to duck or it hit me square in the forehead.

The bus driver who'd brought Diana back to Sanctuary sat in the far corner of the cafe. He, like most of the buses that came and went from Sanctuary, was family to the two red-headed witches in town —Meredith and Hannah. He waved when we came in and rose from his table where he sat sipping a mug of coffee. The scent of the roasted hazelnut blend clung to his shirt.

"How is she?" he asked, stopping a few feet away. Neither Eli nor I were in the mood for conversation.

"She will make it," Eli answered, before I could even open my mouth. "Thank you for getting her here safely."

"Anything for the people who take such good care of my girls."

"We very much appreciate everything you do for the town, Harrison. Please excuse us, though, we have to speak with Rose," I added.

"What about the bus? I can't leave until you boys defrost it for me."

We'd walked right past it without even noticing. Diana was distracting both of us and we needed to get our heads straight before soldiers showed up. "I will make sure it's done by the morning. Do you need a room to stay in for the night?"

Harrison shook his head. "I'm good. Meredith has a

spare room since her sister's in Ada right now. I just wanted to check in with you both before I left for her house. Rose said you were on your way."

I nodded.

"Thank you again, Harrison," Eli repeated.

"I know what it's like to lose someone," Harrison spoke again, his eyes watering. "There's nothing I wouldn't do to have another moment with the girls' mother. Annie was everything to me. I'm just glad you both have a second chance. It doesn't happen often." He rubbed his hands through his bushy head of gray hair and sighed. "Good-night, boys."

We were centuries older than him, but he still insisted on calling us boys. At first, we'd balked at it, but as you grew to know Harrison Bateman, you only grew to care about him more. As many years as his girls had lived in Sanctuary now, we were used to their dad saying just about anything he wanted to. The old warlock had been invited to move back to Sanctuary several times, but he always told Rose he liked being on the outside. That he felt like he was more help that way. We all knew it was because he'd lost his wife here. He just couldn't bear the thought of living in Sanctuary without her. Too many painful memories. The girls, on the other hand, couldn't stand the thought of leaving the town their mother had guarded her entire life.

I could relate. If Rose hadn't made us as guardians over a houseful of crazy women, Eli and I would've drunk ourselves into a permanent stupor. The Sisters were the only reason we hadn't caved in to the grief. There was something about the laughter of women and children that had helped keep us sane throughout the centuries.

"Good night, Harrison."

He waved as he walked out of the cafe. The annoying little bell rang again and I grimaced. The cafe was mostly empty. It was the middle of the night, but several of the Protectors sat along the back wall with the twin pixies, Raven and Maven. Marcus with his mate, Sita, along with Javier, were deep in conversation. Only Sita looked up, a question in her blue irises.

I shook my head.

She nodded and refocused on her group.

Eli started for the kitchen and I followed him around the breakfast bar and through the swinging door. The smell of cinnamon and yeast filled the room.

Rose was alone in the kitchen. She folded a ball of dough on the counter and mashed it down, repeating the process several times. Pans of rising cinnamon rolls were laid out behind her, the source of the spicy, sweet smell.

"How is she?" Rose's voice was soft, but filled with the strength of a leader. She was thousands of years old, millennia older than we were—yet she looked no older than thirty-five.

"Stable and healing," Eli answered, pulling up a stool and sitting across from the counter where she was working. I followed suit and sat next to him on another empty stool.

"And the female vampire? What has she said?"

"Just that Diana has no memory of who or what she is. I get the feeling they struggled to help Diana keep her magick under wraps. Even so, she shifted to dragon form at least twice, from what we've been told. Both times were to protect herself from SECR soldiers. They're tracking her, Rose."

Rose sighed. "I know." She picked up a rolling pin and began to flatten out the large ball of dough she'd been kneading. "They're coming. I've felt Djinn scouts outside the city for the last few hours. But this won't be out in the open; they risk a war with the Texas Republic if they're discovered. These will be skilled soldiers."

"They're still human," I added.

"But they're working with Djinn. Xerxes' reach is growing."

She put down the rolling pin. Picking up a bowl of cinnamon sugar, she sprinkled it evenly across the dough, smoothing and spreading it until there was a generous layer over every inch. Baking helped Rose calm herself. The fact that she had three trays of rolls already done and was working on her fourth said volumes about her stress level.

"I need you two to be focused. The Lycans and Protectors will be able to pick off most of them, but some will slip through. We *must* protect the town. Meredith and her father are here and I've already spoken with them about amping up the power to the wards that protect the buildings. But that will only slow the soldiers. It will not stop them."

"Of course. You know we will do anything to protect Sanctuary."

"Erick also informed me after you both left with Diana ..." She rolled the dough into a long cylinder and started slicing it, putting each roll on the waiting pan to her side. "... that he recognized the vampire accompanying her. He doesn't think she recognized him, though."

"She's that old? There aren't many left their age," Eli said.

"He said she was a shield-maiden from a territory adjacent to his Jarl's. She is one of the fiercest warriors he's come across in all his years. Her betrothed was killed in the same battle that claimed her human life. She was sired by the same vampire who turned Erick."

"And they never met? After all these years?" I asked.

"No," Rose answered, wiping her hands on the apron around her waist.

I added what I knew about her. "She works with the Mason pack currently. As attached as she is to Diana, I'm not sure she will be leaving anytime soon."

"We may need her. It will be good if she stays a while. The Masons are a strong family, but foolish. They know Xerxes is the driving force behind the SECR's corrupt government, yet they continue to risk so much each time they go back East. Hannah knows several of the Masons. She has friends in Ada, where they usually settle for the winter."

"She should be more careful who she hangs out with," I said, growling at the thought of little Hannah Bateman spending time with a pack of Lycans.

Rose smiled at me. "She's a big girl, Miles. They would never hurt her. She goes up there to help with healing."

I knew that. I also knew Hannah and Meredith both traveled back and forth to Ada. It was where their mother was from originally and they still had family there. Sanctuary was blessed that the girls both decided to stay after their mother passed away. Their family had created the warding spells that kept Djinn from being able to teleport in and out of Sanctuary's buildings.

"Hopefully, the girls can help Diana once she wakes

from the healing sleep. She has no memory of her life before three weeks ago."

Rose frowned. "That's strong magick. I promise you both, we will find a way to help her. First, I need you to take the four wolves outside the cafe and set them up with these." She pulled two sets of two-way radios from a cabinet behind her. "Have them stay in the four corner towers of the Castle."

I nodded.

She pulled out a handful of small ear buds from the same cabinet and handed everything to me. I took the radios, put a listening device in my right ear, and handed another to Eli. He followed suit and placed one of the enchanted ear buds into his right ear. At first glance, the tech looked normal—like our mobile phones—but thanks to the Bateman witches' magick, humans couldn't listen in. We were invisible on the heavily guarded networks, no matter which Republic we were in. The Batemans hadn't figured out how to use the Internet undetected yet, but at least we had the modern conveniences of mobile phones and two-way radios.

I rose from my seat and headed for the door. Eli padded quietly behind me.

"Be careful." Rose's warning was soft, but sincere. "None of the soldiers can be allowed to leave the town," she added.

Looking over my shoulder, I caught her deadly gaze and nodded. "I know."

CHAPTER 23

ELI

Killing humans was always messy. People tended to come looking for them. I hated that Xerxes was using them to try and get to Sanctuary. It was bad enough he'd enslaved an entire race of supernaturals, branding them as evil and vicious in human and supernatural eyes alike. The Djinn had not always been hated and feared. But now, stuck under Xerxes' thumb, we had no choice but to kill or imprison them.

I followed my brother through the dining room of the cafe and out onto the front porch. Four Lycans stood off to the side. I couldn't remember a couple of their names, only two had visited the Castle that I could recollect.

"Liam O'Connor," one of the unfamiliar men approached with his hand outstretched. "Brogan is my cousin. I believe Kieran and Douglas said they'd met you previously at the Castle."

"Thank you," I said, shaking his hand. "I couldn't for the life of me recall your names."

The Lycan smiled. "No worries. There are a lot of us to keep track of, especially when we keep taking in strays."

"Rose knows you took more into the pack?" Miles growled softly.

"Aye, no worries there. She knows and has approved each new arrival. Most we've taken in have been extended family to pack members already living here," Liam answered, not letting Miles' attempt at intimidation get him down.

The wolf Liam had called Brogan stepped forward. "Even though some of us haven't been here as long, I can assure you we will fight to the death to protect this town and our families."

My gaze shifted to the blond man next to Liam. His green eyes flashed yellow for just a second and I let my lips curl into a smile. I liked his attitude. That was the kind of man I wanted at my side in a fight, even if he was just a wolf.

"Miles, give them their earbuds and let's show them where they'll be camping until the action starts."

My brother doled out the tech and we headed for the Castle. I reached the massive doors first and pushed one of them open. Miles followed next and then the four Lycans. I closed the door behind the group and then heaved the heavy bar into place. It didn't need to be there yet, but out of habit, I replaced the barrier anyway. Better safe than sorry, though it would take a hell of a beast to even push the door open *without* the bar.

My brother was barking out instructions as they climbed the grand staircase to the right. I followed quickly behind them, catching up in a few strides. Our footsteps echoed down silent hallways. Even the courtyard was empty and quiet. The Sisters probably already knew the shit was about to hit the fan. Their main living quarters were in the lower levels of the Castle, below ground. But they spent most of their time in the outdoor courtyards or the living areas on the first floor.

We climbed two more flights of stairs and split. Miles continued straight with Liam and Brogan and I waved the other two Lycans to trail me. We stayed on the path under the parapet and doubled back toward the front of the Castle.

Each Lycan was assigned a corner tower of the Castle. Liam and Brogan would stand watch in the two back towers, while Kieran and Douglass covered the front. With Lycan hearing and telepathic abilities, any humans approaching the town would be noticed immediately. If Djinn approached first, Calliope and Rose would come on the protected radio signal and let everyone know to be on high alert. Because of the magickal wards, Djinn had to physically enter the buildings in town. No teleporting in and out.

I thanked them for their help and then turned, took the parapet pathway to the back stairwell nearest our living quarters. I stepped down a flight of dark, stone stairs and came out in the hallway that lead to our bedrooms. Miles' footsteps echoed behind me. We were both thinking the same thing.

Diana.

I pulled open Miles' bedroom door and Eira turned her head to face us. "She hasn't stirred."

Miles approached the bedside first and leaned down,

pressing a kiss to Diana's forehead. He moved away, giving me room to do the same. She smelled as sweet as Rose's cinnamon rolls.

I glanced up and caught Eira's gaze. Her jewel-blue eyes sparked and she stood from the chair on the opposite side of the large, four-poster bed.

"Perhaps there's somewhere I could freshen up before this all goes down. I expect the first wave of soldiers to be arriving near the twelve-hour mark, so I have a few minutes before I need to be prepared to fight." She walked around to the foot of the bed. "I haven't seen her sleep this soundly since I met her. Whatever you guys did, it's helping."

It tore at my heart to hear she'd been suffering ... how many years? At least our healing spell was giving her some peace. Would she still be the same woman we fell in love with and married so many years ago?

Wait? "The first wave?"

"It's how the SECR operates. First wave will be small, maybe thirty to fifty soldiers. They can't get more than that over the borders at a time. Texas law will let them send up to fifty for hunting an escaped prisoner, which is what they will have their orders written up to look like."

"Gives them carte blanche to do whatever they want in the Texas Republic," I muttered.

She nodded. "Another reason the Masons hole up in Ada for six months out of the year. Helps with soothing them into forgetting they need to come after us."

"You've been doing this a while, haven't you?" Miles asked.

"Since the walls between the republics were first built. So almost forty years now," she added with a sigh. "It's nothing new. I've always helped. Wherever I lived. I am an ageless warrior. What else am I good for?" She shrugged her shoulders and looked away.

"You've never wanted a mate? How many years have you been alone?"

She rolled her eyes. "No need to go playing match-maker, dragon man. I'm perfectly happy on my own." But the tone of her voice hinted that she didn't speak truthfully.

"I'll stay with Diana," Miles said, catching my gaze.

I nodded and motioned to Eira. She followed me out of his bedroom and down the hall. We had several spare rooms in our wing of the Castle. All of them had their own bathroom en suite.

Pushing open a large, wooden door, I gestured for Eira to enter first. To my surprise, she didn't come back with a witty comment about me holding the door for her. I peered inside and noted that it had been freshened lately and the bed had clean sheets, not that a vampire would really need to sleep.

"There should be fresh linens in the bathroom. If you need anything else, just let me know. There are four Lycans in the Castle right now, just so you know. They're on lookout in the four towers.

"Thank you," she said. "I noticed their scent on you, but didn't realize they were in the building."

I turned to leave, but paused and looked back at her one last time. She was pulling her chocolate tresses loose from its ponytail, reminding me how much I'd missed running my hands through a woman's hair. After Miles and I took charge of the Sisters, our sex lives had become kind of empty.

A casual fling with a visitor or two at the private Castle club or one of the pixies from town, but never more than that. We tried to find regular subs for a few years to release stress ... or grief, but they knew our hearts weren't in it. It wasn't fair to a sub to have a Dom who wasn't focused. Now we taught in the Club once a week, training males from town or visitors how to be responsible and attentive Doms.

The Sisters appreciated our efforts in creating a safe and controlled environment in the club for them to practice BDSM; but neither of us was willing to have sex with any of the Sisters, even though they had attempted to coax us on multiple occasions. The idea that we might father children into the House of Lamidae made it completely unappealing. My brother and I preferred to know our children—should we ever have any.

Which brought me back to the horrifying question in my mind. Did we have a child with Diana? Had that experience been stolen from us along with our wife?

This room had been crafted for the sole purpose of one day being a haven for a son or daughter. Though both of us had given up the hope of Diana's return, the Sisters had insisted when the Castle had been designed that we put a nursery and spare bedrooms in our wing of the fortress.

Maybe the Sisters had held back information all along.

CHAPTER 24

DIANA

I could smell him before I saw him.

The scent of male flooded my nostrils and the beast within me roared to life. I recognized it, but I didn't. Everything was muddy, except the need to touch the male, taste him, and have him completely. Turning my head toward his scent, I opened my eyes slowly, thankful for the dim lighting. It made it that much easier to focus and take in the handsome face staring down at me from the bedside.

He had strong, deep-set eyes, hard brow lines, and a square jaw covered in several days' growth. Black, wavy hair hung forward from either side of his face, easily shoulder length and beautifully familiar. He was one of the men from my dream. No doubt about it ... yet I still couldn't remember his name or how we knew each other—just that we did.

His brown eyes widened, surprise flooding his face like

a man who'd been caught spying on a naked woman bathing. I felt the corners of my lips turn up into a smile.

Heat flowed rapidly through my body and I clenched my hands into fists to keep from reaching forward to touch him. He smelled like heaven. The damned dragon inside me was not helping either. A light sweat coated my body in seconds. I knew what was coming next—ice. Every time this blasted fever rose, my powers overwhelmed me and ice covered the room, froze the bed, the sheets, and the walls. I ruined everything around me.

But nothing happened.

We just continued to stare at each other—silence filling the space between us like fog on the hillside. It just became thicker and thicker, neither of us willing to be the first to break through the barrier.

A click from the doorway across the room drew our attention and I marveled as another man, identical to the one already standing at my bedside, entered the room. He took one glance our way and something akin to a whoop came from his lips.

"When did she wake up?" he asked, rushing to the other side of the bed.

Bloody hell. How was I supposed to watch them when they stood separately on either side of this enormous bed? I flashed my gaze back and forth, studying their faces.

"Just now," the first twin rumbled.

That one. The man I'd seen first. There was a small scar above his right eyebrow. It wasn't much, but at least it was something to start with. I'd never seen such perfect twins before. In my dreams, I'd known they were twins, but seeing them in the flesh and smelling their scents ... it was more than overwhelming. There were so many emotions running through me. Excitement. Arousal. Fear.

"Diana, how are you feeling?" The second twin spoke, drawing my gaze from the first.

Diana? I didn't remember my name, but it sounded ... correct. They had to know me. I would not have had the inappropriate carnal dreams about them if they did not.

"Diana." The name rolled off my lips easily. I liked the sound of it. "What is my surname?"

"Your family name before marriage was Karlson," the second twin spoke again.

"I'm married?" I glanced back and forth. "To whom?"

"To us," the first twin answered.

I gulped and felt the temperature plummet in the room. *Married? To two men?*

"Your name is Diana Karlson Blackmoor," the second twin continued. "We lost you when our kingdom was taken by the Incanti brothers, Kevan and Leif. Do you remember them?"

I shook my head and looked back at the first twin. His eyes had darkened and he was frowning, but not in a frightening way. It was more like he was trying to figure out what to say.

"Where's Eira?" I missed the plucky vampire who acted as my go-between in this strange and unfamiliar world. I prayed to whatever gods were listening that she had not abandoned me.

"Down the hall washing up. Neither of us thought you'd wake from the healing sleep so quickly. Do you feel all right? Any residual pain anywhere?" The second twin rambled on and I watched him refrain from reaching for me at least three times.

At least I was not the only one struggling to keep my hands to myself. Even with the revelation that I was married to two men—two brothers. I wanted them. With every fiber of my being, I craved their touch and so much more. My behavior was that of a tavern wench. This *heat* would not let up.

"I feel tired, but no pain. Why is the room not covered in ice?"

The first twin held out his hand, palm up.

I could feel heat rising from his skin, warming the temperature around me. It was counteracting the freezing cold and ice that normally poured from me whenever stress overwhelmed me. Which was most of the time lately.

"Are you like me?"

"Dragons? Yes," the twin to my right spoke up. "But you're an ice-breather. We're fire-breathers. My brother Miles ..." he pointed to the first twin, " ... and I are born of the house of Blackmoor. We were the crown princes of the Veil before the Incantis betrayed us and stole our home. We would have ruled from the stone thrones as kings once our fathers finished their two-thousand-year reign."

None of it sounded familiar. Not even the name "Miles."

"What is your name?" I asked. It would be nice to refer to them as something besides number one and number two. Or twin with the scar.

"Forgive me," he said. "I'm Eli."

Eli and Miles. I rolled the two names around in my head, but still came up blank. I would give anything to regain my memories. Who I was. Where I was from. If I had a life with these two men, it would be nice to remember it.

"Eira calls me D." I looked up at Eli. His brown eyes softened and he smiled.

"How did she guess?"

"She didn't." I scooted backward against the pillows, giving myself a better angle from which to observe them. It was so strange to lay flat on my back and look up at these two handsome, but gigantic, men. The only thoughts running through my head in that position were nothing a lady should be thinking about. Though they had said we were married. So maybe I shouldn't be so hard on myself.

"She called me D for dragon." I let a small grin curve my mouth.

"Do you want us to call you D?" Miles asked, hesitation in his voice.

"No, it's fine. I'll get used to Diana. I know you know me as this person, but I don't know her. Or anything about you." My words rushed out. I wanted them to know how lost I felt. I didn't think I could handle expectations right now. It was all I could do not to throw ice at anything unfamiliar in this strange world.

Eira had helped me acquire some techniques to calm some of my anxiety, but it was still a learning process. One that Eira had no experience with previously. Maybe these dragons, even if they were fire-breathers, could help me conquer this ice problem.

"I'm sorry. I know you must have so many questions. But, I'm afraid I have no answers."

"It's we who should be answering your questions. Eira said you had no memory of your life before the prison."

"She said she knew a witch in Ada who could help, but when we finally arrived, I was too weak."

Miles glanced up at Eli. "She must know the Bateman family. They're the only witches living in and out of Ada. Hannah would have been there when she arrived. The timeline is right."

I looked first to Miles and then back to Eli. "Do you know the witch, too?"

"Yes, the Bateman family has a long history with the town. Hannah and Meredith travel back and forth regularly between Sanctuary and Ada. Their father lives there," Eli explained. "When you feel up to it, we will speak with her about the spell she'd planned to use. Perhaps when you're stronger, it could help you remember what you've lost."

"If you want to remember ..." Miles spoke softly under his breath.

I turned to him and nodded. "I have to remember. No matter the price. I have to remember."

"Not if it endangers you. We can't lose you. It would kill us," Eli said. His voice broke and he ran his hands through his loose, wavy, black hair. "You don't understand the repercussions, but we will talk about it later."

He sounded agitated and strained. Even Miles was beginning to look upset.

"I'm sorry. I didn't mean to make either of you upset."

"No!" Eli said quickly, reaching forward to brush his fingers down my arm. But just as they touched, he pulled back.

Miles growled. "No, Eli. If you touch her..."

"I know," Eli snarled back at his brother from across the bed. "I didn't think."

But his touch had already started a reaction. My skin tingled. Flames of arousal slithered up and down my arms, spreading across my chest and down into my belly. My heartbeat raced and even my breathing started to come faster and faster. Something I couldn't explain was building inside me. If I didn't touch, taste, and take these men, it would be unbearable. I already wanted to scream in frustration because I didn't know which man to reach for first. Which one wouldn't deny me?

I turned my gaze to Eli, his eyes filled with burning desire. Miles had told him "no" and I didn't want to be told no.

Reaching over I caught his arm and gasped at the shock of energy that passed between us. It was like every place in my body had just come alive for the first time. A moan slipped from between my lips and I tugged him closer.

He leaned forward, but stopped. I released a frustrated wail and threw my other arm around his head, yanking him closer. I covered his mouth with mine and the beast within me roared with excitement. I didn't know the man, but he felt familiar. The kiss started rough, then softened. I pressed my tongue into his mouth and heard a growl vibrate in his chest. He slipped a hand behind my head and crushed my mouth the way I'd wanted to capture his. The soft tenderness turned to an animalistic need.

My body responded to every sound. Every scent surrounding him. He tasted like spice and heat. I wanted more. Not less.

A growl on my left reminded me there were two men in the room, and I was only kissing one.

Eli broke the kiss and backed away. His eyes were wide

and he looked worried that he'd done something wrong. "I'm sorry."

The apology was not directed at me. Nor should it have been. I wasn't sorry and was near whimpering that he had pulled away.

"She's our wife and she's in heat. How can you just stand there and pretend you can't feel the call of your dragon?" Eli said.

"She doesn't know us, Eli. It would be taking advantage." Miles looked down at me. "I can't do that to you. I could never bear you hating me afterward. We're strangers to you."

I heard everything he said. Most of it even made sense, but I didn't care. We might be strangers, but their touch and scent was familiar to me. It felt like home and I wanted it more than I wanted to be left alone to contemplate my existence.

"You bloody hell do not get to tell me how I will feel! I have been through a magickal portal, been shot twice, and now am in the most comfortable bed I could ever imagine with two men who claim to *both* be my husbands ... and they will not touch me for fear of how I will react later! The only thing I want to do is touch both of you. Taste both of you. I've wanted you both every moment I was awake in that wretched ice block of a prison cell."

He didn't say anything. Time froze as we stared at one another. Then, faster than I could react, Miles had me in his arms, crushing his mouth against mine. I moaned in satisfaction and dug my fingers into his thick, black hair. His tongue delved into my mouth and I swept mine into his. He tasted so good. Just as good as Eli had.

Rivulets of pleasure coursed up and down my body. He

had pulled me from the bed and was holding me flush against his chest, my feet dangled in the air. I tried to wrap them around his waist, but the shift I wore inhibited my attempts.

I heard footsteps come around the bed and quickly I felt Eli's warmth behind me, pinning me between them. They were huge men. Their chests broader than any I'd seen on the way to Ada. Not even the soldiers who had chased us came close to their size.

Miles distracted me from my wandering thoughts with a well-placed nip on my bottom lip. "Stay here with us, Diana," he growled into my mouth.

I refocused on him and pulled his hair, tugging him even closer.

My body shivered between them as Eli slid his hands up my thighs, tugging the shift up as he went. Cool air hit my belly and I jerked. He tucked the extra fabric between my breasts and Miles' chest.

Both men growled, refusing to let me budge an inch. My strength was nothing compared to theirs. I was at their mercy and loving it. My temperature soared with theirs and the room became sticky with humidity and the scent of our mixed sweat.

Eli worked his fingers around my waist and then dipped them quickly between my legs from behind. I squeaked in surprise, but didn't object because it felt so good. He slipped them into the opening of my sex, then moved them further forward until he brushed against the swollen nub above my slit.

I squealed into Miles' unforgiving mouth, but neither man let up. Eli's fingers worked my lower half while he feathered kisses along my bare back. Miles still made love to my mouth and lips, occasionally wandering along my jaw line and neck. But he always came back. Perhaps he couldn't resist the cries they were eliciting from me.

My lower body had a mind of its own. If it weren't for Eli's firm grip on my hip I think I would have squirmed away completely. He tortured my slit and then that little nub relentlessly. Something was building inside me, growing and flowering until Miles whispered in my ear.

"Come." He pinched one of my nipples and it was like the world shattered around me into a million pieces of glass. I let my head sag forward against Miles' chest and shouted. Eli pumped his fingers in and out of my slit and I clamped down hard on them each time they entered. The touch of their hands sent me higher and higher. My eyes closed and I saw stars instead of darkness.

CHAPTER 25

DIANA

"I leave to take a shower and you take advantage of her raging libido!" Eira's voice rang from the doorway.

I shivered through a few more waves of the aftershock.

Miles and Eli both growled at my friend and Eli left my side and turned to face Eira. My shift fell down to cover my naked bottom and I pushed against Miles' chest until he let me down. Surprisingly, my fever had abated some and I could think logically about my situation once more. I did however feel the flush of embarrassment creeping rapidly up my face and neck.

"Eira," I said calmly. "Do not blame them."

"I sure as hell will. You can't control yourself. You're in heat like a horny pussy cat." Eira shut the door and headed in my direction, but stopped abruptly when Miles growled and stepped in front of me. She raised the large samurai sword she always carried above her head and snarled back.

I moved to the side and pushed gently. The big giant took a step to the side and huffed his annoyance. Eli stood a few paces closer to Eira and they were eyeing each other like two animals trying to decide which would win. Hands down, I'd bet on the dragon. But Eira was resourceful. I didn't want any of them fighting.

"Stop it. All of you." My voice rang through the room and all three turned to look at me. "I'm perfectly content with my choices thus far. Eira, I can't tell you how much I appreciate you keeping me from leaping on each and every male in our camp over the past few weeks. But these two men are my husbands."

"Doesn't count," Eira snapped, but she lowered the sword to the ground. "You don't remember anything about them except their faces. You didn't even know you were married."

Eli growled again.

"Zip it, you giant fire-breathing windbag. D and I are having a conversation."

I couldn't hold back the snort of laughter. She'd just called a seven-foot giant of a man, who could breathe fire, a windbag and told him to be quiet.

"I remember their touch, Eira. They are a part of me, even if I can't remember our lives together. Doesn't that count for something?"

"Are you sure it's not the heat talking? You have a crazy amount of magick locked up in that body of yours. I'd rather not get turned into a creamsicle because you realize later you made a mistake."

I had no idea what a creamsicle was, but I did notice that her long, brown hair was wet and not combed. She was barefoot and her shirt was on backward.

"Did you run down here?" I asked.

Eira sighed. "I heard you yelling and freaked out. I thought they were hurting you."

Miles and Eli had both relaxed their stances by now and somehow had moved noiselessly to either side of me. Their scent filled my lungs and naughty images of what I wanted to do to both of them danced in my mind. That had to be the heat.

"I'm fine." I held out my hands. "I promise. We are safe here. They won't let anything happen to me."

"They haven't told you yet?" Eira asked.

I furrowed my brows and glanced quickly to Miles and then to Eli. Both men frowned and then flashed an annoyed glare in Eira's direction.

"Told me what?" I asked, holding Eli's gaze.

"The soldiers are coming here. The town is preparing for an assault," Eira shot back before Eli could even open his mouth.

The dragon male snarled, but didn't move toward Eira. Miles didn't budge either, but I could feel the tension between the three. It was like they were vying for the right to be the one protecting me.

I was a dragon. Out of my element and time apparently, but still, I was a dragon. I didn't need three babysitters. I certainly didn't need the men claiming to be my husbands and my only friend to be at odds, either.

"I thought this land was protected—that the soldiers could not come into this place."

Miles turned to me. "They can't, officially. But it won't stop them from sending in small forces by stealth to try and capture you. I'm sure Xerxes wants his dagger back and assumes you have it."

"But I don't." I crossed my arms and frowned. The damned dagger was in a hole, buried where I'd first appeared.

"But you know where it is, don't you, Love?" Eli stated softly.

It was a question, but one he intuitively knew the answer to. There was no way that he could. I hadn't told anyone I'd hidden it. Only that I'd lost it.

"I told Eira I lost it in that little town, before they attacked me the first time."

Eli grunted and a chuckle shook his chest. "The Diana I know wouldn't have taken it with her to the village, especially if she realized how important it was. You're smart Diana. Just because you don't have any memories, doesn't mean you don't have your common sense and survival skills. Look how hard you fought to get back to us. You didn't even know we were here. Not really. You just knew you had to go. It would've been the same thing with that dagger. In your heart you knew it had to be hidden. Protected."

My eyebrows raised, fear lancing its way through my heart. "Will they think of it that way?"

"Probably not for a while," he answered. "It should be safe for now."

"Sneaky little dragon," Eira said, a smile transforming her too-serious face.

In a second she morphed from scary warrior to the friend I'd grown to trust. Now I just needed her to trust these men standing beside me. I might have no memory of them in my mind, but the rest of me, including the beast within, was jumping for joy that we'd found our home.

"Whatever comes, I will help fight. They are chasing me. I am perfectly capable of fighting, just ask Eira."

She gave a small half-laugh. "Maybe as a dragon, sweetie, but you didn't even know what a gun was when I met you, much less how to fire one. And you aren't very good at dodging bullets since we've had to dig several out of you already."

"You just woke from a healing spell. No way in hell are we going to let you fight anything," Eli growled out. Heat rolled from both of them in waves and my body compensated by throwing out its own cooling temperatures.

"If y'all don't cool it off with the hot and cold, it's going to start raining indoors." She laid the flat edge of her sword on her shoulder and smirked. "Since I'm not needed at the moment, I'm going to let you two boys figure out how to order her about. Just a fair warning, she doesn't listen to instructions very well."

I glared at Eira, but she just winked and left the room. The large door clicked shut behind her, leaving me once again alone with my husbands.

"Now what?" I turned around so I faced them both.

"Now we find out how many times you can come in the next couple of hours," Eli said, a wicked grin spreading across his face.

Heat rushed to my cheeks and I looked away, embarrassed that I actually wanted him to try. What they had done to my body before ... it had been magickal in itself.

"Don't be shy now," Miles said, taking a step closer and closing the space between our bodies.

Eli followed suit and suddenly they were both in front of me. Miles lifted my chin and leaned down to press his lips to mine. I wanted to taste him so much, but in the back of my head, I could hear Eira bemoaning the fact that I didn't know either of these men. Yet, I'd already gone so far as to let one of them put his hands inside me. How could I say "no" to a kiss?

But I did.

I stepped backward, separating myself from them both. Instantly I missed the connection of their touch. I belonged with them. I could feel it so deeply in my bones that I ached.

Both men stood frozen. Hurt registered in their eyes, not anger or frustration. Pain and sorrow fairly bled from their souls, which practically tore mine from my body. But, what was I doing? I didn't know anything about them. Anything about me. I just knew they cared about me. Loved me even.

I could feel it in the tenderness of each touch. In the way they had whispered sweet words in my ears as they played my body like an instrument, making it sing just for them. I wanted that again. I felt so safe with them. It was a feeling I could not remember ever having before today.

A single tear ran down my cheek and I watched it drop to the carpet. Then ice started forming around my bare feet. It spread outward toward them. I cried out. Terror filled me. I'd seen my powers kill people. I never wanted to see that again. I could not lose them so quickly after finding them.

"Make it stop," I begged. "Please make it stop." More tears fell, but they froze instantly, pinging against the frozen floor like bits of sleet.

Both men moved at the same time, stepping forward

and pulling me back into their arms. The fears vanished and the ice stopped spreading across the room. I watched in amazement as it all began to melt. The room warmed so much that steam began to rise from the carpet.

"You belong with us, Diana," Eli whispered into my ear as he nibbled on the lobe.

"Embrace what you feel. Even though your memories were stolen, we still have ours. I remember the first time I laid eyes on you in the throne room of Orin. Your snow-blond hair glistening like it was made of pure moonlight. Your sweet scent filled the air and I thought my heart would fall from my chest. I hadn't the words to thank the gods for bringing you to us."

"That is not who I am," I whispered. "I'm more than a pretty painting."

"Aye, we could not have imagined a more beautiful bride," Eli murmured into my other ear. His strange accent fell away for a moment and he sounded like me. "And then that evening at supper, you carried your trencher to the doorway of the banquet hall and handed it to one of the servant's children sitting on a pallet, begging for scraps. In front of everyone. We knew then your beauty was of body and heart."

"For seven days, the palace feasted to celebrate our upcoming wedding," Miles' deep voice continued the story. "For seven days you fed every child who appeared at the doorway before you would eat a single morsel."

I smiled, picturing the faces of the children eager to receive the food. "How many children came the last day?" I asked.

Eli spoke this time. "On the last day of the grand feast,

there were twenty-two children in the doorway. You told them to come to the kitchen entrance every morning from then on and they would have what they needed."

"They were just children. Someone needed to look out for them."

"And you did. The poor of Orin called you *snøen mor*—snow mother," Miles said, sliding a hand down my arm. "The people said whenever you were distraught, your tears would fall in the form of snowflakes. The children were always bringing you flowers, especially before the start of winter."

"Why?"

"Because they thought it would stay warmer longer if you were happy," Eli said, pushing aside my long hair and kissing the base of my neck. Shivers of excitement ran down my spine.

"*Snøen mor.*" I rolled the name over my lips. "What happened?" I asked, leaning back into Eli's firm chest. I turned my face toward his shirt and breathed in deeply, looking for any familiarity in the recesses of my mind.

"We failed our kingdom. A rival family took us completely unaware and killed every Blackmoor in the castle," said Eli.

"Except the three of us," Miles added. "We were publicly tortured, nearly beaten to death and then they hurt you—" his voice broke off and he took a deep breath. "I swear on my life, Diana. If there had been any way to spar—"

I put a finger over his mouth and shook my head. "What happened to me was not your fault. Either of you. I'm here now. I want to find my memories, but even without them, I know I belong to you."

"I vote for making a few new memories," Eli said, nipping at the base of my neck.

The sharp edges of his teeth made shivers flutter across my skin. What he proposed was exactly what I wanted to do.

CHAPTER 26

DIANA

"**I** want you both, but ..." I hesitated. We had obviously done this before, but I had no memory, nor a clue about how to properly take care of two men at once. Bloody hell, I did not even know how to take care of one. I had no memory of intimate relations with either of them. "I do not know how this works."

"Trust your body," Miles murmured, kissing one of my shoulders. "We will not do anything you do not wish to happen."

"I want you both so badly. My body burns for this. What we did earlier helped some, but now it is worse. I *need* with a hunger that does not feel natural."

"Female Drakonae enter a heat cycle every five centuries. It's the one time they're fertile and able to conceive," Eli said, tucking my hair behind my ear and then trailing his fingertips along my cheek.

A baby? How could I commit to something like that

with two men I barely knew? Granted, I trusted that they were my mates. My dragon agreed that I belonged with them ... but a baby? With the dreams that already plagued me about losing a baby—I knew that was what happened now. There was no other excuse for my dreams.

Stepping away from them, I sunk down onto the edge of the bed. Five-hundred years. How old was I?

"Is this what you want? A baby? Now?"

They both knelt to the floor before me, each taking one of my hands in theirs.

"I can't say that I'm not excited by the prospect of our child growing inside you soon, but I know this is much more to take on than you're ready for," Eli said. "It's just that ..."

"That even once everything has calmed down, whether I do or don't get my memories back, we have to wait five-hundred years for another chance," I finished for him, my voice barely louder than a whisper.

A tear rolled from my cheek and froze in the air as it dropped. An exquisite snowflake landed on my arm and melted instantly from the heat of contact.

"Don't cry, Love," Eli spoke again. "We can't even begin to understand what you have gone through, what you're still going through. This world must be a scary place to be thrust into suddenly."

I stared into Eli's brown eyes and then Miles'. The connection between us was so strong. I couldn't deny that I was where I was meant to be; I just wished I could remember what had happened to me. I wanted what they had. The story about our wedding feast made me feel so much closer to them already, but greed made me want more. I wanted to remember their favorite food. Or color. Or what made them laugh.

Instead, I had a mind filled with a fog of pain and confusion. Dreams that didn't make sense. And a nagging feeling that I'd lost more than just my memories in the place they called Orin.

"Make love to me," I spoke slowly. "Please."

Whatever I had forgotten, it was time to push forward. We could face my past together as it came to light. Until then, I wanted to embrace my future.

"If this is our only chance for a family for that long, I don't want to look back and regret not taking it."

Both men's faces brightened and smiles curved their lips upward. "Whatever happens is your choice," Eli said. "I know I speak for Miles when I say we couldn't be more thankful just to have you back in our lives."

"If you're not ready for this," Miles started. "We would never dream of making you regret any choice you made. We are Drakonae. We have lived for millennia and will continue to survive long after those around us have perished."

"How old are we?" I asked, curious again. I couldn't imagine what it would be like to have that many years of memories.

"Eli and I were born nearly three-thousand years ago in the Veil, the world beyond earth. You were born in the equivalent of earth's seventh century I believe, so you would be nearing fifteen-hundred years old."

My jaw dropped and I swallowed. Fifteen-hundred years and I could only remember the last three weeks. "How could I have just forgotten everything?"

"It was not your choice," Eli whispered, pressing a trail

of kisses along the top of my hand and up my wrist. "It was magick."

I closed my eyes and focused on the sensations they were both invoking on my body. Miles was slowly untying the top of my shift and within a moment had uncovered one of my breasts. It ached, and the nipple stood hard and erect as if begging him to tease it. And he did not disappoint. A growl rumbled from his chest just before his warm mouth closed over the sensitive nipple.

I gasped and reached forward, sliding my hand around the back of his head and taking a firm hold of his shoulder-length black hair. Shots of heat radiated from the breast he was nibbling on and my breathing became labored. The spiraling warmth that had blessed my body with a trip to the heavens only a few minutes ago, began growing again.

"We need her on the bed, brother. I wish to taste her sweet body from head to foot." It was Eli's voice calling out the order, but I could barely hear him.

I could only feel. My body was on fire and I wanted more. Needed more.

Miles lifted me, setting me back down in the center of the bed, only taking his mouth from my breast for a moment. Then he proceeded to nibble and nip his way over to the other breast still hidden beneath one shoulder of the thin shift I wore.

Eli crawled onto the bed and situated himself between my legs. Extra heat soared up my neck and cheeks at the embarrassing view of me he had. I tried to pull my halfway spread thighs together, but he put a hand on each and pressed them down.

"Stay open, Love. I have a lot of tasting to do."

Tasting? There?

He must have seen the disbelief in my gaze, because he flashed a brilliant smile before he raised the hem of my shift and his head disappeared beneath it. I bit back a gasp as the heat of his mouth connected with my already throbbing sex. Pushing my head back into the pillows I clenched my fists trying not to cry out.

"Scream and yell if you wish it, Diana. We want to hear you moan." Miles' raspy voice broke through the haze of my euphoria and I moaned a "yes" just for him. "How does she taste, Eli?"

The fire from Eli's tongue abated and his chest shook against one of my thighs as he chuckled. "Sweeter than ever. I've been deprived for too many years."

"We've both gone without her for too long," Miles added before recapturing my tender nipple between his teeth.

"I may never come up for air again," Eli added before lowering his head back to my sex.

I whimpered as his tongue ran from my slit to swirl around the same little nub he had tortured earlier. "Please. Please." I shuddered and squirmed, but they only held me down tighter. It swirled and rose and then fell and then the feelings rose again, but never quite reached the peak I sought. It was as if they could tell when I came close, and then they would back off to draw it out longer.

A growl rumbled in my chest and I tried to push away from their mouths for just a moment of respite. But it was no use. I whimpered and moaned, pleading for them to let me find heaven again. I closed my eyes, waiting for the stars, but Eli denied me once again. I growled again and raised my head to look down at him, but Miles' face blocked my view. He released my nipple slowly from his mouth and caught my gaze. His brown eyes swirled with sparks of glowing orange, like embers of fire.

The bed dipped as Eli crawled over me. I noticed that his clothes were all missing and his impressive manhood stood erect and glistening. I licked my lips wondering what he would taste like. But I didn't get to think long. He knelt between my legs and grabbed my hips, pulling me closer and closer to his shaft. Its velvet tip brushed against my opening and I moaned again, wishing for more than just a touch.

I turned my head toward Miles when the bed dipped again. He had backed away from the bed, and sat down in the high backed chair facing us. Smiling, he gestured toward Eli and I turned my attention back to the brother teasing me with his cock.

He pushed forward slowly and pulled my hips at the same time, sinking inch by glorious inch until he was fully seated. My body stretched to accommodate him and I moaned softly when he started to rock, pulling in and out slowly, then faster, then slower again.

More torture. After a few teasing strokes, I grabbed for his forearms and tried to pull myself against him harder. "Please, Eli."

He leaned forward, slipping an arm around my back and lifted until I straddled him in the center of the bed. He pulled me tight until my breasts were crushed against his bare chest. One of his hands slipped down my back until it cupped my bottom, then he lifted me up and dropped me down on his length.

I let out a moan and dug my fingers into his shoulders. Pleasure tore through my body and I clung to him as he increased the speed of his thrusts until I panted and ached with need.

"Come for me. Now, Diana," he growled into my neck and pushed me down on his cock one last time.

My body shuddered and stiffened. I curled my toes into the sheets of the bed as the stars inside my head overtook me once more. He roared as his seed flowed hot and fast, filling me, driving me higher. My sex throbbed and pumped him until I finally collapsed against his chest, a limp mass of utterly satisfied woman.

He laid me back down on the bed, sliding from my body gently. I moaned at the loss, but gasped for air as my heart continued to race and thump hard behind my ribs.

They weren't done.

Eli moved from the foot of the massive bed and in only a moment, he was replaced by Miles. The scar above his right eyebrow wasn't the only thing I could see differently about them now. The more time I spent with them, the more I realized I could tell them apart just by their demeanor. Eli had a lighter heart than his brother and it showed in the faint lines around his eyes and mouth. Where Eli's eyes sparkled with intrigue, Miles' smoldered with pure male heat.

I wasn't sure I could handle two in a row, but when he stripped out of his clothes in front of me and climbed onto the bed, my mouth went dry and the hum in my body started anew. At this rate I would never want to leave their bed.

Miles' mouth curved into a grin, more wicked than Eli's.

I trembled, not out of fear, but with anticipation.

He leaned over me and undid the last lace strap still

tied on my right shoulder. Then he tugged and carefully pulled the shift down the length of my body until it was completely free. He tossed it off the side of the bed, never once dropping his burning gaze from my eyes.

Moisture pooled between my thighs again and I made a sound that was half-whimper, half-moan. Heat from his body warmed my fevered skin even more and beads of sweat ran from my brow into my already damp white-blond hair.

"I have prayed for this day for so many years." His deep bass voice rolled over me like a soothing blanket. "I have to ask you to forgive me." He crawled over my body and dipped his head, placing a soft kiss on either of my cheeks.

"For what? You haven't done anything ..."

"We lost you. I should've been holding your hand or made you go first when we escaped all those years ago."

A hint of tears made his brown eyes glassy, but not a single drop fell.

I reached up and cupped his face. "There is nothing to forgive." Pulling his head down, I claimed his mouth with mine and moaned. A rumble started in his chest and built as he slid an arm beneath my neck and head. He crushed my lips with his demand and I melted to his will.

Our bodies came together and he thrust inside with one smooth stroke. I stifled a shout, biting my bottom lip. He took the opportunity to nip hard on one of my breasts and I yelped beneath him. The pain only lasted a few seconds before it warmed into something I didn't recognize, but liked.

"Don't hold back," he growled, taking a quick nip out of the other breast.

I yelped again and then moaned loudly when he began to slide in and out of me. He was slow at first, then he sped up and pumped harder. His cock swelled I clung to his body as he made that now familiar and delicious heat curl inside me once again.

He arched his back and thrust deep. "Gods, Diana you feel so good." Then he moved backward, pulling out.

"No!" I begged, left panting and wanting more. How could he stop in the middle?

A chuckle rolled from his chest and he rose up onto his knees.

"Don't fret. We're far from finished. Turn over, love, and get up on your hands and knees."

I struggled to roll over, my arms and legs heavy as lead and about as sturdy as pudding.

He helped me up, holding me by my hips once I'd turned over. His cock impaled me again and I sucked in a quick breath. He was even deeper than before and now as he leaned over my back, one of his hands started to wander up and down my body. He kneaded my swaying breasts one at a time as he thrust in and out of me at a torturously slow pace.

Then his hand moved farther down, exploring the slick folds above my slit. His forefinger circled the throbbing nub Eli had tortured earlier and I jerked against him as a rush of sensations pummeled through my body.

"Oh, oh! Please. Yes," I growled out, not holding back this time. If it pleased them when I spoke and made noises. I wanted to give them as much pleasure as I could. The ways they knew to arouse my body were intense.

The arm that had been holding his massive weight above me, curled around my chest and he tugged me upward and back until I settled across his hips, straddling him backward. I clung to the thick, muscled arm that wrapped diagonally across my body. His other hand manipulated the swollen nub at the top of my slit, making me rock even harder against his rock-hard cock.

I matched his rocking, thrust for thrust, taking in every passionate second of our lovemaking. Higher and higher I soared.

He whispered in my ear. "Come." Then he pinched the little nub.

A scream tore from my throat as he triggered another trip into the heavens. He thrust twice more and then his voice joined mine in a haggard roar that echoed through the enormous room.

Miles held me tight to his chest as he lay down on his side. I sighed and relaxed in his arms, wiggling my bottom until I lay as close to him as I could manage.

He chuckled and nibbled on my ear. "Stop moving or I'll have to turn you around and start over again."

"Is that a threat? Or a promise?" My lips curved into a smile and I looked up, catching Eli's twinkling gaze. He moved from the chair to the bed and snuggled up next to me.

A laugh rolled from Miles' chest. "I have missed you, so much."

"She always was insatiable, brother," Eli added, palming one of my breasts and rolling the nipple between his thumb and forefinger.

I released a long sigh and squirmed until I lay on my back between them. They each sat on their sides, looking down and me and fondling my naked body. The room smelled of sweat and sex and I couldn't deny that I loved it and was looking forward to more. But maybe a short break would be nice. Just to catch my breath and stare in admiration at the men who had just made love to me.

My body was so relaxed and ... cool. My internal inferno was gone. "Will the burning heat come back?"

Eli shook his head and responded. "No, our consummation triggered it to end."

I closed my eyes and smiled. No more fever. And around them, I didn't have the overflowing ice issue, either. Maybe it was just because I was at ease. The ice was always worse the more tense I became. "It will be nice not to feel like I'm on fire and want to throw myself on every male who walks past me."

A growl rumbled in Miles' chest next to me. "If you need to throw yourself onto anyone, just aim for one of us."

I turned to look at his face—so serious and stern.

"What will happen if I land on you?" I asked, desperately trying to keep my face straight.

I heard a muffled snort from my other side.

Miles' mouth curved upward, unable to ignore the obvious tease in my question. "I suppose you'll just have to try it and find out."

"So at any point in the day or night I can leap onto either one of y—"

Their hands fell to my body, finding the most ticklish places, and tortured me until I laughed so hard I couldn't breathe. Luckiest woman on earth. That was me. Against all odds, strangers became friends and I'd made it across an unfamiliar and hostile country and found my mates. Mates that I hadn't seen in over a thousand years. Mates that I wanted to stay in bed with for the rest of the day ... maybe the rest of the week. Bloody hell, I never wanted to get out of this bed, but no one's luck held out forever.

A strange chirp came from the bedside table behind Miles. He rolled over and grabbed a small and shiny black rectangle. The face of it lit up and I could see words written on it, but couldn't quite make them out.

He rolled back to face Eli and me, his smile gone—replaced once again by a frown.

"They're close."

CHAPTER 27

XERXES

"Well?" I glared down at the kneeling Djinn male. Standing from the dining table, I called upon my magick and lifted him into the air with a mere flick of my wrist. Even if he wanted to blink away, he couldn't now without taking me with him—something he wouldn't dare do. The stupid genies were always afraid I had one of those *quppu* boxes in my pocket. Thanks to Rose, I only had a few left. Sirens made them and they were hard to locate and even harder to hang onto. The damn species could make anyone love them at any time.

"We have been unable to locate the dagger, Master. There is no chatter in the town where she was sighted or in any of the surrounding areas."

The smell of his fear filled the room and I smiled. It was good that he feared me. That fear was what kept the entire race under my thumb. Of course the selfish man-whore-of-a-king helped as well. The Djinn just didn't understand how little their king cared about them. And as long as Manda remained in the SECR most of the time, she would never be the wiser.

"Take three more of the guard and go back and look again." My voice deepened as my irritation grew. The last thing I needed was the Mason pack or Rose to discover a piece of the key. If those Blackmoor brothers ever made it back into the Veil, I would never sit on Orin's throne. "And remember, I don't want Manda to see you."

The sniveling Djinn nodded and blinked away without a word. I sat back in my chair to finish the meal my girls had elegantly spread for me.

Taking a bite of a candied date, I frowned. The conversation I'd had with her did not sit well. I had the distinct feeling she was developing her own agenda ... one that did not align with mine. If anyone could become a relevant problem, it was Mandana Farrok.

I shoved the plate forward and one of the castle maids rushed to my side. "Is there something wrong, Master? Can I get you another plate?"

Her voice was smooth. It reminded me of Manda's. Anger rose in my chest like water in a sinking ship. I felt my fangs descend and grabbed the woman by the hair.

She didn't scream and for some reason that only fanned the fire. I snarled at her, flashing my long fangs. My fingers changed to claws and I tightened my grip on the single braid trailing from the base of her skull. With my free hand I traced a claw along her neck and up across her cheek, pressing just hard enough to break the skin.

Beautiful crimson streaks ran down her cheek, and neck, and continued to flow until they disappeared between her heaving breasts. The blood was diluted when her tears mixed with it, but it still ran from the wounds ... still painted her beautiful olive skin with wine-colored streaks.

Sniveling sobs wracked her body and I dropped her to the floor with a thud. "Leave the palace, woman."

"Y-yes, master," she whimpered, crawling backward away from me. Slowly at first, then she turned and climbed to her feet. Her bare feet slapped against the marble floors as she disappeared from view.

I fumed, between her voice reminding me of the one Djinn I couldn't control and that whining soldier with no news at all, rage boiled within me. I needed to hurt something. One of my girls appeared in the doorway, but didn't approach. I'd taught them well and for that, they escaped the wrath of my moods.

"Find me another girl. One that doesn't look or sound like that kitchen maid."

Lily fell prostrate on the floor without a sound.

I walked past her to my suite and collapsed onto the softness of my mattress. Iris and Roshanna appeared at my side and I snarled. My anger would be soothed, but not on them. Neither of the girls cried out or wailed with fear. They were strong and understood what I needed and when. Both withdrew from my side quietly. Iris slipped through the door to their sleeping chamber, a small beautifully decorated bedroom the three women shared. It connected with my bathing hall and bedroom, making them only accessible through my suite.

I lifted my head and watched Roshanna open a chest and pull out a large canvas bag. She pulled it to the side of the bed for me, then bowed and left via the same door Iris had.

"Good girl," I murmured before sitting up and pulling open the bag. My skin tingled and a rush of excitement filled me. The out-of-control rage was replaced with cold focus. Turning the skin of some peasants' back fiery red, even bloody, made my dick harden.

There was a long, black crop laid across the top of the items in the bag, along with a leather flogger, and my personal favorite—a cane.

Lily walked in with a blindfolded woman. Her clothes were heavy and rough cotton weave, characteristic of the poor who lived in the village outside the palace. At one time, all three of my girls had worn the same thing.

The peasant moved hesitantly, but I could hear Lily whispering reassuring lies into her ear to keep her calm. The first time I'd beaten a servant, it'd surprised me when I caught Lily watching with morbid curiosity. Iris and Roshanna didn't like pain, but Lily thrived on it—on receiving it and doling some out. Her excitement fed mine and I watched her pull a lever near the wall to lower the chain that would suspend the unsuspecting female.

The sobs didn't start until Lily began expertly tying rope around the woman's wrists. She knotted it in such a way that a large loop extended out from between the bindings. The loop would attach to the ring hanging from the end of the chain.

The woman was begging now and I took a deep breath, enjoying every terrified shriek. Breaking people was what I liked to do, and this female would be no different. When I finished with her, she would beg to die. But, it wouldn't be me that took her life. That pleasure would be Lily's. Then I would flog and fuck Lily until she couldn't move.

A perfect way to spend the day.

CHAPTER 28

MILES

"You will stay in the suite!" I roared, yanking my pants back on. Diana was wandering around the room, wrapped in nothing more than a sheet, shouting back at me that she could help.

Damn it. I knew she could help, but that wasn't the point. Those fucking soldiers were here looking for her. She needed to stay hidden.

Eli had the same frown on his face that I could feel stretching over my own. The room was hot with our frustration and even Diana's ever-cool body was starting to sweat. The sheet stuck to her in all the right places and I grimaced as my dick hardened again.

"I've fought them before and won."

"You almost died," Eli replied, his voice calmer than mine.

She snarled, but didn't reply. He'd spoken the truth and she knew it.

Eli had always been a better diplomat. I should at least give him a chance to calm her down before I haul her ass down to the Sisters' quarters ... or the club. Chaining her to something sounded good in my mind. Then I could rest assured that she wouldn't come out of the Castle at an inopportune moment.

"Please, Diana. Just let us take care of this quietly. I promise. We've dealt with squads like this before and you don't want to be in the middle of it without training. If you had all your memories and could properly control your powers, this might be a different conversation. But right now, you're a liability to us and to the town."

Her shoulders sagged and she stared blankly at Eli.

Shit.

"Fine. I'll stay in the Castle," her voice was soft, but laced with cold anger.

I heard Eli curse under his breath. It hadn't been his intention to piss her off, but it was too late now. He walked toward her, but she spat out a nasty word and he stopped mid-stride.

The door opened to our room and I could smell the vampire before I saw her. Eira's blue eyes peered at me from around the door. They were ringed with red and she pushed the door wider, crossed her arms over her chest, and waited. She was dressed in her full ensemble— throwing knives strapped to one leg, a pistol strapped to the other, and her samurai sword slung over her back.

Eli left the room first and I followed, pausing briefly at her side. "Watch over her, please."

The Viking ninja smiled and nodded, slinging her long, brown pony tail over her shoulder and behind her back. "I tried to warn you that she didn't follow directions."

I sighed. She had and we'd ignored the warning. So many years had passed since having Diana in our lives. We'd forgotten how headstrong she was, and how fierce. Even without her memories, she was ready to jump into the fray and fight.

The door closed behind us and I glanced over at my brother in the dim hallway light.

"She's in there, brother. Our Diana is there. We have to get Meredith and Hannah to try and help her recover her memories," Eli growled. "I'd forgotten how sexy she was when she got angry at us."

I snorted. "At least I wasn't the only one who wanted to yank that sheet off of her and have my way again."

"If she could only remember, she would've dropped that sheet to lure you into letting her win the argument."

"Me?" I scoffed.

Eli chuckled as we climbed the stairs to the parapet level. "Fine. Both of us would've totally caved."

I touched the earbud in my right ear, turning it on. "All right boys, what's the news?"

"They're about a mile out." I recognized Kieran's voice as it came on the enchanted radio signal. "On foot, we think. Can't hear any engines, but they're approaching from several directions. So they've split their group at least three times."

"Good," Eli answered. "It'll make it easier to get rid of them. Vehicles are hard to burn."

We turned the corner in the stairwell and I continued to the front while Eli turned to the back of the Castle. Wolves had the best hearing on the planet, so good they could hear human thoughts, but dragons had the best eyesight. We could see them coming a mile away—literally.

My footstep echoed softly though the stone tunnel. I made sure to make some noise so the poor Lycan in the tower at the end wouldn't lose his shit. It'd happened before and Kieran still had a scar running down his left arm to prove it. He'd come at me, fangs bared, and before I could announce myself I'd had to swat him down. One of my claws had torn through his arm in the process.

The nasty wound had healed well, but even his Lycan DNA couldn't erase it completely.

"Kieran," I called out, stepping up into the tower room. He was lying on the ground in the center of the room with a grin on his face that stretched from ear to ear.

"Hey, Miles. Feeling pretty good?" He turned his head and I caught the twinkle in his eye.

Shit head. "Listening in to conversations you shouldn't, wolf boy?" I flexed my knuckles and frowned.

He jumped up from his place on the floor and shook his head. "No offense, man, but y'all were loud."

Rolling my eyes, I followed him to one of the narrow, vertical windows. He turned the crank and rolled open the bulletproof window, then pointed out to a grove a trees northwest of town.

"One group is sneaking through the brush out there. Every once in a while, I hear a twig snap. And the foot-steps are in pairs, not fours," he said, answering what would've been my next question.

I leaned forward, looking through the window, and let my dragon come forward. The afternoon sun was bright, but I could still make out the heat signatures in the trees —definitely a human stealth ops team. They crouched as they moved, their body language completely tense and watchful, like a dog that thinks it's safe to come out of the doghouse, but isn't sure.

"Rose, you online?" I spoke softly.

"Yes, Miles. Go ahead. We're in the tactical room above the cafe."

"There's twelve in the group northwest of the town. They're about twenty minutes out from the edge. Are the Lycan families in Meadow Creek already underground?"

"Yes," she answered. "All residential houses are cleared and civilians are in their fallout areas. Every single person is accounted for."

Good. The last time Sanctuary had been raided, a couple of preteens had been unaccounted for and had been caught in the crossfire. It was a terrible day for the town and for those families. The guilt still weighed heavily on him and she must've known.

"Eli?" she questioned. "What's the south look like?"

"Two groups approaching from the south," Eli replied over the com, his voice crystal clear on the radio frequency only Sanctuary electronics could pick up. "Guess they think they'll have a better chance coming through your place." A chuckle came over the line from him and the wolf in his tower. Even Kieran couldn't reign in a snort of amusement.

Rose could flatten them with a wave of her petite manicured hand, but she relied on Eli and me to erase them from existence. Bodies attracted attention. Bones could be dug up at a later date. Dragon fire reduced any material to ash, with the exception of dragon steel from the Veil. These chumps usually had a few blades on them, which we collected from their ashes. Whoever was sending the teams was smarter than they used to be, but it still didn't matter. They didn't have a prayer against us. Xerxes was wasting his manpower—and his dragon steel.

But we didn't rock the boat and we never left the confines of the town. The streets of Sanctuary were set up to resemble a Shamesh star. Thanks to Rose, all our powers were amplified inside it once we added our blood to the sacrificial inscription on the stone above the vault in the center of town.

As long as they kept sending these human teams into Sanctuary, we had nothing to worry about. They couldn't send anything much more obvious or they would attract the attention of the Texas Republic military. That would be a shit storm even Xerxes couldn't contain easily. And even though he was a sick sonofabitch, he wasn't stupid.

"One of the southern groups is veering east. They're spreading out as they get closer," said Eli.

I moved to the eastern window of the tower, opened it, and regarded the countryside methodically. Sure enough, the heat signatures were thinning out.

"Eli, keep your eyes peeled for heavy artillery," I reminded him, waiting patiently for the group that had moved west to exit the tree line. They only had a few more yards of cover. We made sure there was a half-mile of space between the edge of the town and the wild oak groves that were scattered around the stream that circled the northwestern side of the town.

"None that I can see. Calliope, are you meeting us at the door?" Eli asked. "Is Hannah or Meredith coming, too? Or just you?"

Calliope's silky smooth voice slid over the com, "Don't worry, boys. I'll be there. Meredith and Hannah are coming, too. But Hannah is meeting with your guest and

Diana. She wants to try some spell, now that Diana is back to full strength."

"Now?" I scowled.

"Why not?" she asked. "This crap is routine, Miles. It's not like we haven't squashed stealth squads recently. We're on the way. Head down to those ridiculously heavy doors."

I raised my eyebrows as movement at the edge of the tree line caught my eye. A heat signature appeared and then disappeared.

"Miles!" My brother's voice came over the com. "Do you have any hopping heat signatures?"

Shit. Djinn.

Calliope's alarmed voice was next. "Boys, there's someone nasty out there with them. I just felt them. Rose?"

"Keep on track. It's only one Djinn. I can feel it, too. Harrison has the town ward up right now, so they won't be able to blink inside. They'll have to walk, just like the soldiers."

I focused on the group to the west as they stepped from beneath the cover of the trees. My vision changed from heat-seeking to telescopic. "Eli!" I bellowed. "Get down to Hannah and Meredith. Get them inside the Castle now. Grenade launchers! I'll get Harrison."

"No!" Rose yelled over the com, but I didn't listen. "Don't leave that Castle! Miles!"

Guilt drove me faster, than Rose's commanding tone pulled me back. I wasn't going to let the girls lose their father. Rose could scream until she was blue in the face. I'd shift into my Drakonae form and burn them all to ash before I allowed Hannah and Meredith to suffer again on our behalf.

I practically launched myself from the parapet walk into one of the open courtyards, landing with a thump on the soft turf. I ran across the grassy area, throwing open doors in my wake as I made my way to the front of the Castle. The Lycans were behind me. I could hear their footsteps.

Turning the last corner, I burst into the foyer to see Hannah and Meredith bawling and Calliope trying to get them to calm down. We needed them. We needed their magick and the wards they'd created to protect this town. They were the only ones who could activate them. The only person I didn't see was Eli.

"Where is he?" I roared and the two witches gasped through their sobs.

"He went for Harrison," Calliope answered, as the first hit shook the town. The wards were strong enough to keep out bullets and missile launchers, but grenades were a different speed. They traveled slow enough to penetrate the magickal barriers we had surrounding the town, which meant our plan to use the Bateman witches to throw up a shield for us was out of the question. They couldn't survive one blast, much less multiple ones.

A thud hit the door and I yanked it open to find a black-haired, female Djinn dressed in an SECR stealth ops uniform. Even though her violet eyes were shielded by blue contacts, I could smell her. Djinn lived and breathed magick. It clung to them like a sweet perfume, stronger than most other supernaturals.

What my eyes couldn't believe was that her hand was inside Harrison's chest. Eli had one hand on Harrison's arm and was crouched to pounce on her at the slightest misstep.

Something told me this woman didn't make mistakes.

The girls behind me screamed, the pain in their voice wrenching at my heart.

"If anybody moves, I reintegrate my hand and rip out his heart. I don't want to kill him. All I want is the female dragon. Nobody has to get hurt."

"I seriously doubt that."

Kieran inched slowly out of the doorway to stand next to me.

"I meant it, Lycan," she snarled. "Don't come any closer."

"Do you know who am I, Djinn? Who the man crouched ready to tear your throat out is?" I growled.

She narrowed her gaze. "I can blink out of here before anyone could get close. Even your esteemed Sentinel can't make a move while my hand is in this human's chest."

I glanced to the café. Rose stood on the porch as white as a ghost, her eyes glued to the place where the Djinn's arm disappeared into Harrison's chest. But I knew Rose. She would sacrifice Harrison to save the town. To save my brother and me.

We were the only thing standing between Xerxes and the Sisters. Nothing and no one had more value to her than the sect of women she'd protected for thousands of years.

CHAPTER 29

ELI

I watched and waited. The Djinn woman was steady. Her hand didn't tremble and her heart wasn't racing. She knew she had the upper hand and every minute she stalled allowed the soldiers to get closer. I cringed as another grenade struck, and another, and another.

Refusing to turn my head, I hoped the Lycans patrolling the streets were safe and able to take down the SECR soldiers. The protectors were out there with them. It would be slower, but they could get the job done just as well. Soon this bitch wouldn't have any backup at all.

"They're blasting the fallout shelters. The fucking assholes are shooting at the ground," Brogan's voice shouted across the com.

The Djinn's eyes widened, a look of concern passing through her purple-blue eyes. She tried to mask it, but it was too late. I knew.

Lunging, I wrapped my arms around her and tumbled

through a vortex that made my stomach churn. *Bitch took me with her.* We landed on our backs somewhere. I couldn't tell where. Her fist caught my jaw, but I refused to let go of the vice-like grip I had around her neck.

She choked and kicked and we blinked again.

This time landing in salt water. *Fucking bitch.* "You're not leaving me in the middle of the ocean, demon spawn." I kicked with my legs and shoved her beneath the waves, taking a deep breath as we sank into the blue depths.

It didn't last. The vortex opened again and this time we hit and I was on the bottom. Hard rock tore into my back and she writhed in my arms, her voice coming out in choking screeches as she fought for air. She was coughing up saltwater all over my chest.

I took a second to consider my surroundings. The air was freezing and thin. It appeared we were on the top of some gods-awful mountain range. "Jump again, bitch. You don't want to die here."

She started to go limp and I loosened my grip just a hair. I had no idea where I was and I couldn't fly home. The damn satellites would shoot me down before I made it even a few miles.

I lay down on the rocky ground and pulled her tightly to my chest, encircling her body with my arms and legs. My heat would keep us from freezing solid until she woke enough to jump again.

About ten minutes later she wiggled in my arms and I hissed into her ear to jump somewhere warmer or I'd start squeezing harder.

"You bastard!" She screeched, trying to get loose. "They will kill people if I'm not there to intervene."

"Maybe," I growled. "But they will all die in the process. Why were you bluffing about killing the warlock?"

She was silent.

I squeezed her chest harder, listening for the telltale snap of a rib.

She cried out in pain.

"Tell me, bitch. I know you're working with Xerxes."

"Not really," she gasped, a small gurgle in her throat.

"I have to find the dagger. She was the last one who had it. I just want to free my people. If I can threaten his agreement between the damned Drakonae kings, I can free my father ... my whole race. I wasn't bluffing. I would've killed him."

Father? No fucking way did I have Mandana Farrok in a chokehold.

"You're lying. I saw you hesitate when you heard the soldiers were bombing the family shelters."

"Ahhhhhhh!" She screamed and bucked in my arms, wailing when the pain of the broken rib caught up to her movement.

We blinked again and this time we were free-falling through the air. *Fucking hell.* "If you kill me," I shouted into her ear through the wind noise. "Diana will turn and never be human again. You'll never find out where she put the dagger. She and Miles will hunt you to the end of the earth and kill what little is still left of your pathetic race." It was a half lie, but she didn't know that.

I swallowed as another vortex opened seconds before we would've hit the ground. We disappeared through it, landing in the center of Sanctuary.

"Let me go," she begged. "Help me. She's the only way I can save my people."

"No."

She squirmed again, but froze when Rose and others in the town came into our line of sight. Miles stood a few yards from my head. Calliope stood next to Rose and the Protectors stood spread completely around us, their teeth bared and their eyes blood red. Everyone was ready to tear this woman to shreds.

A single female voice rang through the growling and the tension.

"Let her go! Stop! Manda!" It was Eira. She came flying at the group, but was stopped by a tangle of snarls and gnashing teeth. Snarls she returned with a violence that spoke to the years she'd spent fighting to survive.

"Eira!?" The surprise in the Djinn's voice caught me off guard. She took advantage of my loosened grip and elbowed me in the neck. My arms opened and she was gone in an instant.

"Damn it, vampire! We had her. That was Mandana Farrok! She fucking ruled the Djinn for two-thousand years." I jumped to my feet and stormed at the offending woman, but stopped short when Diana stepped between me and her friend.

"It's okay, D. I can handle him." Eira stepped around Diana to face me.

"The hell you can, bitch! You may have saved our mate, but you just cost us one of the most valuable prisoners we could have in this war," I said, allowing the heat from my anger to rise and flow from my body.

"Eli." It was just one word, but when Rose spoke everyone listened—even if they didn't want to. "Let her speak."

I shuddered, trying to push the rage I felt back down

into the beast pacing angrily within. When my thoughts quieted, I also noticed the gunfire and grenades had stopped. They must've taken care of the squadrons already.

"Tell us, vampire. Why do you seek to protect our enemy?" Rose crossed her arms over her chest and waited.

Eira squared up and turned to face Rose, ignoring the ugly glare I threw in her direction.

"Manda works with the Mason pack. She helps us stay ahead of her own troops. I know exactly who she is and she wasn't lying when she said she wanted to free her people."

"She's playing both sides of the fence, Ms. Rennir," Rose replied. "That is a very dangerous place to be in a war."

Eira frowned. "She's not evil. She has saved countless lives, but she can only do so much. Diana made too big of a splash; she couldn't hide it from her people. I don't know why she started coming after her now, though. We never told her Diana had one of the daggers of Shamesh."

"Xerxes did," Rose answered. "She answers to him, Ms. Rennir. She is not on your side unless it is convenient to her. Now she knows how we protect the town and how many of us there are. You should not have interfered," her voice thundered and her eyes flashed white for a brief moment. Then just as quickly, she turned on her heel and walked away.

"Miles and Eli, please take care of the bodies," she called over her shoulder.

I grunted and glanced at my brother. He nodded and grabbed Diana's hand. She didn't object and followed us quietly through the empty streets of the town. As we passed the dead soldiers on the street, I knelt down and let my dragon fire burn from my hands, turning their corpses to ash in mere seconds. We couldn't actually *breathe* flame unless we allowed our body to shift. It was easier to just use my hands. This way felt more respectful to the dead, too. The remains would be carried away on the breeze and no one would be the wiser.

Diana's breath hitched behind me. I hated that she had to see this. But Miles had been right to bring her along. She needed to know what kind of world we lived in now. We might be some of the most powerful beings on the planet, but technology and weapons had caught up to our strengths.

Humans didn't fight with swords anymore.

◈◈◈

IT TOOK SEVERAL HOURS OF TRUDGING UP AND DOWN the streets before we'd cleared all the bodies. Miles and I took turns cremating the remains. Diana didn't speak a word until we turned back toward the Castle.

"Why?" She pulled her hand from mine and peered up at me and then at Miles. "What is going on? Why does everyone want that damned dagger?"

We moved slowly down one of the Lycan residential streets. Luckily, the shelters had held up to the grenades and none of the families had been injured. It was a good fight for Sanctuary, not a soul had been lost on our side.

I motioned to a picnic table situated in the center of the neighborhood green space. Their playground had been demolished. Trees were lying across the swings and the climbing tower had been shattered into a thousand pieces.

"The place you came out of is called the Veil. It's our home. The Blackmoor family ruled it. There was fighting between us and another Drakonae family, the Incanti. They took advantage of our trust and killed our fathers and mother under the guise of a peace talk." I sat down on the table across from her and Miles sat next to her.

"Was my family killed as well?"

"Your immediate family visiting the capitol was, yes," Miles answered for me, his voice softer than normal and choked with emotion. "We thought they had killed you, too, except that we never turned."

"Then they brought you into the throne room and ..." I couldn't tell her. It was a memory I didn't want her to have. I hated the thought that if Hannah succeeded in healing Diana's mind, all the horrors she'd seen and experienced would come rushing back to her like a tsunami of pain.

"What?" she whispered.

"It was terrible, my love," Miles said, wrapping an arm around her shoulder. "What happened that day haunts us more than any pain we've ever experienced, second only to losing you the day we escaped the Veil."

Diana shrugged off his arm and turned to face Miles. "Then tell me what happened or help me remember. I can't do this unless I know the truth—the whole truth. You just burned forty-two people to ash before my eyes."

"We would not be sane were it not for Rose," I said.

Diana looked back to me. "The small woman who told you to let Eira speak?"

I nodded. "She is the Sentinel. The guardian of Sanctuary."

"Did she kill all those soldiers?"

I nodded and watched Diana cringe in horror.

"Was it completely necessary to kill them?"

"Dead men do not tell tales," Miles said, releasing a long sigh. He ran his hands through his dirty, black hair and grimaced. "At first didn't kill them, but they always came back stronger."

"More prepared," she said, her voice flat as understanding washed over her face.

I nodded.

"And the dagger?"

Taking a deep breath, I began. "Sanctuary protects a coven of women called the Sisters of the House of Lamidae. Rose and her people have protected them for over five-thousand years. When Rose came upon us, drunk and lying in a ditch not caring if we lived or died, she gave us a purpose—something to fight for. Until her, we had no hope of ever getting back to you. We assumed the Incantis had all the keys ... the daggers. It wasn't until centuries later we learned Xerxes had one of them."

"It also helped that the Sisters said you would eventually come back to us," Miles added.

"How would they know?" Diana asked, her skepticism evident.

"The Sisters are seers. They can see the past, the present, and the future. Each is gifted differently, but all can see," I answered.

"That seems quite farfetched."

I chuckled and rested my elbows on the table. "I would say that until a few weeks ago, you thought being a dragon was a bit farfetched."

Her lips turned up, just a hint of amusement. "Well said."

"Magick is everywhere in this world, Diana. When the Incanti brothers took over the Veil, they pushed out so many. Killed so many. All magick originated from that land. Every paranormal species once called it their home," I said.

"You intend to go back." She said it as if she knew it was a fact.

"One day. Right now we're honor-bound to protect the House of Lamidae. Until that vow is fulfilled and the spell is cast to protect the Sisters permanently from Xerxes, we stay."

Miles shifted beside her and turned to cup her face in his hands. She didn't pull away and I was thankful for that. "We cannot say how thankful we are to have you back with us after a thousand years. I know Eira has spoken to you about a spell Hannah can try to use to retrieve your memories. I want to caution you. You may not like what you remember. We're perfectly willing to build a new relationship with you ... right now. You don't have to go backward to move forward with us."

Miles' words rang true in my heart. I didn't want her to remember certain moments, but I knew there was more hiding in the darkness than the ugly assault at Orin. But whatever she chose, like Miles, I would stand by her.

The temperature dropped around us and instantly I could see my breath in a fog. "Diana," I soothed. "Whatever you choose, we will be there for you. No matter what."

Her eyes were glassy and tears ran down her cheeks, dropping from her face to the ground in frozen form. Snowflakes whirled through the air around us and I closed my eyes, allowing my heat to radiate outward. Miles did the same and she slowly stopped crying.

The temperature returned to its normal chilly-for-Texas winter, but the wintry mix Diana had conjured was gone. Mother Nature didn't usually visit Texas with anything like that until well after the New Year.

"I have to know," she finally said. "I have to know why I dream about a baby crying. It haunts me every time I fall asleep."

Miles met my gaze. We were thinking the same thing.

Fuck.

CHAPTER 30

XERXES

A crash outside my bedroom door signaled Manda's return. I chuckled and glanced over at Lily, then snapped the bull whip hitting her directly on the left ass cheek. She moaned, wiggling on the spanking bench where I'd fastened her earlier this morning.

I stood from the bed and snapped my fingers. Iris and Roshanna rose from their prostate positions on the floor and waited for further instructions. I motioned to Roshanna and she scrambled to kneel between my legs. Iris didn't move, just as I'd taught her.

I shoved my dick into Roshanna's mouth and buried a hand in her long black hair. She was careful of her teeth and I groaned, loving the feel of her soft, warm lips sucking at my cock. I thrust deep and she gagged, but took all of me.

The doors to my suite burst open and Manda stormed

through. "You lying sonofa—" She froze in the center of the room, her mouth hanging open.

Gods, I wished it was her mouth I was fucking instead of Roshanna's.

I snapped the whip again and Manda disappeared, blinking to the farthest corner of the room.

A wail came from Lily and I rewarded her with another strike to the same ass cheek, leaving a beautiful, red welt.

"Come to join the party?" I directed at Manda.

Manda's lip curled. "You're disgusting."

"And you should knock." I thrust faster into Roshanna's mouth, and groaned as I came. She swallowed every bit and licked me clean.

"Good girl," I said, cupping Roshanna's chin. "Go get me some clean clothes."

She nodded and scurried away, returning moments later with a clean pair of linen pants and a loose robe.

I tossed the bull whip onto my bed and walked to a table next to Lily where lots of toys were spread out. The BDSM culture had grown over the centuries and I was quite impressed with their creativity.

"How dare you give orders to my men without my knowledge," she snapped, walking toward me, her blue-violet eyes flashing with fury.

I loved her passion. It made me want to break her even more.

"Did you get my dagger?" I asked, deepening my voice. Her attitude was starting to wear thin on my nerves. The little bitch didn't think I knew she was playing both sides. Soon she would be the one on the floor begging for my cock and waiting on me hand and foot. I just needed someone to replace her at the SECR ... and I had no one as good as her. Not a single one of her shitty cousins had anywhere close to the strategic mind of Mandana Farrok.

"No, I didn't get *your* dagger. My men didn't follow the orders I laid out and I was nearly taken prisoner!" Her voice grew louder and louder. "I am their commanding officer and they should always answer to m—"

I threw out my arm, grabbing her with my powers before she could blink out. Her passion had cost her today. She'd been careless and slow.

She tried to scream, but I closed her mouth for her and all that came out was a muffled moan. I levitated her from the floor and moved across the room with her toward the spanking bench where Lily was restrained.

I unsnapped Lily's cuffs as well as the strap around her thighs. She stretched and rose from the bench slowly, leaning against the wall as she adjusted to being right-side up again.

"Go get the brass box from the shelf over there," I said, pointing to the far wall.

Lily promptly trotted over and retrieved the box, then stood in front of me holding it, waiting for instruction.

"Show Ms. Farrock what's in the box, Lily. I think she'll be surprised."

Manda struggled against my magick, but barely managed to twitch an eyebrow. A beautifully terrible scream rumbled in the back of her throat when Lily opened the lid to the brass box.

I reached into the container and pulled out a glass bowl of golden rings—enchanted golden rings the width of an eighteen gauge needle. I'd had them crafted especially for her. The inscriptions were tiny, but they were there and would do the job the same. It was the same spell I'd used to keep her father under my thumb for so long. Cyrus merely wore cuffs around his wrists.

I'd decided his daughter needed something with more of a personalized touch. Once the piercings were in place and the spell activated, the magick would eliminate Manda's teleportation abilities, making her much easier to control. Just like her father.

It was hard to run when you knew you would be caught. I could think of several of her cousins who would like the opportunity to exert superiority over the woman who had taken the Djinn throne and ruled like she was a man, like she was better than any of them.

She was, but that didn't matter to me.

All that mattered was obedience.

This would be my world, one country at a time, one government at a time, and I didn't need any cocky bitch to start thinking she could take it from me.

I picked up a heavy clamp and turned to face Manda's wide eyes.

"Should we do your pussy first? Or your nipples?" I asked, grinning wide at the muffled, outraged scream.

"Shhhh, none of that Mandana. I assure you, I'm quite good at it." I turned her to the three women prostrate on the floor a few feet away. "Girls, show her yours."

All three girls rose on their knees and arched their backs. Their silver nipple rings glistened in the lamplight.

"Now show her your pussies."

They arched backward and pulled open their labia, showing off a brilliant line of silver rings that pierced up and down both sides of their inner labia, a testament to my expertise.

Another moan rolled from Manda's chest and I turned

back just in time to catch her terrified gaze. That was the kind of fear I wanted in her.

"I own you Manda Farrock. And if I ever hear of you helping the Mason pack again, I'll chain you to my bed with these." I shook the bowl of metal rings in her face. "And that's where you'll stay for the rest of your miserable life." I grabbed her chin roughly. "Do you understand?"

Tears poured from her eyes as she tried to nod her head.

"Say it."

"Y-you o-own ... m-me."

"Good, girl." I set the box on a small table. "I think I want to start with your breasts. I've just been dying to get a better look at them. Now I have the perfect excuse."

CHAPTER 31

MILES

Miles pushed the huge front door of the Castle closed and Eli set the bar into the hooks. I couldn't imagine anyone but them being able to lift something so large. Really, I marveled that they could. I knew I was strong, but my human size didn't lend itself to feats like that.

Eira was waiting against a wall across the foyer. She eyed Eli warily before approaching. The tension between the two of them was apparent, but that was too bad. She was my friend and they would both have to move past it.

"Are you all right, D?"

"Yes," I said, nodding.

"I'm leaving today."

"No! Why?" I put my hands on her shoulders and tried to hold back more tears. I was crying over everything and it was driving me crazy.

"This is my home now, Eira. It can be yours as well. I'm sure Rose would—"

Eira shook her head. "I have people to take care of and this place has enough guards already. They don't need another cranky old vampire taking up space here." She nodded toward Miles and Eli. "They will take good care of you, D. I can see it in their eyes. And if they don't," she winked at them over my shoulder, "I'll come kick their twin asses."

They chuckled.

I could envision the eye rolling without turning around.

A small woman with blond hair passed through the foyer leading two little girls. One had black ringlets and the other had bright red hair, the color of the sunset starting to paint the sky outside. The little girl with red hair paused at Eira's side and stared at her. Then she turned and caught my gaze.

"She will come back," the little redheaded child said, then walked away with the other child and their adult companion.

Eira raised an eyebrow. "That was strange."

"The Sisters are usually a little strange," Eli responded.

"Of course I'll come back and visit, D. Nothing could keep me away," Eira added and then pulled my hands from her shoulders. I let them sag to my sides and stepped away from the door I blocked.

"I don't suppose you guys would open up that door for me?"

Miles nodded, turning and lifting the enormous bar from its hooks once more. Eli leaned against it, and pushed until it opened just enough to let her slip out.

"Take care of yourself, D," she said, and slipped away into the failing light.

I took a deep ragged breath, willing myself not to fall apart. She was all I knew. My only friend ... well besides the two men who called me wife. But it was different to have a woman to talk to. The ones who lived in this compound appeared as if would take some coaxing to get any conversation out of them.

Eli pulled the door closed and Miles let the bar drop back into place. The finality of the boom shook me to my core. I was here. Now. In this world and I needed to know why. Why had I been locked up for a thousand years? Or had I? I couldn't remember. Not really.

"Is the witch you spoke of ... Hannah. Is she still here?"

"Diana, you should rest. We can talk to Hannah and Meredith in the morning.

I shook my head and nearly stamped my foot like an angry child. *Good gods, what had come over me?* "Now, please. If I've learned anything in the few short weeks since I've been in this world, it's that we only have the present. Anything can happen at any time."

Both men sighed. Eli pointed to the stairwell to my right. "Very well. I think they're in the library with their father."

He came up beside me and I felt heat rush through my body. He put his hand on my shoulder and stopped me. Then he cupped my face in his hands, claiming my mouth with a kiss that could've stopped time. His lips crushed mine and his tongue swept through my mouth, tangling with my tongue in a battle for dominance—one that I did not back down from until he relented and allowed my tongue into his mouth. A moan slipped from my chest and

I felt myself being sandwiched between their warm bodies.

Miles' hands slipped beneath Eli's and he turned me to face him instead, his brother releasing his grip so that I could enjoy his brother's kiss as well. Miles' kiss was harder than Eli's, like he thought it might be our last.

It was as if they were both saying goodbye …

"I'll be fine," I said, pushing away from Miles and starting up the stairs again. "I've been through too much to be afraid of a little spell."

Their feet pounded the stairs behind me as I climbed.

Eli spoke first. "It's a dangerous spell. It could damage your mind instead of restoring it."

"It is a risk I have to take." I reached the top of the stairs and glanced back and forth along the hallway. I had no idea which direction the library was. "If you were a woman, you would understand."

Miles pointed to my left and I started down the dimly lit hallway. "Why is everything so dark in this place?"

"We see better in the dark," Eli answered.

I hadn't really noticed, but now that I stopped and considered it. The bright sunlight at the height of the day had bothered my eyes and I truly had no trouble seeing in the shadowy halls of this fortress. It just seemed gloomy and lifeless.

Perhaps because they had been just waiting all this time … just holding out for me to appear. For a thousand years they had waited. Now I chose to risk my life to find out the truth about a dream—a nightmare really. They would never forgive me if the spell went badly, but I knew I could never live with myself if I didn't try.

Miles moved ahead of me and opened two, beautifully carved double doors. The room they opened into was bigger than any I'd seen so far in the Castle. Books lined walls that stretched up two floors. Two staircases on either side of the room led up to the balcony level. The center of the room was arranged with a variety of leather-clad furniture. An older man with graying hair sat in a high-backed chair across from two younger women, both with bright red hair.

They all stood when we entered.

Miles and Eli led me to another chair across from the young ladies and then moved to stand behind me.

"Diana, meet Meredith and Hannah Bateman," Eli spoke slowly and each girl raised their hand to indicate who was who. "This is their father, Harrison."

I inclined my head. "Hello."

"Are you sure you don't want to wait a few days until the tension from the attack has died down?" the sister who'd identified herself as Hannah spoke up.

"I can't wait," I answered back quickly. "Something could happen and I might never find out what really happened to me. To my child."

Both women's eyes widened and then they nodded.

"We can do the spell here in the library," said their father, standing from his chair. "I'll get the book we need. Boys, you move the furniture out wider so the girls can make the circle."

I stood from the chair and watched as they all moved about the room, each with their own goal. Miles and Eli moved all the furniture to the edges of the room, and the two redheads pulled several jars and pots down from a shelf near the front of the room. Their father climbed the staircase to our right and returned a few minutes later with an old, battered volume covered in dust.

Meredith spread salt on the floor in the shape of a circle. "You need to lie down in the center," she said, pointing at the floor.

I nodded and stepped carefully over the line of salt. Then I lay down, arranging the skirt of the white dress I wore so it wasn't rucked up around my thighs. I didn't mind showing off my body for Miles and Eli, but it made me uncomfortable to do so around the girls' father. The neckline of the thing was already much lower than I was used to, but it was all Eira had been able to scrounge up at the last minute. Otherwise, I probably would've run out into the street still wrapped in their bed sheet.

Turning my head, I watched them mix different bits of unidentifiable ingredients into one of the pots and grind it up. They poured in small amounts of oil and then poured that mixture into a small, black glass.

Their father began chanting something in a language I did not recognize, but I felt a strange spark of energy run across my skin. I tried to move, but found my limbs too heavy to lift. I couldn't turn my head either and I stared at the ceiling of the room, trying not to panic. Miles and Eli were not in my line of vision, but I was too scared they would stop the spell if I asked for them to come closer. Instead, I took a deep breath and closed my eyes.

"I know you can't move," Hannah's voice was soft and near my head.

I opened my eyes to her face. She put her finger into the black cup and then smeared some of the mixture on my forehead, nose, cheeks, and chin. Then she drew something on the top of my bosom with it. The mixture was slimy and cold on my now-sweating skin.

"Just try to relax and take the ride," she said, before standing and leaving the circle.

Suddenly the coolness of the concoction disappeared and my skin burned where it touched. I grimaced through the pain and closed my eyes again. I could do this. I had to do this.

"Diana?"

I could hear the concern in Eli's voice.

"I'm fine," I managed to squeak out.

Pain lanced through my body and I felt myself sink into a familiar darkness. Slowly, the pain disappeared and I saw my dreams—the ones that had haunted me for as long as I could remember. Miles' and Eli's faces floated above me. Clearer now, and I could see they were in pain. Blood ran from their brows, down their cheeks, and even more flowed from wounds to their mouths. *What was I seeing?*

Then it changed. The crying started and my heart clenched. I could hear people arguing. I could feel the pain of labor like it was happening right then and I screamed out for help. The darkness never left. I never could see what happened. When the pain disappeared, I heard a baby cry and a woman's voice telling someone to hide him.

No. No. No.

I clawed at the darkness and screamed for her to bring me my baby. But no one spoke to me. The darkness never left and soon I floated in cold silence again. I sobbed so hard I couldn't breathe. My own tears threatened to drown me.

I gasped for air and suddenly I was back in the library.

Miles and Eli were next to the salt line, straining to cross the barrier, but something kept them back.

"Stop! She's back. Stop chanting."

The voices in the background stopped and whatever had held back my husbands vanished. Eli reached for me first and dragged me into his lap. He smoothed back my damp hair and used his shirt to wipe the grime from my face.

"Are you okay, Love? You were screaming as if something was killing you. We couldn't get to you. It kept us out," Eli mumbled faster than I could keep up as he kissed all over my head and face.

I could feel Miles' presence, too. His hand was on my lower back and he was rubbing his knuckles up and down, slowly, soothing the tension from my body. I relaxed into the caress and leaned over onto Eli's shoulder.

Exhaustion was overtaking me and I yawned. Nothing had changed. I still couldn't remember what exactly had happened. My nightmares had only gotten longer and created even more questions.

"It won't come right away," Meredith said.

I listened, trying not to let sleep steal me away.

"It could come back in an hour, three hours, a few days," Hannah added. "But when it does, it will hit with the force of an ax to a wood block. She will be incapacitated while the memories repopulate."

"And she will be in horrible pain, boys," their father added, his voice soft, but clear. "Be ready for that pain. That is the point where she can be lost to you."

Bloody hell.

CHAPTER 32

DIANA

I followed Miles and Eli down the dimly lit hallway, out a set of French doors, to a stairwell that led down into a green space at the center of the Castle. The winter wind bit at my bare legs, but to me it was only a caressing kiss. I was of ice and winter. It ran in my blood the same way water ran through humans.

I remembered everything—every tiny, painful, sordid detail about the slaughter of the Blackmoor House. How they had tortured Miles and Eli. Raped me. How a woman had hidden my pregnancy from them, and stolen my baby away in the night.

Miles and Eli were right, though. As much as I hated to admit it, I never heard that woman's voice again after that night. There was no proof that my son even made it out of the prison tower alive—except a mother's intuition. Something deep down said he was still there.

We walked along a rock pathway through the winter-dead green space toward a set of white French doors. Before either of them could knock, they opened and a pink face peered out.

"Come in," the small brunette said with a smile. "The Oracle is eager to meet your wife."

Miles and Eli stepped aside and let me enter first. My feet were bare, just like the Sisters scattered through the large sitting area. Even the white dress I wore was just like theirs.

"Please, sit, Mistress," the brunette spoke again.

I sank into the chair she indicated. Miles and Eli moved quickly to stand behind me, refusing the offer to sit down.

"Always stubborn," an old woman in the chair next to me spoke up. She turned and placed her hand over mine. "They never do as we ask."

I gasped at the touch but didn't withdraw. A spark of something passed between us and I knew she was the Oracle.

She smiled. "It is good to finally meet you, Diana Karlson of Blackmoor House. These boys have waited a long time for your return. It seems you have fully returned to yourself as well." She patted my hand and then leaned back in her chair, her sharp blue eyes studying me. "You seek another, though. One who was lost to you many centuries ago."

"My son," I whispered.

"He will choose his own fate."

Tears welled in my eyes. If he was choosing a fate, it meant he was alive!

"Will I see him again?"

The old woman paused, as if trying to decide how to answer. She finally sighed and said, "Yes."

I leaned forward. "Why do you hesitate to tell me good news?"

"His fate is twisted up with ours. There is not a single pleasant path that I can see for him to reach you."

"But you said I will see him again. That means he will come here? Or do I go to him?"

"You cannot cross into the Veil while Xerxes still breathes. We would all die," the Oracle replied, her voice as calm as a summer breeze. "Our fates are knotted together, ice-breather. The fates of both worlds."

It was pig slop! All of it. These women were just rambling about visions to keep themselves safely protected in this fortress. They'd certainly been doing a good job so far. They had a whole town that would lay down their lives for them.

"What's so special about you?!"

"The Sisters of Lamidae are the only beings left in the world that can procreate with a Lamassu."

"All the Lamassu are dead," I objected. "Everyone knows they died when Babylon fell."

The old woman looked past me, up to Miles and Eli. Then she looked back at me. "Rose Hilah, here in Sanctuary, is one of two surviving Lamassu Sentinels."

I felt vomit creep into the back of my mouth. Lamassu and Drakonae hated each other. Our races had fought since time began. There were stories and poems about our battles. How could Miles and Eli be working with one?

"The other survivor is their betrayer from Babylon, her brother-in-law, Xerxes Amir Hilah. He sought to take us then, and he still seeks to take us now. He would use us to create a powerful new species—part Lamassu and part Seer. It would spell the end of both worlds if he succeeds."

I leaned back against the headrest of the chair. I may have missed a thousand years of history, but even I knew what they said was the truth. The Lamassu male could not be allowed to take even one of these women.

"You stand with the Lamassu female because alone she cannot defeat one of her own." It was a statement more than a question, but both men whispered a quiet "yes." It was a noble vow they'd taken. One I would have expected them to find honorable, even if it was with a Lamassu.

My stomach rumbled and I shifted in my chair. I wanted to eat, but I also wanted to hear what else they had to say about this Lamassu female and this strange town.

"I understand your reasons for recruiting my husbands and agree that this is a noble fight. But why haven't we simply gone after this Xerxes and taken him down?" I turned to face Miles and Eli. "Between both of you and the Lamassu female, he wouldn't stand a chance."

"Life is not so simple here on earth, Diana," Miles said, his voice soft and without displeasure. "So much time has passed. We're unable to shift to fight Xerxes. We must find a way to defeat him privately without the general public witnessing anything. The soldiers you encountered on your journey here were only the beginning of what the humans can do now."

"Xerxes also has the Djinn helping him control human armies. He has worked for decades to build his influence in the SECR and looks to soon extend his reach into the Washington Republic as well," Eli added. "I know that doesn't mean anything to you, but think about how many people used to live in Orin when we married, now multiply that by ten-thousand."

I took in a quick breath and leaned back in my chair. That would mean there were ... millions of humans. And the Djinn. They bowed to no one. How was he controlling them?

"No one can control the Djinn, and how do so many people even fit in the world?"

The Oracle smiled, her blue eyes sparkled. "The world is a lot bigger than people thought a thousand years ago. As for the Djinn, he blackmails their king."

"And the humans have weapons now that can cut us down from the sky, from our dragon form. How did they become so powerful? They almost killed me. I know that were it not for our bond, I would be dead now."

"Science has given them the ability to compete on a more equal level with us. Though we have magick and more strength, it is not enough anymore," Eli answered. "They have machines that fly in the sky and can shoot us down. It is not safe to shift. Ever. Not on earth."

"Never?" I turned back to look at both my mates. "We cannot ever shift? How have you lived this way for so long?"

"You grow accustomed to the cage. Find other ways to soothe the beast. Eventually, we will find a way back to our home. Until then, our true nature must be kept a secret at all costs. Most humans in this country have laws against us existing within their borders. You can be executed on sight," Miles answered.

"How the bloody hell are we ever going to beat this damned Lamassu?" I stood from my chair with a snarl. "This is ridiculous."

"The prophecy will honor our vow. We must protect the House of Lamidae from Xerxes until they find the last three Protectors. Once all eight have made their vow to the Sisters, the spell can be completed and the Sisters will no longer be in danger from Xerxes." Eli stepped toward me and touched my shoulder.

I curled my lip, but didn't step away from his touch. I craved it. I'd missed them so much. The last thing I ever wanted was to be separated from them again. If that meant that I needed to honor the vow they had made to protect these women and stay with them until it was fulfilled, that is exactly what I intended to do.

"How do we find these Protectors?"

"You can't," the Oracle said. "Two of our younger girls have had visions of possible Protectors. But it is rare for a novice to have a vision. Usually they only come to the woman appointed as Oracle."

"You?"

She nodded. "We're not sure if the vision she had is valid. It will take time. The fifth Protector was just recently found. It's taken thousands of years to find those five."

"That is not encouraging," I snapped.

The corners of the Oracle's mouth turned upward. "Patience, sweet lady. All will reveal itself in the appropriate time."

I very much doubted it, but I was done listening to their drivel either way.

CHAPTER 33

DIANA

Miles and Eli walked on either side of me down the strange stone-like pathway that lay alongside the large roadway where the horseless vehicles drove. I noticed the large one that had carried me here hadn't moved. We passed by several shops, unlike anything I'd ever seen. One sign read Hardware, another was a woman's name, Calliope Hart. Another just read Market. I knew the market was definitely a place where food would be kept. Though the building across the circle called Rose's Cafe seemed more like a place to eat.

"I don't know about you two, but I'm starving and terribly underdressed." I caught the edge of the strange shoe one of the Sisters had lent me on a crack in the pathway. Miles' hands were on either side of my ribcage before I could even squeak out my surprise.

I brushed his hands away and smiled. "I'm fine. It's just

these strange shoes that woman called flip-flops. I do not see how these are even considered shoes."

Both men laughed. "In Texas, they're one of the most popular styles of shoe. But we'll find you some cowboy boots," Eli said.

I glared up at him. "What in the bloody hell is a cowboy? I have no intention of chasing any cows. Though I really wouldn't mind eating one right about now. I don't suppose you could rustle up a butcher?"

The two giant men who were my husbands proceeded to fall apart like a pair of cackling hens. They grabbed their stomachs as laughter shook their massive frames.

I, however, was not amused. Just because this world didn't make any sense did not give them the right to make fun of me.

"Laugh at this, you over-heated, insensitive cocks!" I waved a hand and froze them in solid blocks of ice that encased them from their toes to their gorgeous necks.

"Diana!" Eli gave me his best pout and Miles merely rolled his eyes.

Not an apology from either of them. Fine. They could melt themselves out.

In the meantime, I needed something besides this shift of a dress to wear and pieces of spongy material on the bottoms of my feet, held in place by a small post I was failing at holding between my toes. Flip-flops indeed. Probably because those who wore them either flipped over or flopped on their faces.

Delicious smells wafted from Rose's Cafe, but the clothes hanging in Calliope Hart's shop window pulled harder, and I carefully flip-flopped down the pathway a few more yards and knocked at her door, completely ignoring the rotation of curses and apologies now flowing from my mates' mouths.

A beautiful face appeared behind the glass of the door. She paused a moment before opening it. Her porcelain skin was flawless. Long, shining brown hair hung in a waterfall braid down to her waist on one side. Her eyes sparkled with amusement and I couldn't tell if they were blue, green, brown, or possibly a mixture of all three.

"Afternoon, honey. Did Miles and Eli get too clingy already?"

I scrunched my forehead, not quite sure what she meant by clingy. "No, they were rude and need to be alone with their thoughts."

"I don't know. Some of those things Eli is threatening to do to you sound like they might be fun. Miles, on the other hand, just looks like he wants to spank your pretty round ass."

Heat rushed up my neck and I took a step back from the strange woman.

"Sorry," she said, holding up her hands. "I forgot you don't speak this century. Right? Women have become more liberated since last you were awake and free."

"I noticed the clothing."

"Yep," she drawled on, throwing another glance toward my husbands. "How long will that hold them?"

"About ten minutes," I replied. "Would it be possible for me to find some decent clothing in this shop? I'm afraid I don't have money, but I'm sure that—"

"Miles and Eli have an account with me. Don't worry about it." She extended her hand. "Calliope Hart at your service, honey. Let's find you some not-so-order-of-the-nymphomaniac apparel."

I accepted her hand and shook it. "Order of whom?"

A soft giggle slipped from her ruby-painted lips. "It's what I call the Sisters of Lamidae." She pulled me up the single stair into her shop and closed the door behind her.

My stomach growled again and I covered my stomach with my hand, hoping she hadn't heard. My body just wasn't cooperating with me. I refused to walk around this town any longer in this slip of a dress. It wasn't proper.

"Oh, honey! Are you hungry? I've got a box of sticky buns in my back room. Bailey brought them over this morning. That girl knows I can't say no to a sticky bun."

My face heated with embarrassment. "I'm sorry. I really need to find something decent to wear."

"Hang on." The tall, curvy woman disappeared behind a swath of hanging fabric and returned with a bright red box. But it was the divine smell coming from within it that truly captured my attention. Sugar. Cinnamon. Nutmeg. Honey. It was like heaven when she opened the lid and I saw the golden brown buns dripping with what could only be some type of syrup.

"Take one," she said, lifting the box even closer to my face. "We can try on clothes as soon as you finish."

"I'll make a mess all over your beautiful carpets." I clasped my hands behind my back and took a step backward.

"Gods, you are something." She laughed and put the box on the counter behind her and disappeared into the back again. When she came back, she had a flat white plate in her hand. "Here." I watched in amazement as she pulled the plate apart and it magickally became two plates.

"Are you a sorceress?"

She cocked an eyebrow and stared at the two plates in

her hand. "Nope. These are paper plates. They come in packs of about fifty." She shoved one into my hands and I turned it over and over, examining it. It did feel like paper, but it had the consistency of something much stiffer.

She opened the red box again and the fresh wave of honey and cinnamon made me forget about my introduction to paper tableware.

"Now will you eat? You don't look like you have in years. Poor thing. We'll have you fattened back up in no time. You've not had food until you've eaten at Rose's Cafe. The brownies are amazing. Of course, Rose is not bad herself. These sticky buns are her specialty. Nothing like them anywhere else in the world."

I continued to listen to her babble on about the different foods and baked goods that were made in the cafe and that there were pixies who worked with Rose. But most of my focus was on each bite of gooey heaven as I demolished two of the sweet sticky buns. All of the food sounded good and I had to admit I looked forward to trying it, but for now I'd be quite happy to just sit and eat every crumb from the box on the counter.

"So, you're looking much better than when I first saw you arrive in town. The boys have been good to you, yes?"

I smiled and put my plate on the counter next to the half-empty box. Those last few were calling to me, but I just couldn't be that rude. I couldn't remember ever eating anything that tasted so perfect. It looked like it would be too sweet. But then the honey balanced out the spice ... and it was just perfect.

"They are wonderful, except that they forget I do not like to be made to feel stupid. It is a problem that has plagued them for longer than I care to remember."

"I'd say being without you for a millennia might put them a bit out-of-practice."

"I agree. Which is why I only iced them up to their necks."

She snorted out a laugh and popped the last bite of her sticky bun into her mouth. Licking her fingers, she put her plate next to mine on the counter and waved me toward several brightly colored racks of clothing.

"I need to wash my hands."

She pulled a strange looking white towel from a yellow container and tossed it my direction. I caught it and rubbed it between my fingers. Suds appeared on my skin from the damp towel.

"Rub it over your hands," she said, holding up her hands as she wiped them clean with the towel. "Then toss over there." She tossed her towel into a black basket in the corner of the room and held up her perfectly clean hands.

I followed suit, astonished by how easily the towel absorbed the traces of honey and sugar on my fingers. But when I threw the towel into the basket after hers, I was just as surprised to find my hands dry in mere seconds.

"It's amazing. What is it?"

"Nothing special. Just a baby wipe."

"A baby wipe?"

"Yeah, disposable cleansing towels. But most people just call them baby wipes. For changing nappies."

I suddenly knew what she meant by baby wipe.

We turned back to the rack of clothing just as a heavy rap at the door rattled the glass windows.

"I believe your boys have thawed out," she said, grinning as she pointed over my shoulder. "Should I let them in?"

"How could you possibly keep them out?"

She gave me a mysterious wink. "I have my ways. That's why they haven't tried to open the door yet."

"I suppose they can come in. They will probably want to pick out the clothing themselves."

"Well, hell no then. A woman should get to pick her own wardrobe after being locked up for a thousand years in a prison tower."

I swallowed a curse. How the bloody hell did she know where I'd been?

"Don't look so surprised, honey. It's a small town and you're the newest bit we have to talk about. Give me a sec, I'll send the boys over to the cafe to order us some food. We can all eat and chat after you pick out the clothes you want."

There was no way this little woman was going to be able to order my two giant mates right off her porch ... was she? But she did. I watched, flabbergasted as they both flashed me apologetic looks through the windows on the door and then strolled down the sidewalk toward the cafe.

She came back inside and closed the door. With a flick of her wrist, curtains dropped across the windows and lights brightened around the room. She could call herself whatever she wanted, but I'd never seen magick like hers before.

CHAPTER 34

ELI

"We hurt her feelings." I kicked a pebble with my booted toe and watched it skitter across Main Street Circle, stopping when it hit the other curb. The afternoon sun glinted off the asphalt and I squinted, not appreciating the sudden glare. "I shouldn't have laughed, but the way she interpreted cowboy just caught me off guard." I called up my dragon's heat and warmed my chilled skin. The sun might be shining, but the breeze was colder than a witch's tit and I wore only a short-sleeved shirt. A storm would hit soon. I could feel the air pressure changing.

"Neither of us should've laughed. It was an idiot move and we deserved the ice block she stuck us in," Miles said, agreeing with me wholeheartedly.

"It was funny though."

Miles chuckled under his breath. "It was fucking hilarious. Hopefully, Calliope's clothes will help. I don't think she was very keen on those flip flops."

I sighed and took in a deep breath of the tantalizing scents coming from the cafe. The sweet scent of honey and BBQ rode the icy breeze. The brownies must've put meat in the smoker last night for it to be smelling so good now.

We reached the door to the cafe and I pulled it open for my brother. Miles walked in ahead of me and ducked his head, narrowly missing the little brass bell hanging over the doorframe.

Several Lycans sat at two pushed together tables to my right and I stepped toward them, recognizing Kieran. "How are the damages to the neighborhood?"

Kieran took a sip from his pint glass and then looked up at me. "About half of the houses along the outskirts are totally demolished. Luckily everyone listened and escaped into the shelters. No one was hurt." His Scottish accent at one time had been out of place in Sanctuary, but now we were all quite used to it. Liam and Brogan said he came over from Scotland a few years ago when meddling humans decided to go on a hunting spree and killed his family.

"I'm glad to hear everyone is safe. Please let my brother and I know if we can help with repairs."

"Aye, will do." Kieran nodded. "I believe Rose already took care of whatever expenses were incurred."

"Eli," Miles bellowed from the counter across the dining room.

I excused myself from Kieran's table and strode across the room to stand at my brother's side. "What is your problem?" I hissed at him under my breath.

"You need to order so we can get back to Calliope's."

"What happen to letting her have time to chill there with the siren?" I grabbed a menu and looked at it absently. I didn't need a menu. I wanted whatever it was they were cooking out back.

"Hey boys," Maven popped up from behind the counter. Her long purple hair was gone, replaced by a bubblegum pink short cut. I knew it was her though and not her twin, Raven. Maven was the flirty one.

I refused to act startled, even though the little pixie had totally thrown me when she stood up. How they snuck around like they did still amazed me.

My brother was less tactful and gave her a half growl of exasperation.

"What's cooking? I could smell it all the way across the circle."

"Depends. We have a lot cooking," she said, a grin spreading across her face. "But I know you guys just want the BBQ."

"We need to order for Diana and Calliope, too. Anything special on this week's menu?" I asked, laying down the red piece of paper with the latest concoctions for the cafe.

"I have just the thing for her after the BBQ. Corinne made her favorite apple pie yesterday and I've got one big slice of it left. I'll be right back." Maven squealed and disappeared through the swinging kitchen door.

I turned around and leaned my back against the bar. The cafe was bustling for the middle of the afternoon. Rose sat against the wall with Erick and Bailey at a table, laughing about something. The Lycans were deep in conversation about rebuilding and what materials needed to be ordered. The door swung open, ringing the damn bell. I didn't like bells and neither did my brother. Something about the way the sound rang out bothered our ears.

Travis and Garrett McLennon walked in. Both nodded their heads in my direction before heading over to speak with Rose. I didn't try to listen in—I didn't need anything else to do right now. All I wanted was to get some food, collect a happy wife from Calliope's shop and figure out how to catch Diana up on a thousand years of history. I had a feeling that we weren't going to get anywhere as a family unit until she felt like she had solid ground to stand on in town.

We just needed to be patient. We could do that. Drakonae lived for millennia. In fact, no one was quite sure how long we could live. What was a little more time?

"Alright, boys." Maven came barreling out the swinging door carrying a large brown paper bag filled with the most delicious smelling BBQ we'd had in Sanctuary in months. The tangy scent of the vinegar in the sauce on the meat, mixed with the sweetness of the apple pie, and the warmth of the yeast rolls. I wiped the corner of my mouth to make sure I wasn't drooling.

"Thank you, Maven," Miles said, handing her about a hundred Texas Republic credits.

Banking changed when the US came apart at the seams fifty years ago. The dollar ceased to exist and now each of the five Republics used currency called credits, named after each Republic. They were still valued about like a dollar had been. Before the collapse, a dollar had barely been worth picking up off the street. Rose didn't charge anyone for food, the money for the meals went to the waitresses like Raven and Maven and the cooks. We all paid for the food when we paid into the town hall from our businesses.

It was an ingenious setup and worked for all of us. Most of us were as old as dirt and had made billions of dollars over the years, Rose included. The Lycan's were really the only ones I knew of that lived closer to a human lifespan—still most would live nearly three hundred years. But they used their talents wisely and made good money, always working together for the good of the pack. They worked hard around the town and Rose paid them well for their help. She had a way of always making sure everyone felt as though they were pulling their weight and deserved the space they took in Sanctuary.

I followed Miles out of the cafe and we trudged back over to Calliope's shop. The wind had increased and I felt the first signs of a wintry mix falling here and there. If the weather continued this way, Sanctuary would be covered in a layer of ice by morning.

"Maybe the weather will keep Xerxes men at bay a while longer," Miles said, rapping gently on Calliope's red door.

"It would be nice. I'd like to spend some time with Diana, without worrying about freak'n grenades being launched through the bedroom windows." I stomped my feet and breathed out some heat, warming my chilled skin.

The door swung out, and Calliope's curvy form filled the doorway. "I hope you are both ready to apologize for being assholes," she hissed under her breath.

"You don't have to rub it in," I grumbled, stepping up and shouldering past the irate siren. Calliope needed to get laid soon. She was only this grouchy when she'd been ignoring what her body needed. "We know we were jerks."

I walked into the center of the store and stopped, breathless at the vision before me. Diana's snow-blond hair was loose, falling in soft waves down her back. The top she wore hung in a deep cowl at the back, showing off her flawless cream-colored skin. The long flowing skirt was light blue and brushed the tops of her toes. The midnight purple fabric of the shirt shimmered in the light as she looked up, catching my gaze in the mirror before her. Those ice blue eyes touched my soul. I could feel her love. I knew we'd been forgiven, but I also knew that she'd been deeply hurt.

"I'm so sorry, Diana," I said softly, setting the bag from Rose's on the carpet.

Miles moved forward with me and we surrounded her.

"Please forgive me, my love," Miles asked. "We forgot so quickly how overwhelmed you must feel right now."

"We were so excited to have you back—to really have you back. We completely ignored the fact that everything about this world is foreign to you," I continued.

She nuzzled her face to the hand Miles had raised to brush through her silky hair.

I ran my fingers up and down the bare skin of her uncovered back and felt a shiver run down her body. The scent of her growing arousal had my dick hard and straining against the crotch of my jeans.

"I have a lot of catching up to do," she whispered. "In bed and out."

The last four words were barely audible, but they punched the air right out of my lungs. Thank the gods we hadn't completely screwed this up.

"Would the three of you like me to just leave for a few minutes so you can get it out of your system? Or can we eat the dinner that Eli so carelessly left in the middle of the floor?" Calliope's snark broke the moment.

Diana began to laugh. A sound I hadn't heard in so long. A sound that I would've done anything to hear again ... and now she was here. She was happy. Or at least beginning to be happy. We had a long way to go. Knowing that we might have a child trapped in the Veil was unsettling, though I tried to remind myself that the likelihood of him or her still being alive was small.

"Let's eat. I can't wait to show you some of the wardrobe Calliope picked out for me. I do hope I didn't spend too much money." Diana glanced up hesitantly. "We did go through a lot of items."

"We have more than enough money to spend on you, love," Miles said, jumping forward to assure her.

A smile stretched across her face and she once again beamed as if the light of the sun radiated from her.

"Miles is right," Calliope added. "These boys could buy the whole shop and not feel the slightest tug on their wallet."

I chuckled as Diana's eyes widened.

"Are you royalty in this world as well?" Diana asked.

I grimaced. It wasn't something anyone knew about us. Not even Rose knew our entire history.

"Royalty?" Calliope drawled. "Should I be calling you Lord and Master?"

She jested with her voice, but her brown eyes darkened with curiosity as the siren in her came forward.

"Miles and E—"

"Diana," I interrupted. "Our past isn't something we like to discuss."

Diana's eyes opened wider and she nodded, understand passing between us.

"You can't just leave me hanging like that, honey," Calliope said, slipping between us to Diana's side. "A girl needs a little juicy gossip."

"I spoke out of turn. When Miles and Eli are ready to talk about our lives in the Veil, then I will do so freely with you first. I promise."

Calliope clucked her tongue like a disappointed mother hen, but a wide smile spread across her face. "Then I will look forward to that day, honey."

She turned back to my brother and me and winked. "Why don't you three take that big bag of dinner and go back and enjoy it at your place. I have a few errands to run." Strolling over to the counter, she picked up three large shopping bags and walked them over to Miles. "These should get her started. Your wife has excellent taste. I think you will especially enjoy the lace."

CHAPTER 35

DIANA

I yawned and stretched out my arm, whacking a pillow in the process. *When did I get in bed?* The last thing I remembered was eating one of the best meals I'd ever had and falling asleep between Miles and Eli on a giant piece of furniture they'd called a couch.

Squinting, I looked around the familiar room. I was back in Miles' bed. Dark paneled walls and crushed velvet curtains blocked out all the sunlight. I didn't think I'd slept that long though. It shouldn't be dark yet.

I walked to the window, pulled back the heavy fabric, and stared out into an ugly gray, overcast sky. Billowing black clouds filled the sky and in the distance I could feel the thunder as it rolled closer and closer to the town. Lightning flashed at the horizon, making itself known as well. A smattering of rain splashed against the window-pane, but I knew it was only the beginning.

Miles and Eli must've carried me up after I fell asleep.

I wished they'd stayed with me. Glancing back at the giant bed, I wondered where they were. They'd more than made up for laughing at me earlier, both of them being sure to explain everything they thought might be new to me. I appreciated it. For me, the worst thing was feeling so out of place. I didn't know how to act. I didn't know what I could say or not say.

My husbands had aligned themselves with this Lamassu, Rose, but they still withheld some of their past from her. How was I supposed to know who knew what? I was so out of sync with them. We hadn't been together except that once to end my heat cycle. I desperately wanted to be with them. Both of them.

Calliope had given me some ideas and I was eager to see if my men would go for it. They were the ones who had built a sex club into this fortress, after all.

I wandered across the room, admiring the various sculptures and furniture pieces Miles had collected for his bedroom. He'd always loved handmade art. Nothing had changed. The bed was custom built and as sturdy as the wild oaks that blanketed the sides of the Brechin mountains back home. He had a lovely mahogany desk set over to the other side of the room and several floor-to-ceiling bookcases packed with beautiful volumes. The floors were covered in soft carpet and the arched ceilings highlighted the excellent architecture of the building.

Pushing open a heavy wood-paneled door, I stepped into a palatial marble palace of a wash room. Biting my lip to keep from squealing like a five-year-old girl, I tiptoed across the cool white marble floors. Nothing could keep me from running my fingertips along the edges of the milky marble counters and the bronze spigots. Two large mirrors had been placed on the wall above each sink. In the center of the room was a shower enclosed only by glass. A bath lay next to it, sunken into the floor.

It was amazing and I wanted nothing more than to strip naked and relax. We had nice washrooms in the palace of Orin when I'd lived there with Miles and Eli before ... but nothing compared to this.

I slipped from the loose clothing I wore and let it drop to the floor in a small pile. Sex could wait a little longer. I needed to take a bath first anyway. It only took a moment to figure out the handles on the large tub and soon I had it halfway full of steaming hot water.

But, before getting into that nice water, I needed to remove the unwanted hair from the rest of my body. I stepped into the open shower, waved my hands over my skin from the waist down, frosting every single one. The air I generated was so cold it crystalized the hairs and they just brushed right off, leaving every inch of me as smooth as the marble floors.

Shaking off the last bit of the frosted hair, I left the shower and climbed carefully down into the sunken bath. The hot water soothed my cold skin and I sighed, relaxing on a seat cut into the side of the bath. Leaning my head back against the rim, I closed my eyes and thanked the gods for getting me back to my mates.

It broke my heart to know I'd left a child back in Orin, but I needed Miles and Eli as much as they needed me. We were linked. Joined by the sacred bond of our people and we existed solely because of each other. When Drakonae mate, it is for life. Some couples are two. Some are three. I'd seen four brothers share one Drakonae female. But when the bond was forged, nothing would break it but death. And the death of one brought on the human deaths of the others. It must've been terrifying to Miles and Eli, wondering when and if the Incanti would choose to kill me. Choose to end Miles and Eli's human lives as well, turning them into vicious beasts without the aid of a human conscience to still their wrath.

I could only assume the Incanti preferred the long-term torture verses finishing us off completely.

It didn't matter now. I was here. They were here. We were safe from the Incanti for now.

"Diana?" Eli's voice called from the bedroom.

"In here," I answered, my voice echoing through the cavernous wash room.

He appeared in the doorway a moment later and smiled when he caught sight of me in the bath. He stalked forward, his gaze drifting down from my face. The water was clear and everything was visible. But, I wanted more than just a fuck. I wanted to play.

If he thought he was going to coax me out of this heavenly water for less than an adventure in this Castle's basement, he was wrong.

"I see you didn't have any trouble with the bathroom fixtures." He sat down on the edge of the bath and slipped his hand beneath the surface of the water, drawing his fingers lightly along my satin-smooth calf.

"None at all." I flicked some water at his face and he scrunched his eyebrows.

"What was that for?"

"You looked dry."

He snorted a laugh and reached deeper into the bath.

I shrieked and slithered away to the other side, narrowly avoiding his fingers trying to slip between my legs. The damn man was trying to feel inside me ... I glared up at his face.

He merely smirked and wiped his wet hand off on his shirt.

"I was just going to see if you were wet, love."

Sneaky bastard. I couldn't help the smile that tugged at the corners of my mouth.

"Where's Miles?" I asked, trying to change the subject and stall.

"I'm not enough for you?" He grinned, feigning hurt feelings.

He was more than enough. And if it weren't for the hot water keeping my skin in a constant blush, he'd know just how aroused I already was. My sex ached and my breasts felt heavy. I wanted his hands on me. His mouth on mine. But I had to control my need. I wanted to play.

Not that I wouldn't be perfectly delighted with a romp in Miles or Eli's bed, but I wanted to experience something they had been enjoying for a good many years without me. The way Calliope had described the submissive role made my insides throb. I wanted to have that experience and I wanted Miles and Eli to know that I was interested in exploring that lifestyle with them. At least in the bedroom. Bossing me around elsewhere was never going to fly. It never had.

"You are more than enough, my love," I drawled out slowly. "But I would really like a tour of your Dungeon this evening."

Heat filled the air in the washroom, creating a thick steam around the tub. His eyes widened in surprise, and I heard a pleased rumble deep in his throat, rolling upward until the air around us vibrated with a sound that could only be likened to a purr.

"Do you know what the dungeon is for? Who told y—" He paused for a second. "Never mind, I know a pretty siren who likes to gossip."

"So you'll show me?"

"You would be required to follow our commands ... explicitly," Miles' voice sliced through the steamy air. My skin tingled from head to foot with excitement as he stepped into the bathroom.

I turned toward him in the doorway and nodded. "I will."

The tone of his voice made my legs feel like pudding. I couldn't wait to see what else he might have in store for me.

"Stand," Miles said, using the same commanding tone. His eyes darkened as flecks of brilliant orange flashed in his honey-brown pupils.

I did as he asked without hesitation, only somewhat aware that I was stark naked and dripping wet. It wasn't like they hadn't seen every inch of me before.

"Good girl," Miles said.

There was something about the way he praised me that sent heat searing through my body, flushing me pink from head to foot for sure.

"I think she likes your Dom voice," Eli chuckled, rising from the ledge of the tub. He held out a hand.

I took Eli's outstretched hand and climbed the stairs out of the sunken tub back to the marble floor of the washroom. Water was still running down my body from my hair, and I was making quite the mess.

Miles walked forward, grabbing a towel from a rack

near the doorway. Eli stepped back and I reached out to take the towel, but Miles shook his head. Dropping my arms back to my sides, I stood still as Miles dabbed and rubbed my body from head to toe, paying special attention to both breasts and the bits between my legs.

"Your pussy smells so sweet. Let's see if you taste as good as you smell." He tossed the damp towel to Eli and ran a hand over my shivering stomach. His fingers splayed wide over my hip and slid lower and lower until he dipped a finger between my legs. I sucked in a quick breath as he entered me and rubbed across that tender bud at the top of my slit. He pulled his finger back and I could see my juices glistening on it. A moment later his finger was in his mouth and he was growling, a look of pleasure covering his face.

"How does she taste?" Eli's voice interrupted my trance-like focus on the top of Miles' head.

"Sweeter than Rose's sticky buns."

Pleasure rose through me like a rushing wave at his approval. I knew how to have sex—really well. But this was different. The tone of voice. The command. It was a high I could become addicted to.

Eli disappeared into a closet I'd not noticed yet. He came back with a satin robe and handed it to me. "Put this on. Say, "yes Master" when we command you."

"Y-yes, Master." The formality was strange, but I was willing to play along.

"Good girl." Eli's voice was warmer than Miles, but still held the same raw power that made every bit of me tingle with excitement like I had when Miles first told me to stand.

I slipped on the robe and tied the attached sash around

my waist. The silky fabric fluttered around my thighs, barely long enough to cover my knees. I was covered, but as transparent as the piece of clothing was, I might as well have still been naked. Surely they planned to allow me to dress. This couldn't be the only thing they were going to let me wear?

Miles moved first, exiting the bathroom with an eagerness that was contagious. Eli gestured for me to follow and then he walked behind me. The marble floors were cold beneath my bare feet—not that it bothered me. I liked the cold. I couldn't feel much of anything except the energy building inside me and the heat rolling off both of my mates in waves. Warmth pooled between my legs as we walked and my nipples pebbled against the slight brush of the satin.

I smiled as we turned and left Miles' room and entered the grand hallway. They really weren't going to let me put anything else on.

CHAPTER 36

DIANA

The sun was setting as we walked down a set of stairs to the ground level of the fortress. It was dim, but not difficult to see with my Drakonae vision. I wondered how hard it was for the Sisters to get around in the low light, but for the most part, I hadn't seen much of them. Though after the attack, Miles and Eli had probably asked them to stay hidden.

"Too many questions in your mind, Diana. Don't think right now," Eli said, his voice deep and smooth as the satin fabric of the tiny robe I wore.

"What am I supposed to do?"

"Feel," Miles replied, his voice carrying clearly over his shoulder.

We walked past a lush courtyard, filled with waving flowers and shrubs. Several small buildings sat amongst the pathways that curled through the garden. The sweet scent of jasmine floated on the evening air and I took a deep breath. Trying to let everything fall away, just as they were asking.

We came to a set of solid double doors and Miles knocked four times and then stepped back. I wanted to ask why he was knocking on a door in his own home, but thought better of it and bit my bottom lip instead. A small partition in the top of the door opened, no bigger than an egg. A few words were exchanged with a woman on the other side before the door on the right swung open.

A tall woman with blue hair the color of Eira's eyes opened the door. She wore the tightest leather pants I'd ever seen and a top that had been cut to cover only the necessary parts. It too was made from black leather. A riding crop hung from a latch at her waist and she held some sort of paper pad in her arms.

"Good evening." She stepped aside, bowing slightly as she gestured for us to enter.

I followed Miles and paused at his side in a well-lit entry. The floors and walls were stone, but the ceilings were beautifully carved wood beams and arched to make the room appear larger.

"Evening, Seely. How is the crowd tonight? Any hiccups we need to address before we disappear with our sub."

The word *sub* made my heart do a pitter-patter and I did my best to keep from smiling from ear to ear. It was difficult. I loved the idea of giving up control. Letting them tell me exactly how our lovemaking would progress. Just the idea of it put my mind at ease. Everything else around me was a mess, but I knew that sex with my husbands would be good, no matter how they chose to go about it. I liked that I didn't have to make any choices. I could just ... let go ... and do as they said.

"Nope, everything is running smoother than molasses. We have four guests in the main hall tonight running scenes, three in the lower dungeon, and two in private rooms. All are repeat visitors and well-loved by the Sisters. We do have one contract completion this evening and it's her first, so I've got several Sisters in the wings to take her afterward and make sure she is settled once he checks out for the night."

I listened. Fascinated and confused by the entire conversation. Now wasn't the time to ask questions. Eli had already warned me to let everything go and to try to just *feel*. I tried to honor that request. There would be plenty of time to pick their brains about the Sisters and the club later.

"You run a tight ship, Seely. Thank you," said Miles.

Eli closed the door behind him and turned. "Have you had to whip anyone lately?"

The woman's face split into a stunning smile and she flashed bright white teeth. Her blue hair rippled in the soft light and she patted the crop hanging from her waist. "Not for a while. But, I've been propositioned by more than one man, begging for punishment. Did you know Master Carter was a switch? Nearly turned my hair pink when he offered to bend over and let me whip his ass."

Eli laughed and shook his head. "That actually doesn't surprise me at all."

"Is the black room available tonight?" Miles asked.

The woman they'd called Seely looked down at her pad. "Yes, black is open." She reached into the pouch hanging next to the crop and withdrew a small key attached to a shiny black disk. She placed the key into his outstretched hand and bowed subtly before sauntering off to attend to something else.

My mates turned to face me and Eli crooked a finger, motioning me to follow.

I took a deep breath and followed him, this time Miles followed behind me. He was so close, I could feel his warm breath on my shoulder.

"Are you ready to have your mind blown?" he whispered over my shoulder. "This is how Eli and I have learned to cope with the cage of being unable to shift. I think you will like it, Love."

My heart raced in my chest and my legs threatened to give way. I was so wet between my legs, even I could smell my arousal. If he'd asked me to turn around right here in the hall and suck him off, I would've.

"Answer him, subbie," Eli said from ahead of me.

"Yes, Master." I spoke the words, but they were no louder than a whisper.

"Speak clearly," Miles commanded.

"Yes, Master," I repeated, this time louder and clearer.

"Good girl," Miles praised.

They were two words that should've made me feel irritated. I wasn't a pet or a child, but the tone of voice used to speak those two words to me made every difference. Instead of resentment, I felt desire, pleasure, and excitement. Heat coursed through me, warming my body from head to foot. I was so pale. The slightest blush would show on my skin. I knew I had to be pink from my bare legs to my face.

We walked quietly through a large hall with several

couples engaging in a variety of activities, from spanking to rope bindings. People were having sex out in the open, in view of whomever walked by. It was a strange atmosphere. Dark floors, dark walls, and music unlike anything I'd ever heard, pumped from the ceilings of the room—a hard beat, animalistic and sensual at the same time.

Everything was controlled, though. Discipline and decisiveness were like perfume in the air. Every move by the people around me was made with precision. Every breath. Every stroke of whatever implement they were using was being done with the utmost care and concern. Even those persons causing a great deal of pain to their partner, never lost focus.

It was amazing to see the couples going through various activities together. I could understand the appeal it held for my husbands. Without the ability to shift and allow our dragon some space, we would become restless and angry. This exchange of power and of restraint would be essential to maintaining control over the beast within.

Eli stopped at a black door, inserted the key, and opened it. He walked in first and I followed, not quite prepared for everything I saw.

My feet stopped moving and I stared. Strange contraptions I'd never seen before were spread around the edges of the room. Whips and paddles and other instruments I had no names for decorated the walls like art. The floor was padded black carpet and at the back of the room a large bed wrapped in black sheets looked inviting.

A tap on my shoulder reminded me Miles was still behind me.

"Inside, love. We'll not be putting on a show for anyone."

I took a few more steps and he closed the door behind us.

Eli moved around the room, pulling several items from the wall and then pushed some lighted spots on the wall. An unfamiliar grinding noise echoed through the space as several different chains and bars lowered from the ceiling.

Fascination wouldn't let me look away. He attached some leather straps to several places on the bars and I shivered as a bolt of excitement skittered down my spine. It looked like a harness that would suspend me in the air.

"Take off the robe, fold it, and place it on the table behind you," Miles said, walking around me to join Eli at the contraption in the center of the room.

I did as told, keeping my eyes on both men the entire time. Cool air rushed over my naked body, raising goose-flesh on my skin from head to foot. I shivered and flipped my long white-blond hair over my shoulder. My chest heaved up and down as excitement built within me. I wanted them so badly; my arousal was dripping down the inside of my thighs. Licking my lips, I took a step toward them, then paused, not sure what they wanted me to do next.

"Come." Miles' voice was deep and commanding. It was just one word, but I knew it was just the beginning of the experience.

Moving swiftly across the room, I stopped and stood between Miles and Eli.

"Any time you feel uncomfortable, say the word "yellow". We will slow down and talk about the experience before proceeding. If something completely overwhelms you use the safe word "red". Everything stops if you say "red" so be very sure before using it. Do you understand?" Eli asked, using a finger to lift my chin. He held eye contact with me until I answered.

"Yes," I answered, nodding.

Miles and Eli guided my arms between several loose straps and made sure my breasts fit between two thicker straps that would support my chest and torso once suspended.

I stepped below the apparatus of metal bars above me and they fastened chains and straps into place. Each man was ever so careful to make sure nothing pinched or rubbed as they raised me up.

I faced the floor as each of them picked up each of my legs simultaneously and threaded them through another set of straps, sliding them to the tops of my thighs. Another set of straps was fixed around my lower thighs, just above the knee. I couldn't see what they were doing, but something was attached to those straps and my legs were pulled apart and fastened tautly, pussy wide for them to see or do as they pleased. Cuffs were placed around my ankles and attached by a short chain to something above me, rendering me almost completely immobile.

My breasts swayed freely below me and I arched my back, feeling strain between my shoulders and my hips.

"Here, love," Eli cooed, sliding his hands around my waist. Another strap followed, supporting my stomach and taking the strain from my back.

I sunk into the support and sighed. It was strange to be so confined and so relaxed at the same time. I completely trusted Miles and Eli. Being restrained during lovemaking was nothing new to me. There wasn't much the three of us hadn't done together in previous years, but these toys were new and the more formal dominant attitude was different. I liked it, but it was a new experience. For once they had me wondering what was coming next.

"I'm tying your hair back with a scarf to keep it from your face. Then you're wearing this blindfold," Eli said. I appreciated the warning and craned my neck to look up at him. He knelt in front of me, a wide smile on his face. "You're so beautiful, Diana. I'm glad you wanted to explore the club with us."

I started to speak, but then considered if it was appropriate.

Eli caught my uncertainty. "You don't have to speak when we complement you, love. I know this is more formal than how we've played in the past. You are doing excellent."

His explanation and extra compliment made my heart swell. I knew at that point, I'd try anything they wanted me to. The title of "Master" was formal and unfamiliar to my tongue, but I liked it. Their domination of me soothed my soul and I released a contented sigh.

Miles grabbed a strap above me and tugged me closer. My body swung in the air. He held me forward and pressed his lips hard to mine, sweeping his tongue through my mouth before letting go. I swung backward and forward several times before my body came to a balanced stop. The free movement of the harness was exciting. I realized how fun this could be as infinite possibilities sprouted in my lustful mind.

I kneaded my breasts and let out a groan of pleasure.

"No one said you could touch yourself. Hands off, subbie," Miles growled. "Those breasts are only for us to play with."

A second later he slipped a blindfold over my eyes, making me feel everything through my other senses.

CHAPTER 37

MILES

I took each of her hands and fastened it to a special latch hanging from the corners of the steel frame. She'd no longer be able to touch herself. Now that her feet and hands were secured, she was completely at our mercy. The knowledge that she trusted us explicitly after so many years had passed, after we'd lost her that one fateful day made my heart swell with gratefulness.

Caressing her face, I leaned down to her ear. "You're an amazing woman, Diana."

Her mouth curved into a smile and she leaned into my hand. "I love you, too," she whispered.

A grin pulled at my mouth. "Say "thank you, Master".

Her cheeks scrunched as her full red lips parted in a large smile. "Yes, Master. Thank you." Her voice was like honey and it made my dick rock hard.

Gods, I loved her so much. There weren't enough words in the world to tell her how much she meant to me.

I glanced up and caught Eli's gaze. He nodded and stepped back.

I shucked out of my pants and took his place between her opened legs. Her thighs trembled under my touch, but it was the scent of her arousal that had my dick standing at attention. Gods, she was so wet and ready.

Eli moved to her face and knelt to the floor. Something chrome flashed in his hands and I knew he was about to test out some clover clamps on her pebbled nipples.

He pinched and pulled a few times, making her squirm and moan in the harness. There was no escape and she hissed when he put the first clamp into place, swearing under her breath. Eli just laughed.

I swatted her ass with my bare hand. "Take the next one without complaint, sub."

"Yes Master."

I ran my hand over the curve of her ass up her lower back, loving the feel of her ragged breathing so early into the session. She was a natural submissive, always had been, and the endorphins from the bondage were hitting her quickly, amping her arousal further.

She tensed for a second when Eli attached the second clamp, but she didn't speak a word. Her submission was beautiful. She wanted to do exactly what we desired.

"Miles, the clamps look so pretty on her pink nipples," Eli said, rising from the floor in front of her. "I think I'm going to add the weights to them. Then every swing and jolt in the harness will give them a good tug."

"Weights?" she squeaked.

I popped her ass again, pleased when bright pink color flushed where my hand had struck. Rubbing away the sting of the smack, I kneaded her ass until she squirmed beneath my touch.

"Please, Miles," she moaned. "Gods, please fuck me now," she begged, her breath ragged already.

I smiled. Taking her was what I intended to do, just not before I made her wait impatiently for a while longer.

"Please, Miles," she begged again. "Eli?"

"Master, love," Eli answered, swiftly attaching the weights to her clamped nipples.

"Master, sor—ahhhhhh!" She writhed in the harness.

I popped her ass again. "Ten for complaining. Count."

"What!?" she balked.

"Fifteen now." I said, trying not to smile, though I knew she couldn't see me.

She made a cute, angry growl, but not another word of complaint fell from her lips.

I picked up a slender paddle from the counter at my left and rubbed it across her pink cheeks so she would know to expect something other than my hand. I raised it and brought it down with a light pop. She tensed into the strike, but a muffled "one" came from her throat.

I kneaded her ass, working out the sting for a few moments before popping her four times, alternating from cheek to cheek. The muscles in her strong legs flexed and her whole body shook in the harness. I knew each movement was costing her breasts though. Eli stood against the wall a few feet away, watching with a smirk on his face.

"Five," she said between gritted teeth.

I continued to paddle a few at a time, stopping between each group to knead her ass and slip my fingers down between her wet labia. *Damn.* Her pussy was dripping.

"You're so wet, Love," I said, making sure she could hear how pleased I was in my tone of voice. "I can't wait to sink my dick deep into your sweet pussy."

"You could now," she offered.

"Not yet, doll," Eli countered from the wall. "You've got five more swats still coming."

I struck her round ass cheeks purposefully, bringing them from a pink to a bright cherry red. She counted the last strike and I heard a sigh slip from her lungs.

"Good, girl." I praised, slipping my hand between her legs again, fondling the swollen throbbing nub at the top of her slit. Her clit was already pushing from beneath its hood and her labia were swollen and ready for me. So tempting. I needed to have just a small taste.

I grabbed the straps around her upper thighs, holding her in place as I knelt to lick her pussy. A loud gasp tore from her lungs as I thrust my tongue deep into her sex. Gods, she tasted so good. Her light musk and sweet arousal made my dick swell further. I wanted her now, but I knew Eli had much more planned.

Eli caught my gaze and I nodded, backing away from her sweet pussy.

"Noooooo," she whimpered. "Please Master, don't stop."

I swatted her ass again for good measure and her attempt to stroke my ego to get what she wanted.

She moaned again as I rubbed her still-pink ass, and began unhooking her ankles and thighs. Once her feet were firmly planted on the floor again we helped her stand straight. Then connected the padded cuffs around her wrists to a bar at the top of the swing frame.

Eli stepped away for a moment, pressing buttons on

the wall to raise her arms higher —until she stood just on her toes. Her back arched and I brushed my knuckles along the sides of her heavy breasts. The clamps would be next, but they were Eli's toys and I would let him have that pleasure.

My focus was lower on her luscious body.

Eli returned to her side and pulled the blindfold from her head. Her bright blue eyes sparked and she growled low in her throat, but she didn't speak. She looked down at me, white swirling in her irises. Her dragon was pushing hard.

"Good girl, Love," I praised her restraint.

I knelt before her, captured her thighs, and lifted them over my shoulders. Eli moved next to me and began massaging one of her breasts. She moaned and bit her lip, watching both of us with a heated gaze. Her sweet scent filled my lungs and I lapped at her sex, drawing another low moan from her chest.

"I'm going to take these off now, subbie." Eli spoke calmly, but we both knew she was about to come apart. A light sheen of sweat covered her body. Her breath was coming in pants and she fought everything inside her to keep from writhing in my grasp.

When he removed the first clamp she screamed and arched her back. Her heels dug into my shoulder blades as I held her in place. The scream turned to a moan as he captured her tit in his mouth and sucked the swollen tender nipple.

I licked and sucked at her sex, distracting her mind further from the pain. As his hands ventured toward the other breast I tightened my hold on her thighs again, preparing for the volcanic eruption that was coming.

"No, no, no," she whimpered, twisting in the cuffs and against my hold.

"It's okay, subbie. I'll make it feel better," Eli said, catching my gaze just as he unhooked the clamp.

I latched onto her clit at the same moment and sucked the swollen nubbin hard. Another scream tore from her lungs and every muscle in her body tensed. Her thighs tightened on either side of my neck and her heels pressed hard into my back. I sucked again, pulling her clit further into my mouth.

Eli had the sore nipple in his mouth and was kneading the other breast.

She arched and fought ... and then froze as her first orgasm crested. I felt the blast of cold and allowed my dragon closer to the surface to keep the temperature in the room even. Eli did the same. Neither of us let go of her until the shudders and moans slowed to a stop.

I licked her slit a few more times, loving the way her thighs trembled against my neck—the way her breath came in pants and the way her creamy, white skin flushed a bright pink. She was gorgeous. Sexy. Mine.

CHAPTER 38

DIANA

I drew in a breath and tried to stand. Were it not for the cuffs and chains holding me upright, I would've fallen into a heap on the red carpet. My body was still reeling from the massive orgasm my mates had pulled from me moments ago.

My nipples were on fire and my sex throbbed, still desperate to have more. I wanted more. I wanted them inside me. Both of them. I needed that connection. Our bond needed it.

So much time had passed since we'd truly been together as one.

Miles left my side and Eli moved to stand in front of me.

"How are you doing, Love?" He caressed my breasts and dipped to kiss me softly on the lips.

"Mmmmm," I moaned, still unable to think coherently.

Every inch of my skin was hot and every pulse point throbbed, reminding me of my racing heart.

My arms were pulled taut over my head and I could just stand on my tiptoes. I dug my toes into the soft carpet and let my head fall forward.

Eli continued to rub his hands over my breasts, down my ribs, and over the mound of my sex. He paused every few seconds and slid a finger through my sopping wet folds. After climaxing as hard as I had, I wanted more. Gods, I wanted more.

Miles hands joined Eli's on my skin and I moaned as he rubbed up and down my back until he reached the curve of my backside. Something cold and slick dripped onto my skin. I shivered as Miles worked the liquid around my tight hole, then an ice-cold smooth shaft pressed against the slicked opening.

"Push back, love. I want you stretched and ready to really enjoy us both," Miles said. I arched into his hand and felt the cold glass of the toy push slightly inside.

While Miles was coaxing the toy into my ass, Eli had his fingers working over my clit. In seconds my breathing was ragged again, and I could feel the spiraling power of another orgasm reaching through my body to claim my consciousness.

A gasp slipped from my lungs as Miles methodically pushed the toy deeper. My muscles gripped the narrow neck to hold it firmly in place. But he didn't just leave it there. He pulled it back and thrust it in again, mimicking what I knew he would soon be doing with his cock.

Then they both backed away and he did leave the toy buried inside me.

Gods no. They couldn't just leave me ... hanging like this.

I couldn't see Miles. He was still behind me somewhere, but Eli turned and picked up something from a table near the wall. It had a short handle and dozens of long leather strands hanging from it like a tassel ... a flogger.

I swallowed nervously. The spanking had been a surprise, but in the end it had made me want them more than I thought possible. But flogging me? How could they think I would enjoy being whipped?

Yanking on the chain connected to my wrist cuffs, I shuddered. The word red came to my lips, but I couldn't say it. The toys were new. The formality was new. But the relationship wasn't. The dominance had always been there when we made love. I trusted these men completely. Called them both husband for four-hundred years before I lost them.

"Breathe, Love," Eli said, his voice soft but still commanding. He'd called me "love" this time instead of "subbie". I relaxed more, knowing he was aware of my anxiety.

He came forward and trailed the leather strands over my breasts, then shoulders, then allowed them to brush across the front of my thighs. The scent of the oiled leather tickled my nostrils and I took a deep breath. He flicked his wrist just slightly and they swung in a gentle arc, thumping against the outside of my thighs.

The leather strands didn't hurt. Not the way he was swinging them.

He raised his arm and the crisscross arc of the strands brushed my abdomen this time. It was hard enough to warm my skin, but caused no pain. The thump of the flogger moved up and down the front of my body until I leaned into each strike. He raised it further, catching just the bottoms of my swaying breasts with the tips of the strands. Then moved to my side and then behind me ... out of sight. I couldn't see Miles either, but I heard him breathing.

My back heated slowly under the soft lashes until it just began to blend together. The steady *thump thump* as he whisked the flogger back and forth over my skin in a rhythm that soothed deep into my aching soul. So much had happened in the thousand years I'd been away from them.

I let the strikes of the flogger strip it away. *Thump thump. Thump thump.* The torture. The mind control. *Thump thump. Thump thump.* The loss of a baby. It was so much to carry.

The strikes fell heavier, but still I arched into the strands —wanting the pain to redirect my mind away from everything I'd suffered. Everything I would have to face again when this was over. But for now ... for now I could just *be* here. I sank to a place in my mind where I was weightless. Nothing existed for me except the sound of my husbands' heartbeats. Their voices. Their hands.

The flogging had stopped. Instead of the drumming leather strands, Miles and Eli circled me, kneading and rubbing my body. I moaned as the ache in my sex throbbed from their careful attentions. Waves of magick rippled across my skin, and I could feel my dragon pushing forward, desperately looking for the same connection I wanted.

Eli bent forward, taking one of my breasts into his mouth.

Miles slid his fingers in and out of my slick folds.

"Please. Please." I begged, not able to articulate what I wanted. But those damned men knew, they were just bent on teasing me to death.

Eli's tongue worked expertly on the one nipple and then he moved to the other breast, nipping and pulling and sucking. I arched my back, pushing closer to his mouth while trying to twist my hips away from Miles torturing fingers. My sex throbbed unbearably beneath his manipulative fingers and I moaned in frustration.

Then Miles returned to the toy he'd inserted into my backside earlier. He pushed and pulled the toy, sliding it in and out so slowly I wanted to scream.

"How much do you want us, love?" Miles asked, nipping at my earlobe.

"Yes, Please. Now, please. Please," I mewled out through their attentions.

Eli pulled back, releasing my nipple from his mouth with a loud *pop*. "He asked you 'how much,' subbie. Answer the question," he commanded, bending down and thrusting two of his fingers up into my wet folds.

I shuddered and gasped for breath. Sweat ran down my temples, and wisps of my hair clung here and there to my slicked skin.

"More than anything," I said, gritting my teeth as his thumb rubbed across my sensitive bundle of nerves.

"I don't think we should make her wait any longer, brother," Miles growled from behind me.

The glass toy was removed from my ass and I gasped for a breath, waiting to feel the velvety smooth skin of his cock in its place. Thankfully he was true to his word and I didn't have to wait long. The warmth of his chest seared my back as he rubbed his cock up and down, teasing me. I thrust my hips back, but Eli's hands grabbed my waist and pulled me toward his chest. He captured my lips with his mouth and thrust his cock up, sinking his full length inside my pussy first.

"Stay still, subbie," Eli ordered, speaking against my mouth as he kissed.

I moaned into his mouth and tried to lift my legs to wrap them around his hips, but he wouldn't let me. I was suspended between their two massive bodies.

Eli grabbed onto my hips and drove up harder, his cock brushed against my womb and I felt the magick of our dragons rising to meet each other. Miles' hands encircled my waist where Eli's had been only moments before. He slowly entered me from behind, his cock stretching my opening more than the toy.

The burn seared through my lower body and I breathed through the pain as I adjusted to being so full. Inch by inch, he pushed deeper. A few minutes later he was fully inside and I felt as though I would come apart the second either of them moved.

I struggled to make myself breathe.

Eli kissed along my neck while Miles nipped and bit the opposite shoulder. A whimper slipped from between my lips and my body shuddered between them as I tried to hold still.

"Good girl, love," Miles growled into my ear.

Then they moved. Not at the same time, but against each other. As Eli pulled out, Miles would drive in. Then they switched. Their thrusts lifted until my toes no longer touched the carpet. I leaned my head backward against Miles' shoulder, breathing and relaxing into the driving forces between my legs. Their bodies were growing warmer and my dragon rose to meet them, cooling my skin so much that steam began to rise from their skin everywhere we touched.

Their thrusts were slow and methodical at first, then they fell into a driving rhythm and the speed and intensity continued to increase. I sucked in air and yanked against the cuffs, but respected the restraints and didn't break them. Only dragon steel could truly hold a Drakonae and nothing in this room was made from the enchanted alloy.

Their cocks slid in and out, driving me closer and closer to another climax. The one that I wanted with every fiber of my being. The one that would satisfy the mate bond between us and our dragons. Being separated for a thousand years had weakened our magickal bond.

Pleasure flowed through me, sending streaks of energy through my body to my fingertips. I closed my eyes and saw stars in the darkness as the world shattered around me like a mirror breaking into a thousand pieces.

A scream tore from my throat as both men roared, driving in deep at the same time. Their hot seed surged into me and they thrust again and again, going deeper each time. My body clenched down to milk every drop from their hard cocks.

Their grip on my body gradually loosened. Miles was the first to pull away. He slid his cock out and I moaned as he left. I felt so empty without him. Then Eli stepped back, pulling his cock from my slick folds.

My toes hit the soft carpet of the floor, but before my arms felt the weight of my body, Miles' arms encircled my ribcage. He lifted me up while Eli unfastened the cuffs.

I reclined into Miles' embrace, his chest hard against my back. "Thank you," I whispered.

Miles kissed the top of my head and said something to Eli I didn't catch. My eyes closed again and I breathed in Miles' musky scent mixed with sweat. If I never moved again, it would be fine with me. Every muscle in my body ached, along with muscles I'd forgotten existed.

Miles carried me across the room and gently laid me on my side, on the bed I'd seen at the back of the room. The sheets were so soft and comfortable. There would be no reason to move for a long time.

I sighed and rubbed my cheek against the sheets.

The sound of running water caught my ear and I licked my lips, hoping they were bringing me at least a small sip. Instead I felt their hands rub up and down my legs, massaging my sore muscles. Something warm and wet touched the inside of my thigh and I opened an eye to investigate. Eli smiled down at me as he wiped my skin clean of their cum that had seeped from my body.

When he finished tending to me, each of them took a moment to clean off in a small bath closet off the side of the room.

I stretched out across the big bed, but didn't come close to reaching both sides. Scooting toward the head-board, I grabbed a pillow and tucked it under my head. My breathing had evened out and my heart no longer pounded in my chest like a caged beast trying to break free. My dragon had calmed.

The bed dipped as both men moved toward me, lying down on either side. Eli fondled one of my breasts and Miles nuzzled my neck. It shouldn't have aroused me, but it did. My nipples pebbled and liquid slicked my sex yet again.

Their nostrils flared and Eli caught my gaze. "Wanton little dragon aren't we?"

I smirked and shrugged my shoulders. "I have a thousand years of missing you both to make up for."

"We intend to make up for every second," Miles said, his voice rough with emotion.

"Good," I answered, turning to face him.

"But we have every intention of letting you get some rest before we start round two," Eli said, dipping his head and pressing a gentle kiss to my still-tender nipples.

"Thank you." I smiled and turned on my side to snuggle into Eli's chest.

Miles sidled up behind me, positioning himself so his somewhat-hard cock rested just against my backside and his hand splayed over my hip.

Sleep came quickly to my exhausted body and I sank into its comforting embrace knowing I was safe in both my mates' arms.

CHAPTER 39

XERXES

A rap at the door and a familiar scent made me smile. Manda was back, along with her two body-guards. She couldn't teleport without them and they were both explicitly loyal to me, most likely because I had their wives locked in the prison beneath this palace. Neither man gave me any trouble and they made sure Manda was on her best behavior. And I hadn't gotten any lip from her since the piercings. Clipping her wings seemed to be just what was needed.

"Come in." I snapped my fingers and my three harem girls scurried to their room, closing the door behind them.

The double doors to my suite swung open wide and Manda strolled in, followed closely by the two guards I'd handpicked. She wore black leather pants, a sheer, red silk blouse, and a nicely cut gray jacket. Her expensive boot heels clicked on my marble floors, and she walked with the confidence of a woman who was not on a leash.

The attitude was a farce, of course.

I caught her gaze and flashed a smile. "How is my pet today?"

Everything about her changed. Her shoulders sank and her steps slowed. The brightness in her eyes had faded to a glassy stare and she directed her gaze from me to the floor. All the independence she tried to believe she still had evaporated into thin air.

That's the way I liked it. She still had spirit, and the guards I'd assigned to her said she tried to slip away from them on a regular basis, but for the most part she just tried to keep to herself when she wasn't in briefings with the defense council.

"The dagger has been located and retrieved, Master." She stood, feet together, head bent, gaze to the floor.

I waved my hand, grabbing her with my magick and yanked her to her knees. She winced in pain, but didn't speak a word of complaint.

"Kneel when you address me, pet. You don't have the pleasure of acting as an equal any longer." I growled. "Where is the dagger?" It was about time the incompetent idiots had located it.

One of her guards stepped forward, taking a knee at her side. He held up a bit of black silk, unwrapped it, and leaned closer.

I took the golden dagger from his outstretched hands and nodded. He immediately backed up, stood, and took several more steps backward. I knew the man feared me. It was no secret what I'd done to Manda and that was on purpose. After I'd pierced her with the enchanted nipple and labia rings, I threw her out of my suite, naked as the day she was born. The guards at my door saw her, and it didn't take long for word to spread that I "knew how" and was more than willing to clip their teleporting wings. No one but Manda knew that's how I controlled Cyrus as well.

"Very good. I'm glad you finally came through with this. I was beginning to wonder who I was going to have to threaten next to get some results." I turned the dagger in my hand, admiring the craftsmanship. For something that was thousands of years old, it was excellently made.

"Get back to Charlotte and await further instructions. I assume you have some new recruits to train, since several units were lost chasing Diana Karlson and the failed attempt on Sanctuary, yet again."

"Yes, Master," Manda murmured, her voice barely audible.

I flicked my wrist and grabbed her by the throat with my magick. Her eyes widened and she choked under my hold, arms and legs flailing as she fought the invisible force preventing air from reaching her lungs.

I put the dagger on the arm of my chair and drew her forward across the floor to my feet, reached inside her jacket and twisted one of the rings in her nipples. She couldn't wail, but tears poured from her wide, frightened eyes.

"Speak clearly and be respectful, Mandana." I opened my hand, allowing the magick to release her neck from my grasp. She sucked in a breath loudly and scrambled away from me on her hands and knees before climbing to her feet and straightening her askew clothing.

"Yes, Master," she repeated, loudly and very clearly.

I smiled and nodded. "Be gone."

One of her guards took her by the arm and the three of them disappeared a second later.

Looking down at the dagger, I picked it back up and sighed. It was time to suck up to the enemies I called my friends. Leif and Kevan were both assholes—worse than I was. But I needed them to believe I was an ally. Therefore, this extra dagger needed to be returned.

"Jahan," I shouted.

The Djinn that stood guard at my door stepped into view.

"Yes, Master," he replied and bowed.

I stood from my chair and walked toward him. "To the Veil, Jahan." I waved the dagger and he nodded, extending his palm. I touched his hand and the world swirled around me. Teleporting always made my stomach turn, but it was the absolute quickest way to travel.

A few moments later we were standing next to the gate, a ring of stones hidden deep within a forest in the Irish countryside. I owned the land stretching in each direction for several miles and it was never disturbed. The air was moist with a fog and cool. A harsh contrast from the searing, dry climate east of the Persian Gulf where I spent most of my time now.

"Be here every half-hour until I return."

"Yes, Master," Jahan answered swiftly, stepping away and disappearing into thin air.

I walked to the center of the ring, sliced my palm with the dagger, and touched the center stone, smearing the blood on its face. The gateway opened and pulled me through. Unlike teleporting with a Djinn, the gate to the Veil was a smooth, almost unnoticeable, transition. One moment I stood next to the altar stone in Ireland and the next I stood on the other side—in the Veil.

Wiping the dagger off on the black fabric it had been

wrapped in, I touched my chest, feeling for the other dagger. The one I wore on a chain around my neck beneath my tunic. The small weapon was a constant reminder of my goals, and *who* stood in my way of reaching them.

A breeze blew across my face, salty and clean. I turned to look out over the Goddess Sea—beautiful, blue, and perfect. Below its pristine waters lay many dangerous creatures, but from here above the cliffs, it was perfect. I took another deep breath of the pure air and turned, starting down the path away from the stones. It was several miles to Orin from the stones and I would prefer to get there before the afternoon sun set, blanketing the hillsides in darkness.

A shadow passed over me from high above. It was shaped like a bird, but when I glanced upward I knew it was nothing with feathers. The wings stretched out bat-like and the tail trailed behind it like a giant python. Its neck was half the length of its massive body, though as high as it was flying it didn't look much bigger than a Cessna. I knew better. It easily had a fifty-foot wingspan and could be just as long from nose to the tip of its tail. Not much different than my shifted form, but unlike a Lamassu, dragons were covered in scales that repelled all magick. An advantage I just couldn't compensate for and had been the thorn in my side ever since my bitch of a sister-in-law took in those two Drakonae brothers. With two Drakonae princes as their bodyguards, the Sisters of Lamidae might as well be on another planet. I would be stupid to go up against them and Rose head on.

The dragon disappeared into the clouds and I continued down the dirt path toward Orin. About a half-hour later as I approached the trade village outside the main gates, the path turned into a gravel road. Most inhabitants recognized me and quieted their obnoxious calls, trying to sell me their wares. But one stall in particular caught my eye. Not the stall itself. Or the clothing they were selling, but the woman standing in front of the weaver's table.

She was beautiful—hair as red as a scarlet sunset and skin that was alabaster white. But her eyes—the windows to her young soul—were bright blue. The color of the Goddess Sea. They sparkled with an innocence that made my dick stand up and take notice. Perhaps it was time to add another woman to my harem at the palace. A Drakonae female would be fun, especially with a dragon-steel collar to inhibit her shifting. Leif and Kevan would be grateful enough to have the third dagger back and I could leave without empty hands.

I stepped toward the redhead with a smile, but stopped when a man stepped out of the tent behind the stall. His brown gaze connected with mine and I curled my lip into a snarl. He had the same wavy black hair and aquiline features of the Blackmoor twins.

Where on the goddess' green earth had he been hiding all these years? He had to be related to the house of Blackmoor.

The large man stepped toward the redheaded woman and moved her aside. I heard him whisper her name—Ísól. He glanced back at me, and I recognized the burning fire of a dragon just beneath the surface. His brown eyes were flame orange. He didn't approach me, but he didn't back down either.

An older woman came out of the tent and rushed to

his side, prattling on about how "he needed to mind his manners" and "would he come help her with something." The Drakonae male broke eye contact with me and followed her back to the tent.

I smiled and continued walking toward the front gate. Taking other people's prized possessions was another of my favorite pastimes. I couldn't wait to see what this Blackmoor brother look-a-like would do when I took away his redheaded wench.

⚜

A HALF-HOUR LATER, I WAS ANNOUNCED AND THE DOORS to the throne room opened. The doors were heavy oak wrapped in a sheet of dragon steel, an upgrade since the Incantis had taken hold of Orin. Personally, I thought it was a bit much. But it could be changed when I took the city from them.

I held my head high as I progressed down the purple carpet that led to the stone thrones. One had been removed from the dias and now only two thrones remained, filled by Leif and Kevan. *I guess they gave up on having a queen.*

"Xerxes, old man. Back so soon?" Kevan called out, chuckling. "Couldn't wait to see us again, I suppose."

I bowed my head slightly to Kevan and then to Leif. "Good afternoon, your majesties."

"What do you want, Xerxes?" Leif spat out angrily.

I held back a snarl. How dare the ingrate speak to me so condescendingly? I'd been slicing men open in battle before he cut his first adult tooth.

"I have come to fulfill a vow." I pulled the black silk

bundle from under my arm and unwrapped it, showing them both the small, golden dagger.

Both the dragon brothers' lips curled up into the hint of a smile.

"We didn't think you would hold up your end, Xerxes," Kevan said, waving his hand at a servant to his left. The man moved quickly, bringing a small, mahogany box in which to store the dagger.

"I always keep my word," I answered.

The servant approached me slowly and held out the open box. I placed the dagger inside it and he backed away, returning to his place at Kevan's left.

"Something else, old man?" Kevan asked, leaning back in the great stone throne.

"I find myself desiring to take with me a female companion from the village outside the walls of Orin. With your permission, I would like to take her back with me when I go."

"Women are an expensive commodity in the Veil, Xerxes," Leif growled. "They're not party gifts to guests. You know as well as I there are too few female Drakonae. And each year fewer are born."

Yet, you've killed at least three wives already.

"I do understand how precious they are, but I am not just any guest, your majesty. Consider it an investment in our continued alliance."

Both Leif and Kevan grimaced, but neither objected. They knew the precarious position they were in. Not only could I come and go freely through the Veil, but I alone made sure Miles and Eli didn't return for their blood.

"Do you have this bitch's name?"

"Ísól. She was a lovely, redheaded woman in the trade village."

"Very well," Leif answered. He turned to a heavily armed guard standing to his right. "Find the woman he seeks and bring her to the stones. Take a collar and cuffs in case you need them."

The guard bowed low and then rushed from the large, throne room.

"In case?" I caught Leif's gaze and he shrugged.

"There are many Elvin in the trade village. The woman may or may not be Drakonae." He smiled. "I do hope that she is just some Elvin whore and I'm not giving you one of Orin's precious few Drakonae females. Peasant or not, we cannot afford to lose even one."

That the woman wasn't a dragon hadn't crossed my mind. But it made sense. With so few available women to breed, it was unlikely the man I'd seen could've afforded to take a bride all for himself. Nearly all Drakonae females were given in betrothal to families with multiple sons to ensure there would be heirs—both male and female.

If the stunning redhead was Elvin, she wouldn't mean anything to the Incantis. The Elves were a race of strong semi-immortals that used to be a nation of great scholars and warriors. Their swords and knowledge were legendary, but over the last millennia, they'd fallen to the status of servants—only because the Incantis hunted them down and killed most of them.

Even if she wasn't Drakonae, I still wanted her. Mostly, I wanted to get that man to follow me through the gate. And the woman he cared about would be perfect bait. He could be just what I needed to undermine everything Rose had built with those damn Blackmoor brothers. I just needed to determine how he was related to them.

I inclined my head in a shallow bow to the two Incanti kings.

Both returned the gesture, dismissing me from their presence.

I held in my disgust and left the throne room quickly, glaring at any of the persons standing about the sides of the room. They whispered and talked about me under their breath, but I could see the terror in their eyes. They knew who and what I was. None of them wanted to have anything to do with me and that's the way I liked it.

It didn't take me long to make my way through the outer courtyards of the palace and back through the trade village outside the main walls. The stall where the redhead had been was closed and abandoned now.

Excellent.

My magick prickled against my skin. I looked forward to the coming confrontation. The only holdup would be the damn guard they'd sent to deliver the wench. The only thing I needed from him was the dragon-steel collar and cuffs he would be carrying.

About a half hour later, the stone circle came into view. The guard stood quietly with a sobbing woman behind him. A smile spread across my face at the scintillating sound of her tears. It made my dick hard instantly. I might need to sample the whore right there on the stone altar.

I approached them and the woman dropped to her knees, begging the guard to let her go. The Incanti guard merely kicked the woman to the side and yanked on the chains connected to her neck and wrists, flipping her onto her stomach. Her face hit the dirt and she coughed, trying to catch her breath.

A loud snap to my left gave away the male Drakonae's hiding place. I reached out with my magick and grabbed him, closing his mouth to keep him from alerting the guard to his presence. The last thing I needed was a tattle-tale running back to Leif and Kevan. I kept that hand low to my side and continued toward the guard.

"Thank you for delivering her, sir. I will take it from here," I said, calmly and without malice.

"Enjoy the Elvin whore," he sneered, handing me the dragon-steel chain. "I put them on her anyway. Just in case you felt the need to chain her up."

"It is much appreciated," I replied, watching him leave down the path I'd just come up.

Turning to the sobbing woman, I growled. "Shut up."

"Please, sir. I'm married. I have a husband. Please don't take me from my home." Her voice was soft and silky, no doubt her pussy would be the same.

I pulled the male forward from the trees. He clawed at the invisible hand around his neck and kicked out with his legs. His mouth struggled to open and yell at me, but all he managed were throaty infuriated roars. I could feel the heat of his dragon building beneath the grip of my magick. It wouldn't be easy, but he could break my hold if he pushed long enough. He was so strong. Without a doubt, the product of a fire and ice mating—the son of the Miles or Eli with their mate, Diana.

"So much for testing out your sweet pussy. I believe I need those cuffs and collar for your husband."

She glanced up and cried more.

Damn, the woman bawled like a newborn babe.

"Please. What do you want? Why are you doing this?"

"Do you know your husband is related to the House of Blackmoor?"

She sucked in a hiccup and shook her head. "They d-died. All of them."

I waved my other hand, unlatching the cuffs and collar from her body. Another flick of my wrist sent them flying toward the male. Seconds later they were firmly attached to him, putting me in complete control with no chance of his dragon pushing to the surface and complicating the situation.

When I turned back to look for the redhead, she was crawling away from me on her hands and knees. I grabbed her by the neck and hauled her back through the air to face me.

Clicking my tongue, I shook my head. "No one said you could leave. Don't you want to say goodbye to your husband?"

Her tears poured again and her whole body tensed under my hold. She was a mere Elf, and nothing she could do would come close to breaking the control I had over her.

"Say goodbye," I ordered, turning her head so she could see the face of the Blackmoor male.

"I love you, Mikjáll."

The male struggled in my hold, his eyes glassy and his face red as he attempted to shout through a closed mouth.

"Good girl." I flicked my wrist and hurled her through the air toward one of the largest outer stones. Her head connected with the rock and the *crunch* of her skull was loud enough for both of us to hear. She fell to the ground at the base of the rock, leaving a trail of blood dripping down the face of it. It was a waste of a woman, but I needed both my hands to deal with ... Mikjáll. That's what she'd called him.

The male screamed in his throat and struggled against my hold and the cuffs, but it was no use and I grew bored.

"It was either dead now, or raped now and dead later. So shut the hell up. We have a bit of a trek to find your long-lost family."

He roared again, his rage coming through in the burning flames of his orange irises. Were it not for the collar around his neck and my hold on his magick, I'd be no more than a pile of ash on the forest floor.

I sliced my palm, then his, and placed them both against the altar stone simultaneously. We crossed through the gate and I released his mouth so he could speak.

"You fucking bastard!" He roared, still struggling against the paralyzing hold my magick had over him. "I'll kill you."

"I highly doubt that. Many have tried and none have succeeded in so many millennia, I've lost count." I studied him carefully. "How old are you, Drakonae?"

He spat at me, but I sidestepped before it could connect with my linen tunic.

"You don't look very old, but I know it's deceiving. Why did the Incantis let a Blackmoor live?"

"I'm Mikjáll Halldór. I have no Drakonae family. What do you want with me?"

"You were named and raised with Elvin." I stepped closer. "How. Old. Are. You?" I squeezed my hand, which in turn squeezed his ribs. I heard two snap under the pressure and he grimaced, fighting through the pain without crying out.

"I am nearly a thousand years. What does it matter to you?" He spat back at me, through his desperate pants for air.

"It will matter to your mother," I answered quietly, relishing the shocked look on his face.

"My mother died."

I shook my head. "Alive and well. And if I know anything about Drakonae physiology, she will feel you coming miles away." I smiled. "And she would do anything to get you back, making you the perfect bait."

CHAPTER 40

ELI

Thunder shook the Castle. I carefully slipped out of the bed, unwrapping Diana's arm from my chest. I didn't want to leave her, but something wasn't right. We were back in Miles' room and the heavy curtains in front of his windows blocked out everything. I pulled them back and scanned the horizon. Menacing, black, cumulus clouds blanketed the sky, uncommon so late in the season. Lightning flashed on the horizon— angry jagged white streaks.

I'd smelled the storm earlier and I'd felt the presence of *something* nearing, but my dick had overtaken my common sense and I'd ignored the warnings my dragon had been prodding me with all evening. It was morning and whatever was coming, we'd now have to face. Whatever it was, it pulled at me strangely. Similar to the bond I shared with Diana, but weaker.

"You can feel it too, can't you?" Miles' voice rumbled from the bed behind me.

I nodded, still watching the approaching storm. The wind was picking up, tossing dead leaves through the air and dashing them back against the cold ground with the fury of a wrathful predator.

"I don't recognize it," I answered softly, looking over my shoulder.

"I do." Diana sat up in bed and darted to the window. "He's here. How could he be here?"

"Who?" I asked, stepping back to allow her access to the window.

"My son. I can remember feeling this bond in the Veil, but I couldn't feel it after I left. It's different than our mate bond."

"It's a familial bond. More like a sixth sense," Miles stated, climbing from the bed. "It's been so many years since I felt one other than yours, Eli. I'd forgotten what it was."

I turned toward my brother. He was right. I vaguely remembered being able to sense when our mother and fathers were nearby. If we could feel a family member, that meant the baby was indeed ours. I took a deep breath and frowned.

Miles nodded.

He knew as well as I that the only way our son would've made it through the gate was via Xerxes. Leif and Kevan, if they still ruled, would never have let him out of the Veil alive.

Diana ran across the room and disappeared into the bathroom. I heard the closet door open and close several times.

"Diana," Miles growled, pulling on a pair of jeans from the floor. "Wait, you can't just go out and look around. We have protocols to follow."

I grabbed my jeans from the floor and shrugged them on as I half-hopped to the bathroom door. She was at one of the sinks brushing out her mussed hair, fully dressed in a purple silk skirt and a white silk tunic. Both were beautiful on her and were exactly her style—feminine and flowing. Except when she was in a fighting mood. Then she wore leather and armor like the fiercest of warriors. I wonder if Calliope had found any of that for her, she'd certainly nailed her everyday look perfectly.

"What are you going to do? You don't know what he looks like ... or his name? What if he's working with Xerxes?"

She turned toward me, her eyes glowing white for a split second before she pushed her dragon back down. "I have to do something, Eli. He's here. I can feel him and it's tearing at my heart."

Her eyes were glassy with tears, and I felt a piece of my heart break for her. This whole thing didn't feel right. We couldn't lose her, not now. Not after everything. But we couldn't abandon our child, either. She was right again—as usual.

"We have to do this together, Diana. Promise me you'll wait for Miles and me to go with you."

"Let's go then," she snapped back, slipping between me and the doorframe.

I huffed and turned around. Miles was standing in front of the bedroom door blocking her way.

A shrill ring sounded through the room, coming from the nightstand where Miles' phone lay.

"Wait, Diana!" he bellowed, moving toward the phone.

She was shaking her head. "Something is wrong. I can feel it."

I lunged, but she was quicker than I was and slipped out before I could grab her.

"Miles," I growled, throwing open the door again and running after her down the long hallway. The front door would slow her down, but not more than a few seconds.

"Rose says Xerxes is close! It's a trap!" Miles' voice shouted from the bedroom. "Stop her!"

I'm fucking trying.

I leapt down the last half of the stairway to the entry of the Castle. The beam that barred the heavy double doors lay tossed to the side on the marble floor and one of the doors had been pushed open.

No. No. No.

Miles' heavy footsteps were right behind me. I stumbled out the door and looked up and down the street.

"Where is she?" He stopped a few feet in front of me, looking back and forth.

I shook my head. She was gone. Someone had taken her.

The door of Calliope's shop opened across the circle and she came flying toward us. "Djinn! There was a Djinn!" Her voice didn't carry across the circle in the violent wind, but I could read her lips.

"Stubborn woman!" Miles roared.

The cafe door opened and Rose came out, followed by several colorful pixies. They all ran toward us.

I just stood still, unable to believe we'd lost her again so quickly. The cold wind whipped my loose hair into my face and I looked down at the pavement.

The end was coming. If he killed her, the whole town would be a pile of ash before the sun rose again in the morning. If Rose killed us now, Xerxes would still get what he wanted.

Fuck.

CHAPTER 41

DIANA

I hit the ground, my stomach heaving from whatever it was that man had done. One second I'd been stepping out of the front door of the fortress in Sanctuary, and now I was in the middle of a grassy field ... It was still close. The air smelled the same and I could hear the thunder from the building storm. The clouds were dark above me and I felt a stray drop of rain hit the back of my neck.

We couldn't be more than a half-hour's walk from the town. That man had been waiting for me. Dark skin, curly black hair, and lavender eyes. *Damn Djinn.* I gathered my wits and my stomach and stood.

He was right there in front of me. I raised my hands to blast him with ice, but he disappeared and I only froze the ground where he'd been standing.

"Where the bloody hell is my son?!" I spun around and came face-to-face with the man I'd stolen the knife from in the Veil. Behind him was a man in irons, beaten and bloodied. He had the same features as my husbands and the bond between us thrummed to life with our close proximity. My dragon roared and I didn't stop her.

My body began to shift immediately.

The stranger lifted his hand as if to grab me but nothing happened. My hands became white claws and my body changed until I stared down at him through my dragon's eyes. I could see his heart beating and smell his fear.

I opened my mouth to speak, but only an infuriated roar bellowed forth. He backed up a step, took out a dagger and held it over my son's heart.

The Djinn flashed back into view from the corner of my eye and I whipped my tail around, missing him by inches when he teleported away again. Swinging my face back around to the object of my anger, I lowered my face carefully until it was level with his. My breath was freezing cold and ice was forming on the ends of his long reddish brown hair.

"I won't die if you freeze me, but he will if I put this dragon-steel blade through his heart. Will you sentence your son to death, Diana?"

I snarled, looking from his calculated black eyes to the brown ones of my son. His eyebrows had risen in surprise. He hadn't known I was his mother. How could he? I hadn't seen him since the day that servant spirited him away after I pushed him from my body.

"It's you I want. Change back and take his place. I'll let him go."

My dragon shuddered. We both wanted to save him, but remembered the other people back in that town. They were counting on me. They were counting on Miles and

Eli to protect them. But I couldn't do nothing. I couldn't watch him murder my son.

"No," my son shouted and grabbed the man's hand, driving the knife deep into his chest. "I won't let him kill you." He looked right at me. "At least I got to see you once."

I screamed. The sound out of my dragon's throat was terrifying and shook the ground around us. Blood poured from my son's chest.

I lunged at the other man, one of my white claws sliced across the front of his chest, but he threw my son at my head and backed away before I could lunge at him again. The Djinn appeared behind him and they were both gone a moment later.

I turned around and around, waiting for him to come back. If I shifted back now and they reappeared, his magick would work on me. Only as a dragon was I impervious to all magick.

I looked down at my son, lying close to one of my large claws. Nuzzling his arm, I huffed and whined. The only thing I wanted to do was cradle him in my arms and tell him how much I loved him.

He lifted his cuffed wrists and stroked the tip of my nose. "Y-you are b-beautiful. I d-didn't know my m-mother was an ice-b-breather," he said, choking on blood as he forced the words out.

A large shadow floated over my head and the familiar scream of a dragon sounded over the meadow. Another was close behind him. My mates had come.

I pushed back my dragon immediately, shifting to human form within seconds.

"Please, fight. I can't lose you again. I don't even know

your name, my sweet boy." I leaned over his body, running my hands over the swollen flesh of his beaten face. His arms were black and blue. Several places were swollen to twice the size they should've been. I knew they were broken and then I knew how painful it had been for him to reach up and touch me before.

Tears poured down my cheeks. I caught them in the palm of my hand and smeared them over his skin. They would aid in healing him faster. Then I dipped my head and breathed softly over the wound on his chest. Ice crystals formed on his tattered tunic, but the flow of blood did come to a stop.

"L-let me d-die. He stole my w-wife from m-me."

My heart broke again at his words, but I refused to let him go. He was my son and he deserved another chance.

"No. You are my precious son. The boy who was taken from me before I could look upon your face."

"I am a grown man. I've lived a thousand years without you."

"Then why did you almost sacrifice your life for me?"

He paused and looked up at the sky. Miles and Eli were still circling above us.

"I couldn't let him take you. He was an evil man."

I covered my mouth to try and stifle a sob. I'd been through so much in my life and yet, this man had driven a blade into his chest, narrowly missing his heart to save me from an enemy I barely knew. From a fate he considered worse than his own death.

"My name is Mikjáll," he added.

I rolled the name off my tongue. *Mikjáll*. It was Elvin, and a beautiful, strong name. "You cannot take your vengeance for your lost wife if you are dead, Mikjáll." I shook my head. "You are a prince of the Veil. Your birthright one day will be the throne of Orin."

He took a deeper breath and looked directly at me. "I am only Mikjáll, son of a weaver. I know nothing of ruling, nor do I want to."

"You are my son and the son of Miles and Eli, House of Blackmoor. You will be a king one day. Never say you are no one. You have a destiny. And it is not to die in this field of grass."

I stood, pulling him up as I rose. Then maneuvered my much smaller frame beneath one of his shoulders. Even with my small size, I still had more strength than most other supernatural beings.

Miles and Eli swooped low, circling closely as I helped Mikjáll back into town, one painful limping step at a time. He would heal completely, but it would take time. The dragon-steel cuffs and collar weren't helping, but at least my breath and tears combined had healed his chest wound enough to stop his blood from gushing.

Once in sight of the town, all manner of people rushed forward and helped me move him quickly through the strange, blue barrier that surrounded the town. The woman I knew as Rose stood off to the side. Her gaze dark and enraged, but the rest of the people swarming around me appeared genuinely concerned about my son's well-being.

I felt the ground shiver as Miles and Eli landed a few yards away. The huge black dragons galloped along several hundred feet before they began to shift back into human form. They never stopped running and reached my side within moments.

"Why didn't you listen?" Eli roared. "We told you to stop. To wait for us!"

"I couldn't leave him. He needed me."

"He's a grown man!" Miles shouted. "A dragon nonetheless."

"So. Am. I," I snarled, handing off my son to a male vampire standing next to me. And then she turned to face my husbands' wrath. "I am Drakonae royalty. A mother. And a wife. He is my son!"

"She didn't shift back," Mikjáll coughed out, hanging onto the vampire's shoulder. "If you hadn't come, she would have let me die. She didn't give him a chance to take her."

Miles' eyes flashed orange and he growled at Mikjáll. "She did give him a chance. He's Lamassu. She endangered everyone by going after you alone."

Calliope stepped forward, attempting to mediate the situation. It was brave, but mostly foolish. "Look, he's gone for now and the rain will be here any minute. Could we please all get inside and argue under a roof? Or maybe just quit arguing and be ecstatic that you're safe and this new, dragon hunk will be okay."

"You're a siren. Why do you care if you get wet? Don't call him a hunk. He's my son," Miles snapped back at her.

"*Now* he's your son, too, huh? Back off, pal," Calliope growled, her painted red nails turning black and lengthening into razor-sharp claws. "Just because you forgot how hard it is to keep up with an independent woman doesn't mean you get an asshole pass with me. Plus there are more Djinn around here making me pissy."

"Hannah and Meredith can't hold the wards much longer," Rose said slowly, her voice even and calm—almost cold. "The Lycan scouts say there are no human troops nearby, but I can feel the presence of dozens of Djinn hopping from one side to the other. This isn't over."

"What happens when the wards fall?" I asked.

"The Djinn can teleport inside the town. Right now they have to walk through the barrier just like us," Rose answered. "We need you three ... now four back inside the Castle protecting the Sisters."

I knew why the Sisters were so valued now. I felt the smallest amount of guilt for putting them in danger. Had he been able to kill me, Miles and Eli would have razed the town once their souls faded away. Everything would have been lost because of my actions.

"I'm sorry."

"I know." Rose unfolded her arms and sighed. "He was your child. I know what that feels like, but if we lose one of the Sisters to Xerxes, you won't be the only parent to lose a child."

"Could you all stop talking about me like I'm an infant," Mikjáll said, trying to stand taller next to the giant, Nordic-looking vampire.

Miles and Eli took him from the vampire, wrapping his arms around both of their necks.

"Let's get moving," Miles bellowed.

I watched my husbands on either side of Mikjáll and sighed. I'd nearly lost everything today. Instead, the gods had favored my plight and spared my family any further loss.

I wasn't about to let a handful of Djinn change that. Storm or no storm. They wouldn't get close to the Castle I now called home.

CHAPTER 42

DIANA

Miles and Eli carried Mikjáll through the Castle and down to the lower level where there were private areas of the club. As we passed through the large hall with the play cubicles, no one said a word. We passed group after group of Sisters, huddled on this couch and that. Babies in their laps and small children were being hushed.

It's a fortress within a fortress.

"Stay here with Mikjáll, Diana." They opened a white door and helped their son stretch out on the large, four-poster bed in the center of the room. "There's food in the kitchen down the hall if you need anything. The Sisters also know where everything is kept, so just ask them if you can't find something."

I grabbed Miles' arm as he turned to leave. "What are you going to do?"

"We're going to the towers. Rose intends to box as

many of them as dare to enter the town, but everything has to be done carefully and quietly. We call out positions on the coms while the vampires do the hunting."

Eli stepped up behind me. "Be safe, Love. We'll be back soon. Take care of our son."

Miles kissed me on the forehead and they both left the room, closing the door softly behind them.

I turned back to Mikjáll. The chains connected to the collar and wrist cuffs clinked with every shift he made. "I'm going to find a pick to get those off of you."

He nodded and then turned away.

I knew he was in pain, but I also wanted him to be glad he was alive and well ... and back with his parents. With me. His mother. I'd missed everything in his life. He was a stranger and that was the most painful thing. I wanted to know everything about him and he didn't even want to look at me.

I slipped through the bedroom door and wandered into the main hall. Tears ran down my cheeks and I sat down on a strangely shaped bench to cry. I'd been holding it back, but now it poured out like water breaking through a dam.

I jumped when a soft hand touched my shoulder. Opening my eyes, I looked up to see the loveliest, green-eyed, little girl with red curled tresses. She couldn't have been more than five or six.

"Don't be sad. The dragons always come back and let us out," her little voice assured me. "I'm Issa, what's your name?"

I couldn't hold back the smile. Wiping my face, I nodded back at her. "I'm Diana. It's nice to meet you."

"Is the man they brought in hurt?"

"Yes, Mikjáll was hurt. Do you know where I might find something long and sharp? Perhaps a hair pin?"

A woman stepped around the corner and stopped suddenly when she saw me. She was dressed in the white shift I now knew was what the Sisters wore most of the time.

"Issa, you shouldn't bother the nice woman. It's not polite. Come, let's give her some privacy."

"She wasn't bothering me," I said quickly, drying the last few tears that trailed down my cheeks.

The little girl skipped away and leaned against the Sister. "Auntie, she needs a hair pin." Then the little girl pulled the woman down and whispered something in her ear. I couldn't hear what she said, but the woman's face changed from a frown to a smile.

"You need a hair pin?"

"I need to pick a cuff lock."

"Ahh, Seely can do that. Issa, run and tell Seely we need her over by the white room."

The little girl dashed away, her red ringlets bouncing with each step.

"She's a beautiful child," I said, trying to break the awkward silence.

The Sister beamed. "Issa is special and has such a big heart. She's my niece. I don't have a baby of my own yet."

"I had a baby."

"The man in the white room?"

I nodded, surprised she knew the man was my son. But then I remembered they were all seers. Born knowing things others had to seek out.

"Don't be unhappy, Diana. Issa said he will come around. The new brother will soften his heart in time."

"The new brother." I repeated absent-mindedly. "Issa said?" I flicked my gaze up to hers. "What do you mean?"

"Issa is a powerful seer. She came to you because of your sorrow. It pulls at her. But she wanted me to tell you not to be sad. Your family will be whole. The baby you carry now will be the bridge to link the four of you together, stronger than ever."

I touched my stomach and took a deep breath. "She's just a—"

"A little girl?" The woman laughed.

"Yes, but she's nearly as powerful as our current Oracle, Arlea. Even though Astrid is being trained to take the position next as Oracle, Issa will most likely also be trained to take that position in the house when she comes of age."

The conversation was interrupted when Issa reappeared around the corner trailed by the Pixie named Seely I'd met last time I'd been down here.

"Diana, my little friend says you need a lock picked."

"Yes, Mikjáll is bound with dragon-steel cuffs. I can't break them."

The pixie shook her ocean-blue hair and opened the white door. "You should come with me. I'm not really in the mood to get melted."

"Of course." I stood from the bench and thanked Issa and her aunt before following Seely into the white room, rightly named for its bright white carpet, walls, and white bedding. Well, it *was* white before we had put Mikjáll on the bed. Now it had smudges of dirt and blood all over it.

"The guys had to choose the white room," Seely muttered, taking in the vision ahead of us. She shook her head and cautiously approached the bed.

I stepped ahead of her. "Mikjáll, this is Seely. She can help with the chains."

He turned his head and I winced at the purple bruises covering half his face. I wanted to heal him. To stop the pain I knew he was in. But the dragon-steel hindered magick.

"Thank you."

"Wow, you look just like them," she said, stopping in mid-stride. "Even with the bruises, no one would mistake you for being anything other than Miles' and Eli's son."

"I wouldn't know," he mumbled. "I barely got a look at them."

"He has your nose, though," she added, catching my gaze and winking.

The tiny compliment warmed my heart. I knew Mikjáll didn't resemble me at all. He was all Miles or Eli. But it still made me feel good to hear the words.

"It's more likely he has Diana's stubbornness," Miles' voice rumbled from the doorway.

"And her heart," added Eli.

I turned, surprised to see both of them.

"The storm has passed, my love," Miles said, walking to my side.

"For now," Eli said, going to the other side of the bed. He sat at the foot and sighed. "Seely, can you break the locks?"

"You know it," the pixie answered. She waved her hand over the cuffs, dropping some sparkling powder inside the lock. The tumblers clicked and the cuffs opened, falling to the bed. She did the same with the collar and a second later it too fell away from Mikjáll's neck.

His eyes flashed orange and he moaned as his magick

surged through his body. He pushed the bonds away and they hit the floor with a heavy thud.

Seely backed away from the bed.

"Thank you," he said, holding out his hand.

The pixie placed her small hand in his and smiled. "Anytime." She looked over at Miles. "Everything good topside?"

"Yes, ma'am," Miles answered.

"I'll let you have some privacy then." She backed away quickly and slipped out the door.

I turned back to Mikjáll, not surprised to see him sitting up and trying to get off the bed. His bruises were fading already. In an hour or two, there wouldn't be any trace of them left.

I reached forward to touch his face, but stopped myself. He wasn't a child. The last thing he wanted was some strange woman hovering over him.

He looked up at me, his brown eyes filled with emotions that made my heart hurt for him.

"I know you want to make up for lost time, but I had a good life. I had a good mother and father. I'm glad I got to meet you three, but you're not my parents and I need to grieve for my wife. I would very much just like to be alone."

I bit my lip and took a deep breath to ward off another avalanche of tears. Instead, I nodded and took Miles' hand in mine.

Miles squeezed it and motioned for Eli to leave. The three of us exited the white room without another word. Eli closed the door behind us and I leaned into Miles' chest, muffling my sobs against his thick sweater. His arms encircled me and lifted me from the floor.

CHAPTER 43

I took a deep breath of Miles' scent and snuggled closer. We were stretched out together on his bed upstairs. Eli lay behind me, his hand resting on my hip.

"I'm sorry." The apology wasn't enough, but it was a start. I had acted rashly and endangered so many people. Children. Families. This town was my husbands' world now. They cared for them as they had when we lived in Orin. I understood that now.

"We know, Love," Miles murmured.

I rolled to my back and took one of each of their hands and placed them on my abdomen. "I'm so thankful to be with you both again. We have a chance to start over. This home that you've made is good. I think both of our sons will learn to love it in time." I hoped Mikjáll would eventually find peace. I knew the pain of losing a spouse, and he had no chance of ever being reunited with his, unlike me.

Eli lifted his head and stared down at me quizzically. "Both?"

Miles hand tensed beneath mine. "How can you know so quickly?"

"A little birdie told me," I answered, stroking his hand gently with my thumb.

The tension melted from both of them and they buried their faces against my neck, both kissing up the sides of my neck to my temples.

"Issa?" Eli asked.

"How did you know?" I laughed, wrapping a hand around each of their heads, pulling them closer.

"She always knows when babies are coming," Eli answered, a chuckle rolling up from his chest.

They shook free from my grasp and Miles moved, laying his head over my abdomen. "She said it was a boy?"

"Yes. Are you pleased?"

He kissed my stomach and looked up, catching my gaze. "More than you could ever know. So much has happened. We have a son we never knew existed. We have you back in our arms where you belong. And now you tell us we have another son on the way."

"Love, we couldn't be happier," Eli added. "The town's safe for now. Xerxes failed. Rose boxed six more Djinn. And we have everything we've dreamed of having for a thousand years."

"I love you both so much."

"We wouldn't have it any other way," said Miles, leaning forward to capture my mouth in a passionate kiss. His tongue plunged deep and he slipped his hands beneath the hem of my shirt, sliding them up to fondle my breasts.

Eli's hands moved lower and I gasped for a breath when I felt his lips trailing kisses up my thigh toward my core. My body tightened under their touch, and that familiar ache began to thrum between my legs.

Ecstasy was on its way, and I needed it.

We were together and starting fresh. For now, I couldn't ask for anything more.

⚜

I hope you enjoyed My Dragon Masters!
Thank you for spending time with me in my world. Please consider leaving a short review. Each one helps tremendously.
XOXO
Krystal Shannan

Turn the page to read part of book 3, MY ETERNAL SOLDIER!

CHAPTER ONE
KILLÍAN

Texas Republic, 2097

NO ONE EVER FORGETS THE CRY OF A DRAGON.

The heartbreaking bellow cut into my chest, strangling my soul with rage-filled agony. Her second scream split the gray Texas sky, nearly sending me to my knees. Searing pain radiated through me as her anguish became mine. I gasped for breath and dug my fingernails into the bark of the tree I stood behind, welcoming the pain of the splinters as a distraction from the burning fire blazing through every cell.

Straight ahead a silver-white dragon, the size of a large house, lunged toward several men about thirty yards south of my position. As far as full-grown dragons went, she was no shrimp. Distinct silver streaks on her otherwise white wings made my heart clench. *I know her.* A thousand years ago, she had been princess in a land called the Veil, separated from Earth by a secret gate. A land I called home. A land all supernatural beings called home before the gate was discovered.

Now I stood on the edge of a Texas field watching the Drakonae princess I thought long dead attack a man I didn't recognize. The shining golden blade hanging from a chain around his neck was familiar, however. Even from this distance, the familiar hilt of the dagger elicited a sudden rush of homesickness.

A Shamesh dagger was as rare on Earth as finding a diamond in a cereal box. I couldn't believe he wore one so openly.

She leapt forward again. This time her sharp claws sliced through the man's chest, leaving jagged bloody streaks in their wake and flinging the chain and dagger to the ground.

Half a second later, the wounded man disappeared through a teleportation vortex with a Djinn at his side.

She roared again and stomped the ground with enough force to shake the trees around me, all the while carefully circling a man lying on the ground. He was a goner for sure if a Djinn didn't return for him quickly.

But no one came.

And no one moved toward the fallen dagger sparkling

in the grass a dozen yards from her position. My hand itched at my side. Desire to retrieve the dagger made me consider leaving my hiding place in the trees for a moment, but common sense and the will to survive overrode that craving, stilling my body and calming my racing pulse.

Just because I recognized her didn't mean it was safe to be in her presence. She was the size of a small apartment building. Nobody and nothing could fight a dragon unless they too were some type of oversized, lethal mythological creature.

No fucking way.

My throat closed up as two enormous shadows glided by, shading the entire grove of trees for several seconds. I peered up and couldn't help the tightening of my chest or the way my heart pounded. I struggled for my next breath. Two more dragons circled, their black, winged forms cutting a swath through the grey-blue sky like something out of an old science fiction movie. Their wings stretched easily a hundred feet across, and their length was equally as much —a magnificent sight. But one that did not belong in the Texas sky. No one knew dragons existed. No humans, anyway. If someone spotted them, they were in for a shit load of trouble.

My heart continued to pound in my chest like the hooves of the wild mustangs that used to roam the Texas prairies. Living through the first purge in the Veil, even though I knew and respected the Blackmoor Drakonae family, had not prepared me to see shifted dragons again. Memories and emotions rushed to the forefront of my mind. Terror. Anger. Hatred. I'd lost everything because of the war between the Blackmoors and the Incanti.

The white dragon, Diana, shifted to human form and helped the bleeding man on the ground to his feet. She carried him toward Sanctuary, cradling him in her arms as she ran. The two black dragons flying overhead, Miles and Eli Blackmoor, stayed in the air and followed her to the edge of town.

As soon as the Blackmoor brothers landed and shifted to human form out of sight, I pulled a sword from one of the leather sheaths strapped to my back and crept from the tree line to where they'd been in the open field.

Kicking through the thick grass carefully, I located the dagger, tucked it into my vest, and moved cautiously to my parked bike. The Djinn could appear again at any moment, and I didn't want to be anywhere nearby when one of them realized the dagger was missing.

I threw my leg over the seat of my vintage Dyna Guerilla motorcycle, turned the ignition, and gripped the clutch. As I gave the custom designed bike a little gas, the v-twin cam engine purred to life. Satisfaction filled me, knowing my hands had modified her from the torn down body of a Harley Fat Bob to the progressive shocks and controls. Besides hunting and killing South East Coast Republic (SECR) soldiers who snuck into the Texas Republic (TR) to kill Others, fine-tuning this machine was my only distraction.

I rode cautiously through the wooded area and made my way to the main road. The small golden blade was cold against my skin. Icy daggers shot through my heart as my mind flooded with memories of fleeing the Veil a thousand years ago.

Even though I was still young by Elvin standards, I had lived through two generations of Blackmoor kings on the throne of Orin. The young twins Miles and Eli, along with their mate Diana Karlson, would've made good rulers for the land had the Incanti family not betrayed and murdered their family, seizing control not only of Orin, but the entirety of the Veil kingdom.

My parents had been killed in the first purge, slaughtered in the fire the Incanti breathed upon those who supported the Blackmoor family. My brother and I had narrowly escaped the second. We found refuge on the Earth side of the dimensional gate, and when news came from people who fled after us, I learned that the Incanti had taken complete control of the Veil and that any surviving non-Drakonae were either dead or serving as slaves.

The painful memories of that day wrenched my heart exactly as they always did.

The attacks had come swiftly and without warning. Thousands had died just trying to escape. My brother and I were the only two in our family to survive. We'd been out in the field behind our home, testing new swords.

Playing.

Goofing off.

Acting like boys a fraction of our age.

Because of that, we weren't in the house when an Incanti dragon incinerated our home and our family. Within minutes, the house was reduced to red-hot ash. Dragon fire didn't leave anything behind.

Hatred pooled in my soul, growing larger and more calculated with each mile of prairie that passed. I wanted revenge. The Blackmoor princes and their bride were a means to my desired ends.

With the appearance of Diana Blackmoor in Sanctuary,

the Veil was up for another dynasty change. With some well-made plans and the dagger I carried, I would make sure the House of Blackmoor rose from the ashes and, with it, revenge for my people and all the others who fled death and the fires of Incanti greed.

ABOUT THE AUTHOR

Krystal Shannan, also known as Emma Roman, lives in a sprawling ranch style home with her husband, daughter, and a pack of rescue Basset Hounds. She is an advocate for Autism Awareness and shares the experiences and adventures she's been through with her daughter whenever she can.

Needless to say, life is never boring when you have an elementary-aged special needs child you are home-schooling and half a dozen 4-legged friends roaming the house. They keep her and her husband busy, smiling, and laughing.

Krystal writes magick and Emma doesn't. If you are looking for leisurely-paced sweet romance, her books are probably not for you. However, for those looking for a story filled with adventure, passion, and just enough humor to make you laugh out loud. Welcome home!

www.krystalshannan.com

Other Books By Krystal Shannan

Vegas Mates
Completed Series

Chasing Sam
Saving Margaret
Waking Sarah
Taking Nicole
Unwrapping Tess
Loving Hallie

Sanctuary, Texas
Completed Series

My Viking Vampire
My Dragon Masters
My Eternal Soldier
Mastered: Teagan
My Warrior Wolves
My Guardian Gryphon
My Vampire Knight

VonBrandt Family Pack
Part of the Somewhere, TX Saga

To Save A Mate
To Love A Mate
To Win A Mate
To Find A Mate
To Plan For A Mate (coming next)

MoonBound
Completed Series
Part of the Somewhere, TX Saga

The Werewolf Cowboy #1

The Werewolf Bodyguard #2
The Werewolf Ranger #3
Chasing A Wolf #4
Seducing A Wolf #5
Saving A Wolf #6
Broken Wolf #7
Hunted Wolf #8

The Moonbound wolves story continues in an epic way through the...

Courts of Draíochta
Part of the Somewhere, TX Saga

Of Spells And Shadows
Of Trial And Torment (coming next)

Pool of Souls

Open House
Finding Hope

Contemporary Romance by Krystal's alter ego, Emma Roman.

Bad Boys, Billionaires & Bachelors
Can't Get You Off My Mind
What's Love Got To Do With It
You're The One That I Want
Accidentally In Love
Must Be Santa (Coming Next)

MacLaughlin Family
Completed Series
Trevor
Caiden
Harvey
Lizzy

CPSIA information can be obtained
at www.ICGtesting.com
Printed in the USA
FSHW02n1255190718
50695FS